Crazed Hearts

He's no fairy-tale prince. But he just may be the hero she needs.

Ren has always danced along the fine line between being a little bit crazy and being overcome by a darkness that's haunted him since his mortal days. As an empath, he prefers to live far from people who would leak their emotions all over him, so he's not expecting the woman who drives right into the heart of his wood. She has a cursed book with her and demons hot on her heels. Even more surprising are her abilities and the reaction Ren has to her.

Aileas is on the run. She just isn't certain if she's running from something real or imagined. One thing is for sure, her brother is dead and she's certain the book she found has something to do with his death. She really starts to doubt her sanity when she meets a hot but somewhat crazed man in the middle of nowhere.

He calls himself Ren, and although he doesn't seem to be out to hurt her, he definitely seems to want something. She just doesn't understand what. She does know what she wants though. She wants him, and the shadows and darkness she glimpses inside him don't matter. At least, right up until he claims to be a guardian angel.

And she thought she was going crazy.

Warning: This title contains soul-sucking demons, kick-ass angels and a hero who is a little crazy and a whole lot sexy.

Tarnished Knight

The mind forgets, but the body remembers. Everything.

One look at Jack Wallace and Perci knows he's going to be trouble. Even surrounded by soul stealers, he's a one-man wrecking crew. What does he need Grimm training for? He's already hell on earth, a warrior bent on destruction. And something...more.

He's too strong and fast to be a mere mortal. Even covered in blood, he makes her forget she's only here to do a job and get out. It's twisted. Sick. She hasn't felt this alive in three centuries.

Born with a natural talent for killing unnatural things, Jack has always known things he shouldn't. The fact that Perci is one of them glows all over her. Giving him an unholy urge to see just how far he can push her before don't touch me melts into touch me there.

When they come together, it isn't careful or cautious. It's heaven and hell, exposing all their raw and wounded places to healing heat, resurrecting memories of a destined love from the distant past. But the evil that destroyed them once before has tracked them here, threatening their second and last chance at forever. Demanding a sacrifice no one—Grimm or human—should ever be asked to make...

Warning: Dark, sexy, a little bit scary—this fairy tale is only for grownups and is best saved for bedtime.

Look for these titles by
Shiloh Walker

Now Available:

The Second Book
of Grimm

Shiloh Walker

SAMHAIN
PUBLISHING

Samhain Publishing, Ltd.
11821 Mason Montgomery Road, 4B
Cincinnati, OH 45249
www.samhainpublishing.com

The Second Book of Grimm
Print ISBN: 978-1-60928-864-8
Crazed Hearts Copyright © 2012 by Shiloh Walker
Tarnished Knight Copyright © 2012 by Shiloh Walker

Editing by Tera Kleinfelter
Cover by Scott Carpenter

Crazed Hearts, ISBN 978-1-60928-079-6
First Samhain Publishing, Ltd. electronic publication: July 2010
Tarnished Knight, ISBN 978-1-60928-231-8
First Samhain Publishing, Ltd. electronic publication: October 2010
First Samhain Publishing, Ltd. print publication: May 2012

Contents

Crazed Hearts

Dedication

As always, for my husband and my kids. I love you all more than life itself.

And for Heidi, who likes a slightly crazy bad boy with a sense of humor.

Prologue

"He isn't ready," Will murmured.

Although he knew he must wrong.

It seemed these things would play out as they were meant to play out, and nothing he did or said would change things.

But part of him, much as he hated to admit it, worried for Ren.

Though it had been decades since his change into a Grimm, the effects of the tortures Ren had endured had yet to completely fade. The losses. The grief. The choices he'd had to make.

They had failed Ren. The Grimms were supposed to protect the innocent, and what had he been when such atrocities had been visited upon him? An innocent, just a child. He'd seen too much and it had damn near shattered his already fragile grip on reality.

They'd failed Ren.

He had failed Ren.

Bringing him into the fold, it should have eased that pain, but Ren kept people at bay, allowing so few close. He didn't allow the bonds of friendship to form and, save for Elle, Ren let nobody close.

And now Elle was lost to him.

He had spent too much of his life suffering and that suffering had left scars.

Could he truly *heal* from those scars?

Mortals say time heals all wounds, but what do they know? They live but a moment and so many took their wounds to their graves.

Ren had lived more than a century. Will had seen civilizations rise and fall.

And both of them had yet to heal.

Feeling the press on his mind, his heart, Will sighed.

"Very well."

There was *one* thing he could take comfort in...shallow though it was.

It was not Mandy that Ren would turn to in the night.

And what sort of selfish bastard did that make him?

An unworthy one. That much was clear.

Chapter One

"Now, Beatrix, I told you a thousand times, if I told you once. If you keep it up, sooner or later Susannah is going to take a piece out of your tail," Ren said, smiling a little to himself.

Behind him, he heard the outraged females snarling and sniping. But he didn't turn around. They hadn't attacked, hadn't drawn blood. If they went that far, he'd intervene. If not... Well, he couldn't always play referee with his lovelies, now could he?

Bo nuzzled his neck and he turned his head and smiled. "Don't look so pleased with yourself, precious." Ren smirked. "They'll come after you next."

Bo gave a slow, lazy blink, looking unconcerned.

Little concerned Bo though. It wasn't much of a surprise.

There was a hiss behind him, followed by a sound of pain.

It echoed through Ren and he swore, grabbing a towel from the counter and drying his hands as he turned around.

The two stray cats he'd taken in off the street were on the floor and Susannah had managed to draw blood from the larger Beatrix. Yes, Beatrix was the older feline, larger and stronger, but Susannah was a scrapper.

He scooped Beatrix up off the floor and sighed as he studied her ear. Bo hooted in Ren's ear and the sound was suspiciously like a laugh. "I'm warning you, you shouldn't look so pleased with yourself," Ren advised again. "Otherwise Susannah might decide to rob you of a tail feather or two."

"Do they really understand you?"

Ren glanced over his shoulder and grinned at his young apprentice. Her name was Mandy. Sooner or later, she'd have to make the choice—become a Grimm. Or not. He wasn't looking forward to it, because for her to *make* that choice, it would mean she was destined for a young death.

Like he had been.

He didn't like the idea of it.

She was a nice kid, and he'd seen too many people die young. Even though she would have the chance to come back...

"Hey."

Shaking his head, he focused his mind back on Mandy. She'd said something. Oh, yes. Yes, that was it.

"Understand the words? Well, certainly some of them do. Many animals are rather intelligent, you know. But even those that don't understand the *words*, they understand my intent." He reached up and stroked Bo's crest. "Like Bo might not understand my words, but knows he knows if he keeps after Susannah, she'll come take a feather or two from him."

"And my lovelies...well, I think they understand me quite well."

Beatrix yowled, her voice plaintive and angry.

Susannah wound herself around his ankles, purring and shooting him hopeful glances.

"Look at her," Mandy said, laughing. "She looks pretty damned pleased with herself."

"Hmm. She is." Ren studied the calico at his feet and sighed. "Mean little bitch."

"Well, to be fair, Beatrix started it."

"Yes, but Susannah eggs her on. I've seen it happen too often to believe she's entirely innocent." The little calico sat down and stared at Ren, a heartbroken expression on her face. She gave him a plaintive meow.

He just laughed. "Yes, my darling drama queen. I see you." Scratching Beatrix under the neck, he carried her to the sink and studied her mangled ear.

Mandy watched from behind with more than a little fascination. "Man, if I'd ever tried to do that to any of my cats, they would have torn the skin clean off my hands," she murmured, watching as he deftly cleaned the cat's injuries.

Ren didn't respond. He was too busy focusing on keeping Beatrix calm.

He'd always had an affinity for other thinking

creatures...animal and human. His family hadn't seen it as an affinity though. They had loved him, but his gift had frightened them something awful. Terrified them.

But then, it had terrified him as well. There had been a number of times when he had tried to kill himself over the so-called *gift*. It wasn't until years later that he finally accepted this strange part of himself.

After he'd become a Grimm, that affinity had become something...more. Perhaps many of the animals didn't understand his words, but he could understand them. He felt their pains and he could ease them as well.

In return, they provided him with companionship. Without them he would have lost himself to the darkness of his mind ages ago.

"Easy," he murmured as Beatrix's pain had her struggling against the gentle hold he had on her mind. "You're fine now, sweet."

And then he was done.

When he released the hold he had on the feline, she deigned to let him pet her and then she focused her eyes on Susannah.

Ren sighed.

These two.

"Betcha it makes you feel like you're raising kids," Mandy drawled. "Did your folks have to get after you like that? Or do you even remember?"

He lifted a brow at her. "Being the doddering, ancient creature I am, you mean?"

She grinned at him unrepentantly and pushed her hair back. Today it was black with royal blue extensions woven through it. She changed the colors almost as often as she changed her clothes.

"Seeing as how you were around when Moses walked the earth, yeah." She settled down on one of the stools and leaned back against the cabinet. Her cropped top rode up, revealing the toned, smooth flesh of her belly. A few months ago, she'd been a bit rounder, nicely curved, Ren had thought.

But he'd put her through several hellacious months of training and those nice curves had melted away. The curves were still there, just not as lush. She was still human though, thus too vulnerable. She didn't have the luxury of a body that would heal all wounds or the added strength. She'd been placed in his hands so he could toughen her up, and he'd done just that.

And she'd repaid his care by driving him utterly mad, taunting him, teasing him and saying... What was that again? Around when Moses had walked the earth.

Ren snorted. "Moses, eh? Not quite, my dear. You're off by a few thousand years."

With a winsome smile on her face, she asked, "Oh, so you're *older* than Moses? Who came before him? Noah? Methuselah?"

Shaking his head, he turned away. He knew what she was doing. It was her way of trying to find out who he was. But really, why did she need to know that? "We're running five miles today," he said.

She groaned.

"Although I've heard the weather is going to be nice. We might try for six."

He chuckled when she started to beat her head against the wooden counter.

It was one way to distract her, he had learned.

Chocolate was another.

But he'd let her have the chocolate after she finished her run.

Motivation. It was all about motivation.

Chapter Two

Don't stop. If you stop, you'll die.

It was one hell of a motivator, she had to admit.

The skin along the back of her neck crawled and the hair there stood on edge. Aileas Corbett knew she was being followed. She'd been followed for weeks, ever since she'd buried her brother. Ever since she'd found that damn book...

She'd tried to ignore it at first. Tried to write it off as grief, exhaustion. Tried to go about her job, her life. Tried to ignore the shadows she saw at night and the weird whispers that echoed through the solitary apartment.

But she couldn't ignore it anymore.

Not after—

No.

She couldn't think about that right now.

Swallowing, she glanced at the damned thing wrapped in a blanket, lying in the back seat.

Damned.

A shiver raced down her spine. It *was* damned.

She'd swear she heard it whispering to her.

She hadn't slept a night through since she'd found the damn thing and that had been nearly three weeks earlier.

"You're going crazy," she whispered, reaching up to toy with the strand of pearls she wore around her neck. "That's all there is to it—you're going crazy."

That was the most likely explanation too.

A psychotic break brought on by grief, lack of sleep and who knows what else. A shrink would have a field day with her.

Assuming she actually stopped running to talk with one.

But she wouldn't stop running. Not until she figured out what to do. And she couldn't figure out what to do until she had this book someplace where it couldn't hurt anybody.

She pressed the heel of her hand against her temple and muttered, "I sound *insane*. It's a fucking *book*. It can't hurt anybody."

It could though. In her gut, she knew it. And the thought terrified her, left her so frightened, so afraid.

You don't need to be afraid, the book whispered to her. *Open me. Use me. I shall make you strong. I shall make you immortal...immortal. You could avenge the death of your brother.*

"Oh, for fuck's sake," she muttered. Reaching out, she turned on the radio, but the only thing that came through was static, static and more static. Sighing, she grabbed her iPod and one of the earbuds. So it wasn't exactly safe. But it wasn't like she was running into a lot of traffic driving through these woods on the way to the cabin her parents had left to her and her brother.

Just her now though... A sob rose in her throat, tried to break free.

She swallowed it down. Crying right now? On these roads? A quick, certain way to get herself killed. The cabin, tucked away in a remote part of Wisconsin's North Woods, wasn't exactly in the most easily accessible area, and if she wanted to keep the car on the road, she didn't have time to cry.

Of course, if she wanted to be *smart*, the last thing she needed to be doing right now was driving someplace so isolated when she knew she was being followed.

The fear tried to press in. Overwhelm.

But before it could, without her even understanding why, there was a warm touch on her mind, on her heart, her soul.

"Everything will be fine," she murmured. "I just need to keep going to the cabin."

That warm touch spread, became a sense of peace, pushing out the dark, uneasy, edgy feeling. A sense that managed to last right up until the time a big black dog—practically the size of a pony—darted out in front of the car.

With a half-scream, Aileas slammed on the brakes.

Ren heard her scream, but he was more concerned with Pan.

"Damn dog," he muttered. Glancing at Mandy, he said,

"Stay up here."

Bent over, her hands braced on her knees, she glared at him from under her lashes.

"Aye-aye, Cap-i-tan," she mocked between breaths.

"Smart arse."

He jogged down the incline.

There was a woman down there. Ren had had about two seconds to notice the fact that she was female, and the fact that she was far too close to Pan. The wolf/dog breed wasn't an aggressive animal, but she was a stranger and Pan considered this *his* territory.

Ren sighed.

He leaped down, covering the twenty foot incline in a silent, single jump. She was being careful, he had to admire that, not trying to approach Pan, talking to the dog in a calm, quiet voice.

"Sit, Pan," Ren said.

The woman went rigid.

Pan growled.

Ren narrowed his eyes and reached out, silently repeating the order with a mental command that no animal could resist. The dog obeyed, lowering his hindquarters to the ground, still staring at the woman with suspicious eyes.

He was tempted to do the same with the woman, but he hadn't tried to impress a command on a mortal in decades, more than a century to be exact. He wasn't about to do it now.

"He won't attack," Ren said, keeping his voice light, crisp. "You best get in your car, run along."

She turned around and studied him, her eyes narrowing. "Run along?" she repeated.

Her tone was offended.

Her eyes were dark brown, shot through with slivers of pale gold.

Around her long, slim neck, she wore a strand of pearls. He wanted to see her wearing nothing but those pearls.

Her mouth was quite possibly the softest he'd ever seen.

When he looked at her, Ren was certain the very earth beneath his feet shifted. He wanted to stare into those eyes for a very long time. Then he wanted to cradle that face in his hands and take his time as he kissed that mouth and learned it, explored it...

He sucked in a breath as the punch of hunger hit him hard and fast. Hunger, need, something too intense for him to describe.

Her eyes widened as she stared at him and he saw something...was it an echo of what he felt? There was something in her eyes. He sensed it dancing just beyond the shields he didn't dare lower.

He couldn't risk that.

He didn't need to lower them to see some things though. Like the way her pulse was pounding against the fragile skin in her neck. The way her nipples hardened, pressing against the thin worn flannel of the shirt she wore.

Slowly, he breathed in through his nose, wondering what she'd smell like.

And that was when he realized something else.

Something rather pressing. It cleared the fire in his blood, the fog in his mind all too quickly.

She had the stink of death, destruction and demon hanging in the air around her.

Around her.

But... He closed his eyes, dragged the air in, tasted it, rolled it around on his tongue... The smell was not on her, but it was damn close.

She hadn't been tainted...*yet*. But there was something very, very wrong. And it was close. Far too bloody close and on his land too.

Ren's gut clenched and he had to do it—had to risk it. Bracing himself, he lowered his mental shields. He was prepared to feel an onslaught...from her. And while he felt *something*, it wasn't the sheer rush of madness he'd been expecting. Pushing past that, he reached farther—a mental net, casting it far and wide.

What he came up against had him all but snarling in fury. The bizarre, unexpected hunger of a few moments ago forgotten, he looked back at the woman, trying to figure out just how in the hell she was involved in this...clusterfuck.

That was the only way to describe it. A clusterfuck.

"Did you just tell me to *run along?*" she said, completely unaware of his impending mental explosion.

"Did I? So sorry. My apologies. If you'd like to stand in the middle of the road while my dog growls at you, please...feel free." Ren bared his teeth at her. *Although, my dear, you're not going anywhere,* he thought mentally. "Have a care though. If you hold out your hand to pet him, he might bite it off."

"Where in the hell did you come from?" she asked, eyeing him suspiciously.

"I was out hiking," he said, gesturing toward the hill. He lifted a hand and whistled. "Me and my sister."

Mandy peered down at him from the top of the incline a minute later. He could see the disgust in her eyes and if he wasn't so disturbed by the ever-darkening ripples he could feel moving through the air, he might have been amused by the silent *fuck-you* he saw in Mandy's eyes.

"Your sister. Hiking."

"Hmmm."

She started to back away, eyeing him like he'd grown an extra head and razor sharp teeth. Ren acted like he didn't notice, but he mentally commanded Pan and the dog obediently padded forward and placed his bulk in front of the door of the car. She couldn't go traipsing off. Somehow she was in this mess up to her pretty neck, which meant she was in danger. He couldn't have that, even if he wasn't feeling strangely, almost insanely protective of her.

"Why would you hike around here?"

Now that he could answer.

"Oh, because I live around here, that's why." He flashed her a grin, tried to temper down the raging maniacal edge and pretend to be friendly, perhaps even charming. Did he remember charming? No. He was quite sure he didn't. He didn't know if he'd ever known charming. Well, other than a prince, of course. Still, he really didn't want to show the crazier side of his nature. He needed to keep that under wraps.

"Just over the rise, a few miles down."

Up said rise, Mandy was swearing as she started to make her way down. Tripping, too and not particularly happy. But as she moved to the busted, uneven road, she fell silent, picking up on something.

The mortal wouldn't pick up on Mandy's tension, but Ren had spent months with Mandy and he knew her well.

Well enough at least.

The look in her eyes was one of fear...and resignation.

She was staring not at the woman though.

She was staring just past her, at the car.

Ren shifted his gaze, focused on the car.

Yes...there. There it was, he realized. He lowered his shields, and that was when he sensed what Mandy had sensed.

That black, nasty vibe.

Something shuddered, twisted from the car.

Could a whisper have a stench, a feel? Could it make the air quake and wrench around you?

It seemed so.

"What have we here," he mused, narrowing his eyes.

The whispers grew louder—an ocean of them. They flooded his mind, flooded his soul.

The darkness... It was all but reaching for the woman, trying to wrap itself around her like a boa constrictor.

Like hell, Ren thought.

He extended his gift, touched one of the distant minds in his territory. It was a bear cub, perched high in a tree and trembling, shaking. There was a smell in the air the cub didn't like and Ren understood why.

There was a car drawing closer to them that had some unpleasant bastards in it. They looked human on the outside, but that was it. Soul-sucking monsters. Orin. They fed on souls, stank of death and evil.

He watched through the cub's eyes for a moment and then returned to himself.

"Holy fuck."

Reaching up, he touched the leather band he wore around his wrist. It held a silver medallion in it. Under his touch, it pulsed once with an answering warmth, but he didn't know if that was any sort of reply. Two women with him, and his animals. One of the tomes.

And it seemed this woman had *orin* trailing after her. Either

her, or the book. Perhaps both. Ren wasn't sure and there was no way for him to know. The minds of the *orin* were too alien for him to connect with, and they had nothing that even remotely resembled human emotion.

It made his skin crawl to think they might be after *her* directly.

They can't have you, he thought, his mind teetering dangerously close to that dark, dark edge. Too close.

What in the hell? He pulled himself back under control. He needed to focus, needed to think. Needed to get these two women someplace far safer than here. Back to his home. They'd be safe there and he could deal with this mess. Then he could figure out what was going on with—

Later. Problems now, woman later, Ren.

"Mandy, love, we're going to have company. Rather soon," he murmured, pitching his voice low.

Still, the woman heard him.

Standing just a few feet away and staring at the dog who still blocked her path, she froze.

"What?"

Ren looked up and met her eyes. "Beg your pardon, my dear?" He gave her an absent smile and shook his head, like he wasn't sure what she was asking about.

"What did you just say about company?" she asked, forcing it between gritted teeth.

He blinked and reached up, scratched at his chin. "Company...did I mention company?" He looked at Mandy. "My dear, did I mention us having company tonight? Did you say we were having company? Why did you tell me that you'd invited a friend? We haven't set the house to rights or anything."

Mandy didn't smile.

She was too afraid, although she did a fine job of hiding that.

Chapter Three

He was insane, Aileas realized. She might have thought he was an idiot, but there was a biting intelligence in those eyes.

No. He was just insane.

That's what it was.

He was insane.

And looking at him made her knees go weak. Made her heart race. Looking at him made her feel strangely like crying and laughing. She wanted to throw herself against his chest and just wrap her arms around him and sigh, because she *knew*, she just *knew*, everything would be okay now. *Everything...*

Which meant she was probably as crazy as he seemed to be.

She'd cracked under the strain of her brother's death.

And this guy... Well, hell. He'd cracked under something.

No other way around it.

She'd clearly heard him say they were going to have company.

And then he was off and rambling about whether they were having company, picking up the house? All the while there was a light in his eyes, the light of a warrior. The light of a man preparing to go to battle and commit bloody mayhem.

Open the book. Just open it. Once you do, he can't hurt you.

She flicked a look at the man. Hell, he wasn't going to hurt her. He might be a little...weird, but he wasn't dangerous.

Well, not to me at least. She wasn't sure how she knew *that*, but she did.

Wind came blasting down the road just then and she shivered, rubbing her arms. Shit, she was cold.

She needed to get out of here.

Now.

Forget the crazy guy—even if he was kind of hot—forget the woman. She needed to be gone, and *now.*

Although her heart screamed at the thought of walking away from *him.* Her gut pitched at the idea of leaving him and her spine crawled as though it recognized that walking away from him meant nothing more than certain death.

Stupid, stupid. He's just a guy and he can't help you any more than anybody else.

She went to back away. She needed to get out of here.

He looked up.

His dark gaze met hers. Black brows settled low over his eyes and he sighed, shook his head. The strange, almost unbalanced light in his eyes faded and he gave her a sad, tired smile. "Sorry, lamb. It's too late for that."

"Too late for what?"

"For you to run. If you run, they'll just find you again."

Then he glanced at the woman with him. His sister? Yeah, right.

Abruptly, she realized what he'd said. *They.*

She stiffened. "What are you talking about?" she whispered, her chest tight and aching, her voice raw.

He shifted his gaze back down the road. "Them."

It just wasn't right, Ren decided.

Orin driving in a bleeding Lexus.

They should be in a fucking hearse.

Absently, he tugged the sleeve of his shirt down, making sure the leather cuff on his wrist was concealed.

Wouldn't do to give away the surprise and all.

"Mandy," he murmured.

She slid him a nervous look. He beckoned to her and waited until she was close before he murmured into her ear.

"I need you to get her back to the cabin. Away from this, and do it fast."

If at all possible, he wanted Mandy away from this fight. She was too frail, too mortal. Too easily broken.

And this other woman... Well, Mandy might break, but at least she could fight. This other woman though. She was mortal. Simply mortal and had no idea what was coming for them. And the thought of seeing *her* broken was enough to enrage him. And that was never a good idea. Ren and rage—never a good mix. He did bad, bad things when he was enraged. He didn't have time for a quick cool off either.

He watched the anger, the denial, the fear, dance across Mandy's face.

"You want me to *leave* you here? Alone?" she demanded.

When she pulled away, she was shaking her head. "You're nuts," she said flatly. "Just insane."

"Yes, very often. But not right now. Not yet, at least. Right now, I'm just being realistic." He tapped a finger on her nose and then looked at the car as it crept closer, inching along at perhaps five miles an hour. Why the fuck were they taking so long? "You're mortal. So is she. I'm not. They aren't good enough to end me, and you know it. They'll find it out soon enough. I'll cover you long enough to get her safe and then I'll get away."

Mandy hissed in a breath between her teeth and glanced at the woman.

"Fine," she snarled. She stormed over to the woman and reached out, grabbing the woman with a steely, unrelenting grip. "Come on—we do *not* need to be here right now."

The woman stared at Mandy as though she'd lost her mind.

No, not yet. Mandy was still entirely too sane and she'd stay that way for a while. Pity. Was easier to do this job if you had a few screws loose, in Ren's opinion anyway.

The woman jerked away from Mandy. "Oh, you're dead right. Don't want to be here, thanks. But I think I'll *drive*."

Mandy smiled and then reached into her back pocket.

The blade flashed in the dappled light filtering through the trees. The sound of the woman's gasp rang in Ren's ears. For the briefest moment, he felt stirred to catch Mandy's arm, and what foolishness was that? He knew what she was about. It would take too long to drive to his cabin—the car might move faster, but he'd deliberately built in a spot that wasn't easily accessed by a road.

They could be there in minutes on foot, if they knew the way, which Mandy did.

Trying to drive there, without knowing the way? That could take hours. Days. Never...

Mandy straightened and met the woman's gaze. "You're *not* driving. We're running, and we're doing it now," Mandy said, her voice flat, uncompromising.

"Are you fucking *crazy*?"

Mandy sighed. "No. Not yet," she said, echoing Ren's thoughts a little too closely for comfort. "He is though. Come on. We do not want to be here... *Fuck.*"

Ren heard the strangled tone in Mandy's voice and whipped his head around and stared.

She was doubled over, gripping her stomach, her face pale, sweaty, her eyes almost glassy.

He knelt in front of her, cupped her face in his hands. "What is it?" he asked quietly, forcing her to meet his gaze.

She blinked, her lids lowering over her eyes. "I...I think I might have just screwed us. Or me and her, at least. It's not just the one car, Ren, and it's not just the *orin*. They've got... Oh, fuck." She shoved him away and puked, emptied her guts in one violent, endless stream. "Empath. They've got somebody like us with them. He's been blocking us out. That's why we didn't feel them coming. It's *not* just the one car. There are more, and they are too close."

As the Lexus slowed to a stop behind the woman's car, Mandy straightened and grabbed her blade. Then she reached inside Ren's jacket, pulled out the bladed weapon he'd gotten from a friend a few months back. "Will the animals fight if you aren't here?"

Ren glanced around, studied Pan. Although they had yet to emerge from the shadows, other wolves awaited his summons. "For a bit, love. But it's a moot point—I *will* be here."

"No." She shook her head. "If I hadn't gone and slashed one of her tires, we could put her in the car and just track her down. But now you have to get her out of here."

The *her* in question stood by, staring at the Lexus, an odd, frightened look in her eyes.

They hadn't opened the door, hadn't climbed out.

Waiting, Ren realized.

Just how many others were there?

A chill raced down his spine. Reaching down, he closed his hand around the leather cuff on his wrist and sent another silent summons. *Come on, you wanker. Get your arse down here.*

Mandy reached up and touched his cheek. "Take her, Ren, and go. Get her to your place. They won't take you on there, will they? They know better."

"If they could find it... Well, it would depend on how badly they want *her*," he murmured. Then he glanced at the car. Was it her? Or the book? The fucking book. Had to be one of them. "I can't leave you, though. You're not ready to take on one of them, much less..."

"I know that." Terror flashed in her eyes. "But *I* can come *back*. I have that option. I've got the choice and you and me both know I've already made it."

She looked at the other woman.

The mortal.

The innocent.

An innocent woman who'd somehow had a book fall into her lap. And she'd resisted it. The demon tomes weren't that easy to resist—the evil was a stain, one that leeched out and infected damn near everything after a time.

"*I* can come back," Mandy said. "*She* can't."

"Not like this, damn it." He could feel them...too many of them. Bloody hell, too many. Another car was drawing near too. He could hear the low purr of the motor. "No, Mandy. You're not ready for this."

"I'm not ready for *this*, but I *am* ready for that choice." Her voice shook as she added, "It's my right to make it, and you can't take it from me."

Then she shoved him and started to spin the staff, warming up her arms. "Now get the hell out of here, or she's dead meat. They are getting closer..."

Grief.

It had been ages since he'd felt true grief.

But it tore into him now like jagged, gnawing teeth.

Staring through the mist, he watched.

He knew what awaited.

"I can't just watch this," Will said softly.

The voice that answered wasn't just spoken. It was felt.

It is her choice. Free will, my son. Free will. You cannot take the choice from her.

"Free will," he bit off. Spinning away, he pressed the heels of his hands to his eyes, as though that might help block out the vision of what he knew was coming. "She's *choosing* to die in a very bloody, painful way—is that what you're telling me?"

She chooses to become more. It is her choice.

"No. There's an easier way for her," he muttered. He lifted a hand. He could go to her. She was just a mortal, after all. It was an unfair match. He'd help—

He froze.

Literally. His entire body was frozen by an outside force.

If you go now, her fate is sealed. You will save her life, but she will never again have the chance to become what she has chosen to be. She will never be as she should have become. Would you take that choice from her?

Then, as simple as that, Will was free.

Sagging to his knees, he stared at the floor.

White hair fell, shielding his features.

"It isn't right," he whispered.

But what good did it do to rail against it?

Slowly, he forced himself to his feet and made himself watch.

If she had the courage to die like this, then he would make himself watch. He would be no less courageous than her.

Ren turned away from Mandy, vicious, horrid anger raging inside him. With one punch, he shattered the glass of the woman's back window and he reached in, grabbed the cloth-covered lump in the back seat.

A discordant song rang in his head when he touched it, and he wanted nothing more than to drop it, soak it with gas and burn it until not even ashes remained.

And he would do that—later.

But for now he looked at the woods and sent out the

summons.

Animals came.

From the ground, snakes slithered.

From the trees, birds flocked.

From their dens, bears and foxes crept.

"Guard," he ordered them. But he knew it would change nothing. They would die.

And so would Mandy.

Looking back at her, he said, "I'll be back once I have her safe."

"It will be too late," she said, her voice trembling. "Now get the hell out of here, before I realize that I've become as crazy as you. I'll slow them down the best I can. The ones who still have something human in them...those I can do something about."

An evil smile curled around her lips and she started to spin the bladed staff.

As Ren turned toward the human, he heard a car door open.

"Let's go," he said, his voice short and brusque.

"Go?"

She glanced past him to Mandy. Her eyes went wide and horror flitted across her face. She lunged, but Ren grabbed her arm. She struggled against him.

"Damn it, they're—"

Ren swore and released her arm. She stumbled, a little dazed to be freed. Then she glanced at him.

She never saw his punch coming.

The blow was just enough to knock her out, but not enough to do any lasting harm beyond a headache. Ren caught her before she could drop to the ground. Keeping the book tucked under his arm, he tossed her over his shoulder.

A high-pitched scream—male—rang through the air and Mandy laughed. Ren took off running. He could run, and he could do it fast. But it wouldn't be fast enough.

He watched the woods through the eyes of his creatures and even before he made it halfway home, he knew it was too late.

Mandy fell.

Chapter Four

Will awaited him.

Clothed in white from head to toe, he looked almost luridly pristine.

"Why the hell didn't you arrive sooner?" he growled, shouldering past the older guardian and laying the unconscious woman down on the couch. He dumped the book on the floor, careful to keep it covered. He'd burn it, and then he'd burn the ashes. And if there was anything left of the ashes, he'd burn those as well. Maybe piss on them.

Slowly, he turned and looked at Will.

The other man stood there. His hair, as white as his clothes, fell straight and smooth to his waist. His eyes were clear and pale silver. His brows were as white as his hair.

Just the sight of him infuriated Ren.

Will's ageless face was smooth, unreadable.

Fucking bastard had about as much feeling as a lump of clay. Nothing inside him, Ren thought. Not a damn thing, even though he'd spent a year or two with Mandy himself. Bastard came down from his mountain on high and actually worked with the girl, and he felt *nothing* over her death.

He had to know. Bugger knew every fucking thing.

Pain clawed at Ren. It exploded and he launched himself at Will. Will did nothing to stop him and they crashed through the solid oak bar. Glass shattered and wine bottles exploded. Ren felt bone crunch as he drove his fist into Will's face. "You heartless fuck, why didn't you come?"

Will didn't answer, didn't move to defend himself.

He struck him again, and again, the rage tearing at him. Dark, black memories of another girl he'd been helpless to save rose up, taunting him, merciless and cruel. Visions of Mandy's fallen body, the memory of Rose... With each one, he struck Will harder, harder.

Then suddenly, he started to cry. Pulling away, he sat on the floor, hardly able to think past the pain ripping through him.

"Oh, fuck, Mandy. She was just a kid, Will. Why didn't you..."

The words froze in his throat, all but choking him. The memory of a small, heart-shaped face, big, dark eyes lingered in his mind. A sweet, mischievous smile and a voice like an angel...until a devil had taken her.

Her screams...

Rose.

"Fuck, fuck, fuck..."

It was like he was living through that time all over again...

A hand touched his shoulder.

Ren wanted to knock it away, but he didn't have the energy.

"Mandy made her choice," Will said quietly.

Ren looked up.

Blood splattered Will's face, staining his perfect features, the pristine white clothes. Blood, dirt, grime and wine. The older man looked a bit less angelic now.

Ren shook his head. "She couldn't have wanted to die that way."

Will crouched down in front of Ren and reached out, tracing his hand along the thin, nearly invisible scar that ran along the underside of Ren's neck. Ren knew he'd gotten the scar when his mortal life ended, but he didn't know how.

He didn't remember those events...nor did he want to.

"You didn't die easy. Even now, after more than a century, you hide from it," Will said quietly. "For some reason, it is our fate to go screaming into death. So few of us go easily, Ren. But she went not just willingly, but with a courage many of us cannot claim. To save a woman she doesn't even know."

"And alone. She died alone."

"Yes." There was an odd note in Will's voice and Ren narrowed his eyes, studied the other man's face.

It struck him then.

Rather blindingly, he realized.

"You wanted to be there. To stop it."

"I could not. If I had gone, it would have interfered with a choice she had made. It was not my place," Will said, and there was a world of rage in those simple words.

Slowly, Will rose and held out a hand.

Ren stood, and as he did he grew aware of the pain in his hands. It was fading already, but for him to even be aware of it... Studying Will's battered face, he said, "It seems as though I should feel sorry for that."

Will lifted a brow that was now russet with blood. "Does it?"

"I'm not."

With a grim sigh, Will said, "Oddly enough, neither am I." Then he looked past Ren to the woman sleeping on the couch. "I know my duty, and I know it well. But never has it been so hard to remember it. The guilt of this... If ones like us could die from guilt alone, I think this might kill me."

"We need to go...take care of Mandy," Ren said. Then he looked past Will to study the woman who'd brought this darkness to his woods. "I...I have to go with you. I have to. But she might wake. The book..."

Will shook his head. "She will not." He moved to stand by her, touched his fingers to her brow. "Not for a time, at least. She'll be safe here, and none of them can sense the book here. As you well know. She's safe from its taint. If she was going to fall to it, she would have already done so."

Then he looked at Ren. "Do not blame her, Ren. She carries no blame in this."

Ren's lips peeled back from his lips in a snarl. "No, she's just traipsing around the countryside with a demon tome—the picture of innocence there."

"All is not as it seems, Ren. You've lived long enough to know that."

Ren knew his home was secure.

It was protected by more than just mortal security. As he slid outside, the warmth that hid his presence from the world—and the world from him—closed around the woman who slept inside.

Tucked inside his home, even Mandy with her talented empathic skills would have a hard time locating her now.

Or rather...she would have.

Now she was dead.

"She is not dead," Will said. "She sleeps."

"Come off it," Ren snarled. "She's dead. We die, and He brings us back. I don't need poetical nonsense to comfort and ease me. She died bloody, and she died alone, and she..."

His voice trailed off. Sighing, he skimmed a hand across the smooth skin of his scalp. "I need to move past this for now. I don't want Mandy waking to this. I'll rant and rave and have my merry, psychotic little breakdown when she's off acclimating—how does that sound?"

Will gave him a half smile.

Even from yards away, they smelled it.

Blood, shit, urine. Death.

The animals had crept off to die away from the fight. One of the foxes was still lying there, panting, even though something had torn into him—literally. Crouching beside him, Ren drew a blade and murmured, "Thank you."

The fox's liquid eyes stared into his. He held the small animal's gaze with his, kept him distracted, kept him from feeling the pain. The fox didn't feel it, but Ren did. He kept it from showing as his gut turned to fire and ice, as everything inside him screamed out in denial at what felt like death.

He wasn't dying, but his body didn't *know* that—it felt like it was dying and his body reacted accordingly—heart racing, lungs tight, adrenaline crashing through his system...and the pain, centered exactly where the little fox had been hurt.

Despite the pain, despite the adrenaline rush and the false sensation of death, Ren's voice, his hand was steady as he stroked the little animal's head. The fox gazed at Ren in fascination, adoration. Once the animal was no longer feeling the pain or the fear, he pierced the creature's heart with his knife, ending the pain. He couldn't have healed the fox—the damage was too severe.

"You handle it easier than you used to," Will said quietly.

Ren drew a folded cloth from his pocket and cleaned his blade. "No, I don't. I just no longer let it show." All his life, he'd felt a kinship with the creatures that walked the earth, creatures that flew, creatures that crept along on their bellies, and with humans. He just felt more at ease with animals than with people.

After all, they'd always welcomed him. Always accepted him.

While his father...

Now, mate, you can't go thinking down that path right now, he told himself.

Not wise. Not at all.

They neared the rise and Ren's gut gave one viscous twist. With his lips peeling back in a snarl, he leaped down, clearing the earth in one leap.

Will beat him to it.

The *vankyr*—bloody, beastly demons—turned their blood-stained faces to them and grinned. Ren bent down and grabbed his staff from the ground. Specially designed, bladed at both ends, it fit in his hands like it had been made for him and him alone. And it had.

One *vankyr* leaped for him. As he buried the blade in the heart of the demon-possessed human, the rage threatened to consume him. He could see, somewhere in the back of those monstrous eyes, the remnants of the mortal soul.

The mortal, trapped, an unwittingly and unwilling prisoner, went screaming to his death. Forcing the words out, Ren said, "Have mercy on him."

It was hard to force the words though. Demons couldn't take one who was completely unwilling. It simply did not happen—somehow, this man had done something, said something that had opened him up for possession. He had no idea it would lead to this, had no idea he'd become the weapon in a horrific murder.

Nonetheless, it had happened.

Nonetheless, the blood of Ren's friend stained his face, hands and mouth.

They'd fed on her.

While bile rose in his throat, Ren spun around and faced

another.

And another.

And another.

There were ten in all—a lot for the *vankyr*. Seemed like overkill. *Vankyr* were good for nothing but destruction anyway.

As the last one sank to the ground, Ren muttered to the dying soul trapped inside and then looked for Will.

The old Grimm wasn't hard to find.

He was where Ren would have expected him to be.

Mandy...

Dear Lord.

Her body had been...savaged.

There were no other words for it.

Vankyr weren't known for their refined tastes—rape, pillage, plunder...feast. That was all they wished. Living. Dead. It didn't matter. Ren had one thing to be grateful for—Mandy hadn't been alive for much of this. There simply wasn't enough blood.

And her face, oddly enough, was peaceful. Peaceful, and thankfully untouched. That was a memory he wouldn't have to take into the nights with him.

Her eyes, lifeless, were locked on the sky overhead and there was a faint smirk on her lips. Like she knew a secret none of her killers knew.

Ren reckoned that was even the case.

None of them would survive the week.

He'd hunt them all down.

He had to swallow the bile churning up his throat. He'd seen ugly things, but what they'd done to her...

Ren shook his head. "You can't bring her back here."

"No." Will's voice was soft, almost eerily so. Flat, emotionless. Carefully so.

When the other Grimm looked up, there was a screaming, empty hell in those dark eyes.

The fury there...

"Do you see?" Will asked, in that strange, quiet voice. He wasn't looking at Ren. It was like he was seeing something else...something other.

Ren suspected he knew just what Will saw too.

The older Grimm's gifts were varied...and endless.

Ren imagined he was seeing every awful atrocity done to her. As it was done.

A cold wind danced down his spine.

"Do you see what they've done to her?" Will whispered.

Crouching down in front of Will, Ren reached out, touched the man's shoulder. "Yes, I see, old man. I see. But she doesn't have to. She wasn't here when most of this happened. She didn't see it, she doesn't know what happened. She won't ever know it."

Something sparked in Will's eyes. Those silver eyes flashed.

Power rolled from him.

Ren gritted his teeth as it struck him. "Tone it down, old man. Take her now...she's waiting to come back. You said she'd made her choice and she can't very well come back without you, now can she? You're kind of like that old bastard Charon in the ancient Greek legends—the one who guides the boat on the River Styx? Except you don't ferry people to Hades. You ferry the Grimms back to life, and you can't bring Mandy to us if you go and...well, have a nervous breakdown. That's my territory anyway."

Will lowered his head.

White hair fell, hiding his face.

When he looked up once more, a mask had fallen and that ageless face was unreadable. Will rose and looked around them, studying the devastation on the road. Bodies—thirteen of them. Between Will and Ren, they'd killed ten *vankyr*, which meant Mandy had killed the other three.

Ren was prepared to have the mess of cleaning it all up dumped in his lap, but to his surprise, Will lifted a hand. A flash of white came, blinding Ren. When he could see again, it was to find the area meticulous. All signs of death, destruction and devastation were gone. Even the bodies of the animals who'd died at Ren's call were gone.

All that remained were the cars. The woman's car was unmarked—even the window he'd busted to get the book was whole, untouched. And the tire Mandy had slashed was fixed as well.

Just a few feet away lay Mandy.

As Ren watched, Will knelt by her side. With a gentleness that might have surprised some, he gathered her lifeless, broken body in his arms.

"Will..." Ren's voice faded and he closed his eyes, made himself banish the images of Mandy from his mind. If she came back to train with him, he couldn't have those memories in his mind. There was no telling what the transition would do to her gifts and he didn't want his memories to become hers as well. "Will she return here?"

Will flicked a glance at him and then shook his head. "It is unlikely. I think you're about to go on a different path. I'm going to have a few others come out. They'll be here within a few hours. The woods won't be empty for the next few nights and I'm not leaving you here alone."

"I can handle myself," Ren said, scowling.

He didn't want anybody crawling through his woods, even if they were fellow Grimms.

"It's no longer just you," Will reminded him, cradling Mandy's lifeless body. To Ren's surprise, a faint, bittersweet smile curled the other man's face. "Life is all about doors, you know that? One closes. Another opens."

Then, before Ren could process that, Will was gone.

Chapter Five

As he drew nearer to his home, Ren reached out with his senses and knew that the woman, this nameless intruder, still slept. He couldn't feel much from her beyond that unless he really lowered his shields. He didn't really want to do that.

It had been ages since he'd used his abilities on a mortal. He was probably a bit rusty.

Which suited him nicely.

He didn't want to be in touch with mortals. Most of them had caused him nothing but pain in his years before he'd left his mortality behind.

Even those who hadn't caused him harm directly had been somehow tied to pain and suffering. His sister, his mother.

Mandy—

No. He wouldn't blame the girl. She'd made the decision she'd needed to make for her, and it wasn't like he had truly lost her, had he? He'd see her again in time, and they could find that friendship again.

Friendships were something he had too few of. Friends were even harder to come by than lovers.

Aw, but hell, it hurt. The loss of her was going to be an ache in his heart. Having somebody there to talk with, it had done something to ease the darkness in him, and because of Mandy's empathy, she hadn't *leaked* all over him.

He might not connect well with human emotions as he once had, but human emotions—well, they were a lot like odors. They collected. And he was tuned in on their frequency. He didn't have to connect with those emotions for all the baggage to drive him to the edge.

He was already insane. Having that pressing in on him...

As he circled through the trees to his home, he tried to make himself quit thinking about the emptiness that would await him once he'd divested himself of his unexpected guest. Tried not to think about the odd, empty sensation it left in his heart when he thought about her leaving. She'd leave, after all. She'd have to, and he'd be alone.

Again.

An empty home. What of it? Not like he wasn't used to it. He did best solo anyway. It was how he'd spent so much of the past century. Just the occasional job with Elle, and that was a thing of the past now that the pretty princess had reunited with her prince charming.

Fucking wanker.

There was a rustle of sound where there shouldn't be. Ren knew these woods and could glide through them in complete silence. Easing to a stop, he waited near a tree and cocked his head, listening.

There was a reason he hadn't gone straight to his home.

The divine protections around his home would keep any of the demon-possessed from finding it, so long as he wasn't fool enough to *lead* them there.

Ren touched the cuff at his wrist. Some didn't need that extra connection. He did. Reaching out, he closed his eyes and waited.

His consciousness brushed against something alien, evil...cunning. And all too clear-thinking.

Orin. Curling his lip, Ren opened his eyes and stared into the trees, shifting only his eyes, looking for the slightest movement that would betray the enemy's location.

Fucking *orin.* He loathed them. All of the demons that crept through from the netherplains were evil bastards, but many were creatures of sheer chaos, mindless lust, or so focused on a blind hunger. Ren could dispatch them without letting emotion interfere.

But the *orin,* there was something worse about them.

They were evil. But they were thinkers. There is something worse about an evil that thinks. Something worse about an evil that can look you in the eye and calmly, coolly plan on sucking the soul out of everybody you love, everybody you come in contact with, slowly killing them from the inside.

Orin—the closest thing to vampires in existence, and

nothing romantic about them, no matter what modern romantic fiction might say...and Ren should know. The whisper of memory tried to come in him, but he shoved it aside, shoved it down.

Not here. Not now.

Slowly skimming a finger down the staff still stained with Mandy's blood, he leaned a shoulder against the tree. He had a need to taste some blood of his own. Perhaps he could see the appeal of vampires. He wouldn't feast on the blood of his enemy, but he'd damn well feel the slippery warmth of it on his hands.

The *orin* moved past the tree, not even sensing Ren's presence. Ren used his staff to tap him on the shoulder.

"Hello there. Looking for Grandma's house?"

The once-human body was now nothing more than a vehicle for the demonic host, and he spun with a speed no mortal possessed. Ren remained where he was, flashing a toothy at the *orin.* "Lost?" he asked. "Not a good place for it."

The *orin* pounced.

They were vicious creatures, and knowing death was imminent only added to that.

But Ren wasn't just vicious—he was pissed.

In under thirty seconds, he had the *orin* under him on the ground. Feeling the demon scrambling to escape, he twisted his staff and pressed the blade to the fragile wall of the human's chest. "There isn't anybody close enough for you to jump to," Ren murmured. "You're well and truly out of luck."

The *orin* snarled and tried to push against whatever protected Ren's sorry soul. It wasn't the first time a demon had tried to push into one of the Grimms. Although it left Ren with a nasty, oily feeling, like slime clung to him inside and out, it had no effect and only weakened the *orin.*

Sagging back into the human, the *orin* whispered, "Your little protégé wasn't very good. She didn't last five minutes. You should have trained her better. How long did she have her wings?"

"Hmm. My little protégé didn't have her wings...yet. But you, you bloody dumb-fuck, sent her off to get them." Patting the *orin*'s cheek with the flat of his hand—hard—Ren throttled down the rage before it could peek through. "She was still mortal, you see. And you gave her what she needed to get the wings. Death. Score one for our side, mate. Now...let me talk to your ride."

"Too late for him. You can't get me out unless I want out and you already made it clear there is no place for me to jump."

Ren used the flat of his hand again, but this time wasn't a tap. He slapped him. Hard. "Now. Or instead of piercing this blade through your heart and being done with it, I'll start somewhere farther south. You're well and truly inside the body. You *will* feel the pain."

The *orin* sneered at him. And instead, he pushed himself *up*, impaling his chest on the blade.

It wasn't but a few seconds later that the heart stopped beating.

The mortal's soul was fading even as Ren whispered, "Have mercy."

There was a strange look of peace on his face, terribly at odds with the decidedly *non-peaceful* shriek the *orin* gave as it too, died. It didn't go quietly into the night, that one.

Rising, Ren wiped the blades of the staff off as best as he could. He couldn't retract them until he'd cleaned it—if he mucked the thing up, Rip wouldn't be so accommodating about providing him with a new one.

He lingered over the body a moment. He'd have to deal with it, but not now. Sending out a silent request, he made sure the creatures knew not to come near. It would tempt some of them terribly, but the taint clinging to the body would likely be enough to throw even the most determined predator off. Providing the predator had a nose stronger than a mortal's, and animals did.

This man, he even smelled of death. The *orin* had done some terrible things while living inside his body.

Had he known?

Had he been aware?

Most of the Grimms didn't think so, but Ren wasn't so sure. Too often, he'd gazed into the eyes of the men and women he'd been forced to kill and he'd seen that silent, screaming agony.

Like your own...?

Ren shook his head, shrugging the voice off.

Best to get back to the house now. Perhaps he would even have a bit of good fortune smile on him and the other demons would come looking for their fallen comrade, deal with him.

But then again, perhaps he was more insane then he thought.

London, 1884

"*Oh, please, doctor, is there nothing more you can do for him?*"

Thomas rolled onto his side and curled into himself, pretending he could not hear his mother begging, pleading.

For him.

Begging yet another doctor to try and save him.

I do not need to be saved.

What he needed was simply a knife and a few minutes alone.

But they wouldn't give him that, not since the last time. She had found him, and he regretted that. The pain in her eyes, and the pain he'd felt coming from her...

Squeezing his eyes closed, he tried not to think on it. Of it. It did no good, truly. Something tickled his chin and he looked down, found the small mouse on his bed again.

Hearing his mother's footsteps behind him, he curled in closer and used his hand to hide the little thing. It bothered her terribly to see the little animals that came to him. Almost as much as it bothered her when he told her he could feel her pain, her pleasure...just as he'd known the man who had been coming to court her had also been looking at Thomas' little sister with a wicked, wicked eye.

Perverted, evil bastard.

She hadn't wanted to believe him, but the love she had for her daughter wouldn't let her disbelieve him, and she hadn't let the man come calling again. In truth, Thomas knew she *did* believe him and that scared her more than anything else.

Unnatural.

Yes. It was. He knew it wasn't natural—if it was natural, it wouldn't hurt him the way it did. All the pain he felt from others felt like it would split his skin, turn his insides outside and leave him hollow, dying and drained.

He hadn't asked for it.

He hadn't wanted to feel it when his father lay sick and dying, wasting away inside. Thomas had almost died that summer too, from a sickness none of the doctors understood. Thomas had tried to tell them—*it eats away at me. I feel it on the inside.*

And then his father died. Thomas did not.

After that though, he felt the pain of others more acutely. People, animals, it didn't matter. It frightened his mother terribly. As he grew from a skinny boy to that gawky stage just before manhood, the terrible curse grew stronger and it started to drive him mad. Bit by bit, until he could no longer leave his home.

Then he could no longer stand to look upon one who wasn't of his family.

It wasn't until the man had come calling on his mother, and laid eyes on his sister, that Thomas forced himself to leave the room. For the first time in weeks, perhaps even months.

He hadn't wished to, but he had no choice. He'd felt the man's evil, like a stain that would spread over their entire home. Cursing it, damning it.

Mother couldn't let that man come back.

She couldn't.

Mother believed him, though she never said the words.

She wouldn't let the monster near Rose, and that was all Thomas needed.

But the monster came back anyway.

Weeks later.

Mother had all but forgotten him in her determination to find a "cure" for her son, somebody who would make him forget his insane notions that he could feel the emotions of others, that would make him forget his unhealthy devotion to the small mammals that came and went at all hours of the night.

The monster returned. He wore a different face, but he *felt* the same. Thomas had known he was there. Thomas had known. But Mother wouldn't believe him. Mother wouldn't believe him, and then, it was too late...

North Woods, WI

She still slept when he came into the house, but he didn't have much time.

Not the time he needed to make sure the book was well and truly eliminated. They didn't burn as easy as a sodding book should burn, after all. It was like whoever had crafted them had found some ungodly way to resist the laws of physics.

Burning them required patience, time. Extra gasoline was preferable and Ren intended to make sure this bastard burned like wildfire.

So instead of attempting to do it, he wrapped it with care and tucked it in a specially crafted space under the floorboards in his room. None of the demonic could sense anything about his home, so unless they stumbled on it through sheer dumb luck, they'd never find this place. And he'd make sure his guest didn't find the book.

He was also going to have some extra eyes on his home though. Already the nocturnal creatures were on the prowl. If anything, anyone out of place came near his home, he'd know.

It was likely they wouldn't bother with the book at this point. It wasn't like there weren't more. By now, they'd know what he was, and for the most part the demonic were cowards. They wouldn't openly face off with the Grimms, because they never won.

Even as that thought circled through his mind, he felt something ripple along his senses.

A familiar, warm presence.

Followed by another familiar, not-so-welcome presence.

Elle. Michael. Then...Rip and Greta.

Farther off, there was another, and another. Another.

Seven in all, and three he didn't recognize.

Will had been rather serious about sending others, it seemed.

Seven Grimms.

In his woods.

"Turning my home into the Enchanted Forest, Will?" Ren murmured as he rose and moved to the window. He saw a familiar, dark head of hair moving through the trees toward his home.

Greta, with her man Rip at her side.

She'd been the one to bring Mandy to them.

He sensed the echo of her grief.

And for a brief moment, he knew he needed to share that. At least that. Slipping out of the small bedroom he kept for guests, he used the balcony door to leave the house after one quick glance at the sleeping woman.

"It was quick though," Greta said, looking at Ren as though she needed that reassurance.

"It would have been." He wished he could tell her something to ease the pain, but she would know if he lied. And pretty lies were still just lies. Greta would take an honest truth any day, he knew that much.

He *should* know that much about her. They were friends, of a fashion. She had helped train him after all. Her gift was akin to his, in a way. Although he couldn't coerce people like she could, he could manipulate emotion. They tried to pair people with similar gifts together for a time.

She hadn't been his only trainer, but she had been easier—relatively speaking—to work with than others. More, she'd probably been his first friend. He looked at her and gave her a tight, strained smile, then met Rip's solemn face.

"She's with Will now," Ren said.

Rip's mouth twisted and he said, "I wish I could say that was comforting."

"Actually, it kind of is," Greta said. "Will is...different with her."

"Less of a bastard or more?" Rip asked.

She smacked him lightly. Then she scrubbed her hands over her face and sighed. "This never gets easier. Hundreds of years, and even knowing she will come back, it still hurts." She leaned against her husband, studying Ren with knowing eyes. "Are you going to be okay? Want me to hang around tonight? There's enough of us combing the woods that I won't be missed if you need an ear."

"Hey, I'd miss you." Rip squeezed her and nuzzled her neck, then glanced at Ren and gave him a smile. "But I'd understand too."

Ren shook his head. "It isn't necessary." He caught Greta's hand in his and brushed a kiss against her fingertips. "But thank you."

Chapter Six

Aileas came awake just as the door opened.

She barely heard it, and if it wasn't for the rush of cold wind washing over her body, she might not have awakened at all.

There was no sound to give him away—no floorboards creaked and there wasn't even the quiet brush of clothing rustling as he walked, but she knew he was there.

Standing there, and watching her.

Keeping her eyes closed and her breathing slow, she waited.

Couldn't open her eyes and look at him, not yet.

She was too fucking terrified.

As long as she didn't move, she was fine. Granted, her heart raced like a car doing the Indy 500, but so what? It wasn't like he...could...hear...

Abruptly, her heartbeat sped up for reasons she couldn't understand. What was he doing?

"If you're going to pretend to be asleep, would you like me to move you to my bed? It's more comfortable."

Huffing out a breath, she opened her eyes and met the dark, unsmiling eyes of the man she'd encountered in the forest.

Those eyes—hell, they were just plain unsettling.

They looked black.

Logically, she knew they weren't. They couldn't be jet-black, but she couldn't discern any visible pupil, they were that dark.

And she had the feeling they saw clear through to her soul, had the feeling he was fully aware of her terror and...other things.

"So are you awake or should I put you someplace more

comfortable while you decide?"

Aileas scowled. "It's pretty obvious I'm awake."

He shrugged lazily. "Well, if you decide you'd rather be asleep for a while, then be asleep."

"I can't just decide to *be asleep*." And there was no way she could sleep now, not with him standing so close, watching her. "Who are you?"

With a queer smile on his lips, he murmured, "I'm called Ren."

Odd phrasing there. Called. Not *my name is...* Nervous, she swallowed and sat up. She edged away from him, farther down the couch. Once she had put some distance between them, she glanced around the airy, spacious cabin.

It was brightly lit and open. The floor plan was laid out so that the dining room, living room, kitchen and bedroom were all one huge area. A long counter separated the kitchen area from the rest of the room and she could see the gleam of copper pots and pans hanging from a rack on the ceiling.

On the other side of the floor, just across from where she sat on the couch, she could see the bed—and damn, what a bed. It was almost the size of a lake. The bed was tucked under a window every bit as large as itself, and she could see the woods through the glass.

There was a skylight over the bed too, and some part of her heart sighed in wistful envy. She'd always wanted a skylight over her bed so she could stare up at the stars as she drifted off to sleep.

Along the far wall there were a couple of doors, a bathroom, she supposed—she *hoped*. Maybe another bedroom. But she already knew there wasn't anybody else in the cabin with them.

Call it gut instinct. Call it women's intuition, whatever.

But they were alone.

How in the hell had they gotten here? She remembered the drive up here. Remembered almost hitting one giant-ass dog. This guy. A girl. And then things got very, very fuzzy. The girl. Where was she?

A smirk twisted her lips. His...*sister*. "Where's the other woman? Your sister."

He lifted a sooty-black brow. "What sister? I don't have a

sister."

Aileas gaped at him. "The woman. You know, the one you left standing by my car after she slashed my tires. The one you left down there with a bunch of crazy..."

"Crazy what? And left standing where? I found you wondering through the woods." He cocked his head, looking rather intrigued. "You've quite the imagination on you."

"I'm not imagining this," she snarled.

"Well, I don't have a sister." Then he frowned, his gaze shifting off to stare into the distance. "At least not anymore. I had a sister, once. She died, a long, long time ago."

She opened her mouth, that automatic apology on her lips, but it died, faded away. How many times had she wanted to scream when people had said, *Oh, I'm so sorry for your loss.* Sorry. They were sorry. What good had that done her?

Sorry. Such an empty word.

It meant nothing. Frowning, she edged away from him and stood. "You're telling me you don't have a sister. That there wasn't a girl with you when you found me on the road. What about the dog?"

"Dog? No. I don't have a dog. And what's this about a car?" He rested his chin on a fist and studied her face. "Maybe you cracked your head. As I said, I found you wondering around the woods, looking rather...well, out of it. Maybe you hit your head or something. Do you know your name?"

"I didn't hit my head," she muttered, reaching up to touch her head. As soon as she realized what she was doing, she jerked her hand down. She hadn't hit her head. Damn it, she'd seen *this* man with a woman, and a dog near her car.

The book. Damn it. She started to prowl around the room. He'd grabbed the book, and considering how easily he'd found it, and the way he'd handled it, so careful not to touch it, it was like *he* had recognized the nastiness of the book too. If she found the book here, then that was proof...proof of what though?

What did it prove if she found the book?

But the book was nowhere that she could see. It didn't mean anything though. She'd been unconscious—there had been plenty of time for him to hide it.

"Take me to my car," she said quietly. He'd broken the window. He could hide the book, and he could pretend no woman, and no big-ass dog had been there, but he couldn't act like he hadn't busted out that window. Even if he'd had the foresight to get it repaired—*if* he could do it that fast out here in the boonies—there would still be shattered, slivered glass, right?

Although how had he broken it like that?

With just a single strike?

"Your car." He gave her a puzzled, disconnected smile, a slightly crazed smile. "You have a car." Then he shook his head and muttered to the ceiling, "I should have thought to look for a car, of course."

"You've *seen* my car," she snapped out.

"No. Sorry, love."

He didn't know why he was needling her, truly. Maybe just to relieve the rising tension inside. Pretending to be the crazy bastard—or at least crazier than he was—had always amused him. But there was something about the way she looked at him, as if she couldn't quite decide if she wanted to smack him or what, it was a nice...distraction.

Just a distraction, of course. It didn't do much to ease the ache in his heart, and it also didn't do a damn thing to ease the vague, itchy restlessness he felt every time he looked at her.

Best thing for that would be to get her out of here, but that couldn't be done tonight.

Maybe he should have taken Greta up on her offer after all. A third person here could have proven a better distraction, and Greta, when she wanted, had a soothing way about her.

He moved into the kitchen, leaving her staring at his back. "I can't take you out looking for a car just yet anyway. It's getting late." He waved vaguely toward the windows, glad it got dark earlier in the woods. Although he had no trouble navigating the woods at night, he wasn't about to take her out into the darkness.

He wasn't sure how many demons waited.

Some, he knew.

He could feel their presence, an itch on his skin. He hadn't raised his personal protections—couldn't afford to, not while the possessed humans were still around his home. Had to protect his intruder, after all.

Even with the extra Grimms out there in force, this woman was his responsibility.

His.

The word echoed around in his mind. Echoed. His hands started to itch. Heart started to pound. The longer he looked at her, the worse it got.

His.

She stood there, shifting from one foot to another, her eyes big and dark and velvety soft. "I need to get to my car," she said. "I need to get out of here."

"Yes, yes." Although he wasn't hungry, he busied himself getting something to fix out of the freezer. Steak. Easy enough. Potatoes. A salad. He wasn't hungry, but he should eat and she needed to. "I know, you want to find this car of yours, but it's late and we can't very well go trampling around through the woods at night if you're not sure where we're going, now can we? Do you even know where you left it?"

She opened her mouth. Probably to argue with him again, insist that he'd seen the car. He knew the exact moment when she decided not to bother. This was a bit he'd played often—he knew almost to the second how long he could push a person before they decided it wasn't worth it, and they'd try another tactic.

He could feel the edginess coming off her, but it wasn't panicked. Good. He didn't need her thinking he was going to slaughter her in her sleep. That wouldn't make for a restful night. He didn't mind her being uneasy, but terrified, no.

"You like red?"

She blinked. Those big brown eyes shifted from irritation to confusion. "Red?" she repeated. "As in the color?"

"Well, it is a lovely color." He imagined she would wear red rather well. Red satin against that pale, pale flesh, those pearls lying against the vivid color...

Then he frowned, wondered where that thought had come from. Turning it aside, he crouched down in front of the small wine-chiller. The wine chiller that had been crushed when he

55

and Will had their little...tussle.

All undone now. Will, Ren knew. Although Will's clothes had still been stained with the blood and the wine when he disappeared with Mandy earlier.

Grabbing a bottle of red, he showed it to his guest. His still-nameless guest. "Red," he repeated. "Do you like red? And I still don't think I know your name."

"Aileas," she murmured, eyeing the bottle in his hand.

"Aileas." He smiled as he echoed the name.

She lifted a brow at him. "I'm impressed. You didn't butcher it."

"I've heard it before," he said, shrugging. It had been some time—years, actually. "Not here, of course."

"Hmm. I thought there was an accent there. You're not American."

No. No, he wasn't. Lifting the bottle, he asked again, "You like red or not, Aileas?"

"Yes, I like red." A polite smile curled her lips. Then she scowled, wrinkling her nose. "Screw it. No. I don't really like red wine, unless it's sweet. It always makes me feel like somebody crammed a dozen crackers in my mouth and didn't bother giving me any water. Now if you have sweet wine, yes. I like *sweet* red wines."

"I'm making steak. You can't do sweet wines with steak...Aileas," he murmured her name again, just to feel it on his tongue. He really did like the way it felt. It felt like...home almost.

"Says who? If I'm drinking the wine and eating the steak and I don't care if I'm eating a steak and drinking a sweet wine, why can't I?"

Ren cocked a brow. He had to admire that logic, even if she was completely wrong. Kneeling down, he reached inside the chiller again. The muscat wines there had been picked out by Mandy, but Will had already said she wouldn't be returning here.

Might as well see somebody enjoy them. Somehow, he suspected his guest—Aileas—needed a glass of wine.

He sure as hell needed one.

"What the hell," he murmured. "If you'd like to have your dessert with your steak, why not?"

Her eyes lit up as she saw the silver label on the bottle he sat on the counter and he smiled a little.

Those eyes...they tugged at him. "Like that one, do you?"

"Yes."

Reaching for the corkscrew, he opened the bottle of wine and poured her a glass. From the corner of his eye, he saw her rubbing at her head, frowning. Through the low-level shields he kept up, he could feel her vague unease. Wondering now if she *had* hit her head—despite the fact that she was actually very convinced she hadn't—if she did have a head injury, and if she should be drinking the wine.

He sighed and lowered his shields. It had been years, decades...longer, since he'd attempted to use his gift on any mortal. But she couldn't be running off on him. He'd have to stop her and that would frighten her more. She couldn't leave his home tonight. Too much danger in the woods. And although he had it under control, his temper was balanced on a hair trigger tonight. He didn't need to tangle with her and risk setting it off.

As he poured the wine, he took a deep, slow breath and centered himself. He'd need to touch her.

A quick touch, make sure she was open. Should be, otherwise he wouldn't be able to feel this much from her.

As long as she was open, he could plant a gentle, easy suggestion for her to relax. Trust him. Rest through the night. It would be quick and easy, nothing he couldn't handle. He might not use his gift, but they'd seen to it that he was trained. That was one thing he hadn't had much choice with. Calming a tired, nervous woman who already looked exhausted wouldn't take that much, surely.

Come morning, he'd get her pretty ass out of these woods and figure out how to handle the demons who'd set themselves on her tail.

He had a score to settle with them anyway.

Setting the wine bottle aside, he turned and gave Aileas a small smile. Easy. The one he used when he was dealing with his animals, or the few times he had to handle children. Not the crazy, just-this-side-of-maniacal smile that had made grown men piss in their pants.

"Your wine," he said, strolling over to her. He handed it to her and casually, easy as you please, he hooked his arm through hers, guiding her to the table. "Why don't you sit in here a bit, keep me company while I cook? Not too often I have company, you know..."

As he spoke, he pushed. Oh, she was open.

And holy fuck, the pain inside her. It screamed at him. A loss, like a bloody, gaping hole. Fear, gnawing and deep. Determination. He also sensed that taint he'd felt earlier. But it was light, just hovering on the surface...like the book had been trying to sink its evil inside her. It clung to her skin, but it couldn't get any deeper.

Her soul...it was strong.

It called to him too, damn it. The same way her eyes did.

Ignoring that deep, relentless tug, Ren planted a suggestion, buried it inside her heart. *You can relax here. You are safe. You can sleep and nothing, nobody, no thing shall harm you. I will keep you safe.*

Her subconscious resisted. *You can't.*

She hadn't felt safe in a long, long time.

I can, he promised. He wanted to do more than that, actually. He wanted to cuddle her close, run his hands through that silken, dark hair and promise her all sorts of nonsense...not just that he could and would protect her, but more. So much more.

Mentally, he jerked himself back, slightly stunned at the path his thoughts were taking.

Getting a little off tangent there, mate, he told himself. *Way off tangent.* He just needed her calm. And asleep. So she didn't rabbit on him. That was all.

But he didn't believe it. Not even for a second.

You are safe, he whispered inside her heart again. *Safe, I swear on my soul.*

Then he retreated. It was the best he could, he told himself.

Retreating, pulling away from her, it was something he did not want to do.

Only seconds had passed.

When he looked into her eyes, he gave her a smile and pulled out the chair, let her sit.

Just seconds. Mere seconds.

Yet, as he moved to the counter to work on dinner, the ground beneath him no longer felt quite so...steady.

Chapter Seven

It felt too easy sitting here.

Watching him.

Easy, almost natural.

Part of her realized she needed to be out of here, out of here and gone. Running. Hard and fast away from this place.

Someplace *safe*.

Not away from him, exactly.

He wasn't a threat to her. She didn't know how she knew that, and she also wasn't sure how she knew that he'd help her if he could.

Aileas just knew there was a threat, and it wasn't some bump on her head.

Absently, she reached up again and touched her head, searching for that nonexistent bump. She hadn't hit her head. She knew she hadn't. She hadn't hit her head, and she damn well had seen him on the road with a woman, and the dog—shit. Not a dog—more than a dog. Part-dog, part-wolf, if she knew anything about animals, and she should considering they were her life's work.

Assuming she could ever get back to her life.

If she could ever stop running...

She lifted her glass and sipped the cold, sweet wine, letting it roll down her throat and warm her belly.

She was so tired of running.

"How do you like your steak?"

Looking up, she met Ren's eyes. Such dark, dark eyes. Full of secrets. And pain.

"Excuse me?"

"Your steak," he said again, angling his chin toward the small countertop grill. Then he grinned, strong white teeth flashing at her in a wide grin. "Please don't tell me that you're vegetarian. I don't have much to feed somebody who doesn't eat meat."

"Oh, no. I'm a carnivore. Ahhh...medium rare," she said, forcing a smile. That grin of his should be illegal. It made him look like a pirate. Pirate... That kind of suited him. With that smooth, naked scalp of his, that dark swarthy skin, he looked a bit piratical. Maybe give him a patch. A gold hoop in one ear, and a parrot on his shoulder.

Her mind started to wonder and she could see him standing, legs spread on the deck of a ship. But it wasn't a parrot on his shoulder. It was an owl. In the middle of the day. Didn't make much sense, but then again, this was a daydream. Daydreams didn't need to make sense. He turned and murmured to the owl, his voice soft and low. Sad. The owl nuzzled his cheek and a smile curled his lips.

"...salad?"

Aileas jerked and the daydream shattered around her. Looking up, she saw him standing just a few feet away, holding a glass bowl in front of him. She found herself eyeing those large, long-fingered hands. Elegant hands, she realized. Very elegant...very nice...

Her mouth went dry as she imagined feeling those hands gliding over her body.

Her heart started to race.

Oh, shit.

The wine. Had to be the wine.

All two drinks she'd let herself take.

Maybe she had hit her head.

A crazed thought leaped into her mind and she looked down at the wine appalled, wondering if he'd drugged it.

A sharp breath escaped him and she jerked her gaze up, saw something flash across his face, something that look like a mix of outrage, disgust...and hurt.

She had the strangest feeling he *knew* what she was thinking.

But then it was gone and he gave her that polite, oh-so-meaningless smile. "Would you like some salad?" he said.

Salad. He was asking her if she wanted salad and she was

sitting wondering if he had slipped her some sort of date-rape drug.

Shit. Swallowing, Aileas shook her head and looked away.

He moved away and she found herself watching from the corner of her eye. His back was rigid and the look on his face... Shit, he looked like somebody had slapped him. Hell, like *she* had slapped him.

But it wasn't like he knew what she was feeling.

That would make him...

Like me.

Abruptly, she sat her wine down. Her hands were shaking. *Shit.* Most of her life, she'd been keenly aware of the emotions of others. Too aware. She'd been diagnosed, misdiagnosed with ADD, ADHD, medicated, overmedicated, all in attempt to control something that had terrified her parents. Her parents had never understood, but fortunately, her grandmother had helped her figure it out, and helped her figure out how to handle it.

She didn't have ADD, ADHD and she didn't need drugs.

She had trouble with school because she was too easily picking up on the emotions of others. Once she learned to block those emotions, she'd done fine. Her parents assumed she'd outgrown it, and she was fine with that. There had been a few others she'd come across who had her weird knack for reading people. She'd always been able to sense them. They gave off a low-level vibe, and there was often a careful absence of emotion, because many of them, like her, either had learned to shield or they were taught.

But this guy...

She licked her lips and once more reached for her glass of wine, but this time it was more to keep her hands occupied. She didn't want the damn wine, but she needed something to touch, something to fiddle with. She couldn't risk drinking it though—

"It's not fucking drugged," he snarled and metal clanged as he hurled a knife into the sink.

Aileas flinched at the sound.

Then she leaped to her feet, gaping at him.

Shit, he can read me.

"Yes, I can fucking read you, and a damn sight better than you can read me. So if it's possible for you to shield even a little bit better, I'd appreciate it because I've had one bloody bitch of a day and I don't need you thinking I'm a bloody psychotic rapist on top of the shit I've had to deal with today," he bit off, his voice growing more clipped with each word.

Blood rushed to her face, then slowly drained away. Stiffly, she said, "I'm sorry. But I don't really *know* you, do I?"

"Well, I don't know you either, but I'm not sitting here worried that you're going to wait until I'm asleep and try to rob me blind."

She narrowed her eyes. "It's hardly the same thing, I think."

"True." With his back to her, he turned on the water and then washed his hands. When he turned around to face her, that lean, saturnine face of his was expressionless, but those black, black eyes burned with emotion. Too much of it, she thought. It danced over her skin like fire, stinging her, leaving a fiery trail in its wake.

"I'll tell you what. I can prove to you easily enough that I'm not a threat to you, seeing as how you've got a bit of an unexpected surprise inside of you. Then will you stop staring at your fucking wine like you think I loaded it with roofies or whatever the current drug of choice is for perverts?" he asked, his voice silky, soft.

She folded her arms over her middle. "You can prove to me you're not a pervert."

"Sure. Similar gifts, lamb," he said. Then he shoved off the counter and came to stand just a foot away. He held out a hand, his palm up. "I can't tell you that I've never hurt a woman in my life, but I can tell you that I've never forced a woman, never drugged one, and I don't plan on changing that now. Touch me. If I lie to you, you'd feel it. You'd know it."

Hell. Aileas swallowed and lowered her gaze, staring at his long-fingered hand. Elegant hands. Poetic hands. She didn't need to touch him to know the truth.

Plus, shit, if she touched him now he was going to pick on something else she'd rather him not know. Considering the crazy-weird thoughts circling through her head, she was really better off *not* having him pick up on that. She'd been on an emotional roller coaster from the time she'd looked at him and if he could read her that easily...?

Her breath caught in her throat "That's not necessary," she said quietly. "I'm sorry."

She braced herself to meet that hot, stinging fury as she looked up.

But when she met his gaze, that hot, stinging fury...it wasn't there.

No, his eyes no longer burned like a black, angry hell.

They were warm and soft, a black velvet night, and the heat she felt rushing through her own blood was echoed there.

Shit, shit, shit.

This was bad. Things would be better if one of them could keep their distance. Him being pissed off was actually probably the wiser call. She was tempted to do something to set him off, but she suspected he'd see through it too fast.

She was barely aware of the shift of his moods, while he could read her like a wide-open book.

"Why do you suddenly want me angry again?" he murmured, reaching up to brush her hair back from her face. He caught one thick curl between his thumb and forefinger and toyed with it.

Aileas scowled. "Just how can you pick up on so much?"

He shrugged. "I'd say habit, except I don't know if that's it. I prefer not to be around people much and I keep them blocked out when I can. I don't know. You're...easier to read than some." He wrapped the captured curl he had around his finger, focusing on that task as though it fascinated him.

"Easy?" she echoed. *Shit.* Nobody had ever called her *easy* to read—even her grandmother had been hard-pressed to penetrate her shields, and her grandmother had taught her everything she knew. "Nobody has ever accused me of being easy to read."

"Hmm." He looked away from the curl to gaze into her eyes. "I've never drugged a woman."

The force of his gaze was practically a drug in itself, she thought, licking her lips. She didn't point that out to him though. Wasn't really his fault God had given him eyes like that, right?

"Okay. I'm sorry." She tried to look away, but she couldn't. The grip he had on her hair sort of limited just what she could do, unless she wanted to leave some of her hair in his hand.

Besides, she really, really didn't want to pull away just yet.

"Why would you think I'd do that?" he asked, his voice gruff now, and there was a flicker in his eyes. A flicker of nerves, of sadness, of pain.

"It was...ah..." She blushed, unsure how to explain that she didn't know why else she'd be feeling like this around him. Why else she'd be so willing to stand this close to a man she barely knew...and so eager to think about him touching her, so eager to think about touching him.

She didn't know him. At all. And...

Her heart started to race.

Oh, shit.

She tried to pull away and this time, when he wouldn't loosen his grip on her hair, she started to panic. She reached up to tug his hand away, but that light contact, her bare skin to his, was all it took to deepen that surface connection. What fragile shields she had left in place buckled and broke.

His wavered. She could feel them shifting and swaying, and behind them, she glimpsed something else.

Heat.

It rivaled her own.

That one coherent thought slammed into her mind just as Ren's brows dropped low over his eyes. "Aileas," he muttered, his voice whiskey rough and low.

She might have been embarrassed to have some total stranger be so completely aware of the naked need she felt. Except she felt the same from him. His hands came up and cradled her face and she knew *exactly* how he felt. Naked, raw need burned inside him.

Under it, there was a raw, screaming pain.

It felt like a mirror of her own.

She wanted to soothe it.

But more...she just wanted *him.*

As his mouth came down on hers, she pushed up on her toes and met his lips. Him. She wanted *him.*

He tasted like wine and life and heat and man. She shuddered as he pushed his tongue into her mouth. She bit down on him gently as she slid her hands down the front of his shirt and then under the hem. The skin of his torso was hot, sleek and smooth. She wanted to see it, feel it under her hands and her mouth.

Pulling back, she fisted her hands in his shirt and worked it up. Her mouth went dry as he obliged her, stripping the shirt away and revealing a lean, rangy body, subtly corded with muscle.

Oh. Oh, man. He was a soft, golden tan from the waistband of his low slung jeans and up. His belly was flat and firm, the muscles of his chest defined, leading up to the kind of shoulders that looked liked they'd been designed just for a woman to rest her head on.

Or stare at. Or maybe stroke her hands down.

She couldn't decide which one to start with.

She decided to compromise. Leaning forward, she put her hands on his shoulders and stroked them down his arms. She learned the feel of his muscles, loving the play of them under his skin as she pressed her mouth to his. She caught his lower lip between her teeth and tugged on it. He groaned and caught her head between his hands, holding her still.

"Minx," he muttered. "Bewitching minx."

Bewitching...bewitched, maybe she was one of the two. Bewitched, most likely. Or insane, maybe.

That might explain it.

Might explain why she was all but ready to devour this man she barely knew.

Her heart was racing. Completely, utterly racing, and she couldn't get enough of touching him. Or tasting him. He muttered something against her lips, something she didn't understand, and she didn't care. It drove her insane, because when he was muttering he wasn't kissing her and that meant she couldn't taste him as well. But then she realized she could kiss other parts...like across the finely carved bones of his face, down along his jaw to his neck, along those shoulders she'd just been admiring. She bit down at the spot where his neck and shoulder joined and his body stiffened against hers, those elegant hands gripping her hips.

"Aileas."

She barely heard him. Flicking her tongue against his skin, she scraped her nails against the flat circles of his nipples. When he shuddered, it sparked the growing heat curling through her.

Ren's brain was about to explode. He was certain of it. Explode...or maybe just melt.

How had this happened? So fast?

One moment he'd been about ready to snap—he had even felt the rage building inside him and he'd been about ready to send out an emergency call for Greta, Rip, Elle...hell, even that smug bastard Michael.

Anybody else, just somebody to watch over Aileas so he could get the hell out of here. He couldn't leave her here alone, but he couldn't *stay* here either, not when his temper was this on edge...and then she'd looked at him. He'd caught a glimpse of those warm brown eyes, caught the echo of ravenous hunger inside her. And it clicked.

She didn't feel hunger like this.

No more than he did.

Not this easily, at least.

But he looked at her and felt it...and suddenly he could understand why she wondered if maybe something had been dumped in her wine.

Her hunger sparked his, and every time he touched her he felt the echo of her pleasure in his own body. When he kissed her, he felt her pleasure as acutely as he felt his own, and he knew she was feeling it as well. This was the pleasurable side of their shared gift, although she might not entirely understand *what* she was feeling.

It was overwhelming, to put it mildly.

Overwhelming...and almost exactly like a drug.

Cursing, he tore his mouth away. When she would have closed the distance between them, he closed his hands around her upper arms, holding her at a distance.

"You don't want this," he rasped, swallowing, fighting the need to pounce on her, tear her clothes off, fuck her blind. "You don't know me enough to want me."

Her eyes, burning hot and so hungry, stared into his. "Do I need to know everything about you to know I want this?"

"You should," he said. Darkness stormed inside. The things he'd done...they twisted him, haunted him. "You should know something more than the fact that I've never drugged or raped a woman. It's not much of a character reference."

"It's a damn good start," she said. Then she lay a hand over his heart. That simple gesture all but sent him to his knees. Not just because her hands felt so right on him either. Although he had to admit...he did like the way her hands felt.

When she touched him, that aching, gaping empty place inside him...it contracted, shifted...and he'd almost swear the emptiness started to close up and heal.

Insane, but it seemed just her presence did something to soothe the ragged wounds that had festered inside him for decades.

Her gaze lifted and met his. "For some reason, I touch you...and I feel whole. It makes no sense to me, but there you go," she said quietly. "It's insane, I know it. But it feels *right* to touch you." She leaned and pressed her lips to his chest and whispered, "It just feels right...and that matters to me a little more than a character reference."

Well, then. Perhaps she did know, to some extent. Still...

Trying to clear his mind, trying to think past the fog, he stared at her. He was stroking the satin soft skin of her arms, he realized, up and down, and drawing her closer without even realizing it.

Close, so close, she was leaning against him, her slender weight braced against his own. Her breasts were a warm, wonderful weight. The pearls she wore were trapped between them, warming between their bodies and he found himself remembering the very first moment he'd laid eyes on her—only hours ago, really.

He'd seen those pearls, and wanted nothing more than to see her wearing those and nothing else.

Focus, Ren. Think. Stop touching her and think...

But that wasn't easy, especially when she wouldn't stop touching him.

His eyes crossed as she scraped her nails down over his skin and ran them along the waistband of his jeans. Oh, bloody fuck.

"Aileas," he muttered.

"Ren." She nipped his lip again and then leaned back. "I spent most of my life doing the smart and safe thing. I don't feel like doing the *smart* thing right now, and I already know this is perfectly *safe*. I feel it."

Then she reached for the hem of her shirt and stripped it off.

It fell to her feet and as she reached for the strap of her bra, Ren tried to get his brain functioning once more.

Brain. Function. Mouth. Speak. Body. Move.

From the waist up, she wore nothing. Nothing but those pearls.

They hung between her small breasts, and what little functioning brainpower he still possessed abruptly died.

With a hand that shook he reached out, traced one finger down the strand of pearls. He could feel the heat of her skin, and as he drew close to one breast, she sighed and arched closer, but he didn't touch...no, not yet.

Think.

Function.

Think.

Move.

Finally, he managed to move...to reach out to her, draw her back against him. He moved back as he did so, and kept moving back until he bumped into one of the padded leather bar stools. Sinking down on one, he kept one foot braced on the floor to steady himself. Then he boosted Aileas up. He needed to taste her, needed to get those sweet, plump nipples in his mouth.

They were tight and hard, rosy pink. When he took one in his mouth, she cried and wrapped her arms around his neck, one hand cradling the back of his head, her fingers dancing over the naked skin of his scalp. Using his tongue, the edge of his teeth, he toyed with one nipple, then the other, driving her closer, closer. It was the sweetest torment, and through their shared gift, he felt the echo of the pleasure.

A strange, hot coiling sensation settled low in his gut and he realized it was an echo from her.

Close to coming.

Swearing against her flesh, he pulled his mouth away and then stood her up between his feet, stripping her jeans away. Once she was naked, he pulled her close again. But when she went to fumble with the button of his jeans, he turned her around, pressed her back against his front. *Not yet, not yet...*

He pulled her into his lap and smoothed his hands up her thighs, nuzzled her neck. Gathering her hair, he pushed it over one shoulder, baring her nape. He raked it with his teeth as he cupped the heated flesh of her sex in his hand.

She was molten silk, liquid fire. When he touched one gentle finger to her entrance, she moaned and jerked, bucking against him so hard, he ended up wrapping one arm around her waist just to keep her steady.

Her hands came down, gripping his thighs. When he pushed a finger inside her, her head fell back on his shoulder, a gasp hitching out of her.

"Fuck, you're sweet," he muttered thickly, staring down the expanse of that pale, perfect body, watching as he stroked her.

Sweet...sweet didn't even touch it. The strand of pearls glowed against her skin, and unable to resist, he took them and teased the erect tip of one nipple with the cool, hard beads. She shuddered.

"The first time I saw you, I had this wicked thought...seeing you wearing these," he muttered against her ear. "Just these."

As he flicked his thumb against the knotted bud of her clit, he continued to torment her with the pearls as well, working her until she was twisting and gasping in his lap, panting and straining.

The need to come became a painful ache, one he shared with her.

Her nails bit into his thighs through the heavy denim of his jeans as she moved against his hand.

"Damn it, Ren...please!"

A split second later, his harsh groan mingled with her cry as she started to climax, and he damn near followed.

Damn near came in his jeans just feeling the echo of her pleasure.

She was shuddering in his arms, shaking, so wild and hot. Groaning, he scooped her into his arms and carried her across the floor to the bed he had under the window. He told himself this wasn't wise. He told himself she wasn't thinking clearly, and he already knew he wasn't.

But he didn't fucking care. He stripped out of his jeans and joined her on his bed.

He really did like the sight of her there. He hadn't ever shared this bed with anybody before. Hadn't ever wanted to bring a woman here. But he did like the sight of Aileas on his bed. He loved how her body looked against his sheets, how the pearls around her neck glowed against her soft, lovely skin.

Stretching out on top of her, he cupped her face in his hands. Her lashes fluttered open and she gave him a wide, wicked smile as he pressed the head of his cock against the entrance of her sex.

"Weren't you just now thinking we shouldn't do this..." she teased, skimming a hand up his side.

"I'm very often wrong," he muttered. Then he linked their hands as he linked their bodies, slowly pushing past the initial resistance of her body.

She was tight, but so welcoming, so wet. Each time she started to tense up, he eased back, working his way deeper with slow, easy thrusts until her slick, sweet heat gloved all of him.

Perfect. So fucking perfect he couldn't stand it.

Sucking in a desperate breath, he pressed his brow to hers. "Aileas...I think maybe *you* put something in the wine."

A slow smile curled her lips. "Hmmm. If I did, I need to make sure I get more. I think I could get used to this."

As Ren started to move, he knew he could get used to this.

He could even come to need it...need her.

Tangling a hand in her hair, he stared into her eyes as he started to move. She moved with him, her body gliding in perfect rhythm. The sweet, slick tissues of her pussy gripped him, hugged him, milked him...an erotic, maddening torture.

He licked her lower lip, bit it gently, smiled when she whimpered.

When he shifted his angle just *so*, he felt the reaction ripple through her body, because it rippled through him as well—from his scalp straight down to soles, tightening every inch in between. Snarling, he shifted higher on her body and pressed more firmly against her so that each and every thrust hit that spot.

Her nails tore at his back and he felt the pain of it, loved it. She cried out, arching up. Canting her hips higher, he pushed his hand under her ass and lifted her up, drove into her harder. Harder.

He would have feared he'd hurt her—soft and fragile—but she wrapped her legs around his hips and cried out his name. He felt that mind-numbing pleasure burn through her. Burn through her, tear through her...consume her...just as it was consuming him.

The climax hit him with breath-stealing, heart-stopping intensity, and if he had been mortal, he didn't know if he would have survived it.

As it was, he was weaker than a baby when he rolled to his side and curled up against her. As shudders racked her body, he wrapped an arm around her middle, pulled her close. Burying his face between her breasts, he tried to think of something to say.

Anything.

But there were no words.

There was nothing but the warmth and the wonder of her in his arms. This woman he had known just hours...and all he knew was her first name, and the fact that he'd found her driving around with a demon tome in her car, and demons on her tail.

That and the fact that he'd just had the most blissful experience of his life—either life—with her.

Lifting his head, he opened his eyes, tried to force himself to say something.

But her lids were closed.

And her chest moved in the slow, steady rhythm of sleep.

Reluctantly, a smile tugged at his lips. Reaching out, he

caught the corner of a blanket and snagged it, pulling it up over them. As he lay down, he heard the click of claws gathering around the bed, felt the presence of his friends.

He touched their minds.

Sleep out of sight tonight. In case she wakes.

Then he gave into the call of sleep himself.

Chapter Eight

Crazy dreams.

She'd been having crazy dreams ever since that book had fallen into her hands.

In some of them, she'd gone and turned into a fucking nympho, having sex as often as she could, wherever she could, with whomever...and sometimes, several whomevers. She'd never been into adventurous sex, but those dreams, sometimes she wasn't just having sex with a guy—sometimes it was two or three guys, or even a guy and a couple of women. It wasn't just the sex that made her so uncomfortable though, it was the way it *felt*...like somebody was almost pushing on her. *Needing* to push it on her.

There were other dreams like something had settled inside her and was riding her, feeding off her rage, off her jealousy, off her anger. Once she'd been sucked dry, it reached out through her and found others through her, friends, family, lovers.

Dreams where she was nothing but a monstrous rage, lost inside herself, and she needed to hurt as much as she needed to destroy. Needed to tear, and rend, and feed...even thinking of *those* dreams was enough to have her ready to empty her stomach, so she tried not to think about them.

In other dreams were those voices that offered her endless promises, showed her some incredible life. She could be young, strong, healthy...for always. For a price, just a small, simple price.

Such confusing, horrid dreams.

But they were just dreams, and even as real as they felt, Aileas had no desire to live forever, and she wasn't so stupid to believe she could have youth and beauty without a major cost.

This dream though, it felt different.

It didn't seem to be about her at all.

There was nothing, nobody that Aileas recognized.

She didn't even recognize the *time*.

Two children, a woman.

There was a woman, and there was something familiar about her, but Aileas couldn't figure out what.

There was a man...at least he *looked* to be a man, but something about him screamed *monster*. Something about him screamed *wrong*.

The children, a girl, probably just dancing on that verge between childhood and young adulthood, twelve, perhaps thirteen, and a boy, a year or so older. He was taller, but he looked ill. Skinny, almost to the point of being scrawny, with huge, bony wrists and hands, shoulders that looked too big for his gaunt frame.

The woman was petite and she looked terrified, so terrified, wringing her hands and looking back and forth between the man and the children.

Of them all, only the boy stood tall and unbroken.

And his eyes, dark and compelling, they tugged at some memory, but Aileas couldn't quite remember *why*.

There was strength in him. The kind of strength many grown men didn't possess. So skinny, so tired, and although the boy looked weak and frail and sick, he didn't back down as the man came circling around him and the girl, closer and closer, eyeing them the way a dog would eye a bone. The boy pushed the girl behind him, protecting her, and the man laughed...like this had amused him.

The man reached for the boy, but just as his long, snakelike fingers would have touched the boy's arm, the dream shifted, then shattered.

The last thing Aileas remembered seeing was the long, greedy shadow extending from the man's fingers. Like something trying to reach *inside* the boy...

She came awake with her heart knocking against her ribs, a cold sweat on her body and her breath rattling in and out of her lungs.

Fear gripped her, and for long, long moments, she didn't know where she was.

The warmth of the arm around her waist was oddly soothing, but she knew it *shouldn't* be.

It was a man's body behind her, and she knew damn well there wasn't a man in her life, so why was there one in her bed?

Except...this wasn't *her* bed. That was a problem.

It was a lot nicer than her bed, cradling her like a plush, yet somehow firm cloud. The blankets were thick and soft, and the linens smelled a little like lavender and herbs and a lot like warm and sexy male.

Still, that didn't explain how she was in some guy's bed.

She chanced a look down, saw the dusky-skinned arm around her waist, and the black leather cuff at his wrist. Some bit of memory started to wiggle free. She remembered seeing that cuff. She hadn't focused on it an awful lot, but she remembered it. Remembered that arm it was attached to, the hand...the body.

The spit in her mouth dried up and she swallowed, trying not to panic.

Holy shit, she'd just had sex with a guy who really wasn't much more than a total stranger. *Holy shit.*

Ren.

She'd spent the night in bed with Ren.

Gorgeous Ren with the mysterious black eyes, the wicked pirate's grin and a way of pretending to be slightly off his rocker. An act. It had to be act, right?

Oh, shit.

She needed to get out of here.

She dared a glance at the skylight over the bed and was startled to see bright swathes of sunlight streaming in.

Sunlight.

Good.

That was good. It meant it was morning. She could find her car. Get the hell away from here.

It was daylight and she could find it in the daylight, no problem.

She just needed to get away...

Behind her, he sighed and shifted, pushing his knee closer to her thighs, almost wedged between them. That damn near had her whimpering as it pressed his cock against the crevice of her butt.

Get it together, Aileas. She could do this. Get away without waking him, without alerting whoever was on her trail...

The book.

That voice was an unwelcome whisper in her mind as she went to put her feet down on a cool hardwood floor. *He has the book. You cannot let him keep it. He will do terrible things with it. Bring the book with you. Only you can keep it safe.*

Safe...she couldn't keep it safe. The damn thing was driving her insane. She didn't even know what was real or not. She'd fallen into bed with a man she didn't know, she'd up and abandoned her life, she was hearing voices, all kinds of crazy shit that hadn't started until she'd found that damn book buried among her brother's possessions.

And why in the hell did she need to keep a book safe anyway?

She was having a hard enough time keeping *herself* safe lately.

Besides, she couldn't even hope to find it, not without waking him up.

Slowly, she took one step, then another. The floorboards creaked under her feet and she winced, darting a quick look over her shoulder. In the dappled sunlight coming through the skylight, he looked relaxed, his eyes closed, the arm he'd curled around her waist still there, as if he still held her while she slept.

Part of her wanted to be back there—*right* there, pressed against his chest.

Safe. You want to be safe? Go back over there and lie down. He'll keep you safe.

Something punched through her mind, penetrating the wispy barrier that sometimes protects dreams from the waking mind. It superimposed over Ren's sleeping face and she saw the boy from her dreams.

Shifting to protect a young girl from a man who was a monster.

Ren.

Aileas swallowed.

Shit, she really was going insane. Tearing her gaze away, she focused once more on the door. She needed to get out of here. Find her clothes. Get out. Find her car. Get out.

Find the book, the silky seductive book whispered. *Find me...look. I will help you.*

"I *can't*," she whispered, her voice harsh.

She didn't even realize she'd spoken outloud.

Yes, you can. I'll show you.

Against her will, she felt something tugging on her, drawing her gaze. Back to the bed.

No...*under* it.

Look.

No.

Ren waited until she'd crept away from his bed and into the bathroom before he opened his eyes.

That internal battle of hers had damn near exhausted him, and she didn't have near the resources to fall back on that he did.

Sighing, he sat up and listened as she moved around in the other room, scrambling to gather up her clothes. Something pecked against the window and he glanced over, saw Bo there. He opened the window and smiled as the owl flew in and settled on his shoulder. He winced a little as the talons dug in. "Watch it there," he murmured.

Bo eased up on the pressure and rubbed his crest against Ren's head. "Yes, yes, I know."

He held up his arm and Bo hopped onto it. "You need to be out of sight," he murmured. "I have to go see to her."

Bo gave him an injured look, but Ren ignored it and took the owl to the room that had been Mandy's.

Aileas was already on edge. He could feel it.

Oddly enough, it didn't have him hovering on the brink the way mortal emotions always did. He wanted to help...soothe.

Protect.

As he came out of Mandy's room, he glanced back toward his bed and shot the space below a dark look. What he needed to do was burn that blasted tome. But first...Aileas.

There was a pair of trousers over the back of a chair and he grabbed them, tugged them up over his naked hips before he moved into the main part of the cabin.

Curious to see if she'd slip away, he lay back down just before she opened the door. He closed his eyes, listened as she emerged.

Judging by the state of her thoughts, there was no question...yes, she was going to just slip away. At least that was her plan.

Sorry ,love. We can't have that.

Grimly, he opened his eyes and climbed out the bed, watching as she scurried around, unaware of him.

She was trying to be quiet, and if he had still been mortal, it likely would have been quiet enough.

Bracing a shoulder against the bedpost, he hooked his thumbs in the pockets of his trousers and watched as she scrambled around looking for her shoes. The worn denim jeans she wore clung to her nicely rounded arse. He spent a few seconds admiring the view as she crawled around looking for her shoes and muttering.

When she straightened up, she was flushed and flustered and it only got worse when she finally sensed his presence.

Her spine stiffened and she turned slowly, staring at him across the expanse of the living room.

"Taking off so soon?"

"I need to," she said, her voice unsteady.

Ren nodded. He'd heard the book calling to her. If something that was supposed to be inanimate had been whispering to *him* like that, he'd want some distance as well.

Still, he couldn't let her leave.

Not until he knew she was safe.

Even then, he didn't think that he'd *want* her to leave.

That was another matter altogether though.

Entirely.

"What about whoever or whatever is after you?" he asked quietly.

She stilled, the blood draining out of her face. "Who said anything was after me?"

Ren snorted. "Oh, come on, love. Do I look like a fool?"

Aileas just stared at him.

"You're running, and you're running hard." Ren pointed at her. "When you run that hard it's because something is chasing you. What are you going to do...run until you're too tired, and then collapse? Then what will happen to you?"

"Maybe there's no reason for me to run anymore," she said, her chin jerking up.

He lifted a brow. Oh, was she hoping that leaving the book with him would deflect their interest? Part of him wondered if he shouldn't be insulted, or hurt. Except he knew he was far more equipped to deal with the problems. Aileas was far more perceptive than the typical mortal, and gifted. That empathy of hers probably gave her some knowledge—she *knew* he was more equipped to deal with the book. On some level, even if she didn't acknowledge it.

Except Ren didn't think it was just the book the demons wanted.

They had her scent now and they wanted *her*. They wanted the book, but her too. The fact that she'd resisted the book as long as she had probably just made her that much more enticing.

Ren didn't like her being an enticement to demons.

He didn't want her touching his world at all.

"And what if you're wrong?" he asked. He hated watching that fear creep into her eyes, but fear could keep a person alive. He should know. Fear, rage...ugly, nasty emotions, but they could keep a person alive for a good, long while. "What if you're wrong and the moment you leave this house, you walk out there with a target on your back?"

She set her jaw. "Are you proposing that I stay here for the rest of my life?" she asked, jerking a shoulder. Sinking down on a chair, she put her shoes on, giving that task a rather focused amount of attention.

"No. But perhaps you could tell me what's going on. Perhaps I can help."

She stilled. Without lifting her head, she glanced at him through her lashes. "You can't."

"How do you know?"

She just shook her head. "Trust me. If I even tried to explain it, you'd think I'd lost my mind."

Ren laughed. He shifted around and leaned back against the bedpost, staring straight ahead. "Lost your mind," he muttered. Oh, that was a rich one.

Half the known world had more or less considered him the poster child for insanity, and perhaps they weren't so far off in some ways. There had been a time...a period of weeks, months, even years, that were lost to him...where he had been lost to insanity, lost in a darkness so complete that it was a miracle he had emerged with any measure of sanity left.

Will, damn him, had pulled him out of that hellhole, but his grip on sanity had been so fractured—hell, his very humanity had been fractured at that point.

Turning his head, he met Aileas' gaze. "Trust me, there's nothing you can tell me that would surprise me, and nothing you can say that would make me think you'd lost your mind."

"You're wrong," she muttered, rubbing her hands together.

"Try me."

"No." She grabbed her jacket from the floor and shoved her arms into the sleeves. "I need to go."

Uncoiling from his relaxed pose, he sauntered over and blocked her before she could reach the door. "That's not a good idea," he said. "It's not safe."

"You can't *keep* me here."

"Well, actually, I could. But I won't." *Not unless you force me...please, Ali. Don't force me.*

"I just don't want you leaving when I know you're going to walk into a world of hurt. You *do* have something after you, you know. You've felt it, sensed it." He studied her soft, dark eyes, watched as fear shifted and swam in their depths. "And I can tell without even touching you that I'm right."

He laid a hand on her cheek. A double bolt of sensation struck him—the feel of her skin and the intensity of her fear slammed into him. One flooded him with need. The other flooded him with rage. "I'm right, aren't I, Ali?" he whispered, stroking his thumb over her lip.

She closed her eyes and swallowed.

"Tell me what's going on. Let me help." *Trust me.*

"You'll think I'm crazy," she said, forcing the words through clenched teeth.

He smiled. "No. I can promise you, I won't." Dipping his head, he pressed his brow to hers and murmured, "Look at me."

Her lashes lifted and once he could look into her sad, troubled eyes, he said, "Let's strike a bargain. You tell me what is going on. And if I'm wrong, if you surprise me, if I start thinking you're losing your mind, I'll let you walk out that door without a qualm. I'm telling you the truth, and you can feel that, I know you can. But if I'm right, if you don't surprise me, you stay here...and let me help."

"And how will I know..." She scowled, her voice trailing off.

Through their physical contact, Ren felt it when she answered her own question.

Just as she felt the slow, gradual rise of his desire.

He'd woken wanting her, but the insidious whispers from the book had quickly dampened that, and her own fear, her determination to leave had killed the rest of it. All it had taken was to touch her again and he wanted her again. Here, right here.

Right now.

And once she agreed to stay...

He caught her lower lip between his teeth and nipped it gently. "Do we have a bargain?"

"It's a strange bargain, you know. If you suspect I'm insane, you should be pushing me to a psychiatric hospital, not out the door on my lonesome."

"Not an answer, Ali."

She sighed and leaned against him, resting her hands on his chest. He felt the echo of the dull flush rising up to stain her cheeks red. She really, really didn't want to tell him.

He stroked a hand up her back. He wished he could reassure her, but he wanted—no, he *needed* her to trust him with this. Needed it like he needed air.

She pushed away from him with a sigh, moved over to the chair and curled up on it, drawing her knees up to her chest. She gave him a sour look. "You know, I realize in a few minutes you're going to be looking at me and saying so long, have a nice life, but I really hate to think that some guy I had fantastic sex with is going to look back and think 'man, that chick was *insane'*."

Ren scooped her up in his arms and then sat down in the chair, wrapping his arms around her to keep her from pulling away. "I won't," he said softly. "Now, start talking."

The words kept trying to stick in her throat.

Aileas stared at the wall, wishing he would let her go. It was so much harder to do this when he was touching her. She kept her mental walls up, blocking him out because she couldn't stand to feel it when he started thinking she'd lost her mind.

"It all started when I found this book," she said softly. "I found it a few days after my brother died. At first, I didn't think much about it, just threw it in one of the boxes to take to my house and sort through. Everything at his place was such a mess. It wasn't like him. He used to be so... Well, he was kind of a neat freak. Obsessed even. One of those types who never have a thing out of place, never had a speck of dust. But not lately. It was like he just wasn't himself the last few weeks before he died. Anyway, I found the book when I was going through things, and for some reason, I couldn't leave it there. It didn't feel right leaving it in his place, or tossing it in with the stuff for Goodwill. He had it buried in his closet. I took it to my place. That first night, I started having nightmares."

"What kind of nightmares?"

Aileas shivered. "Awful ones. In some of them, it was just like I was some kind of raging nympho. But in the other ones, I was almost like a monster. The things I did... Fuck, even in the dreams, it made me sick. Each night, it got worse and worse. And the book whispered to me in the dreams." She lifted her hands and pressed them to her temples, but it did nothing to ease the ache there. "Driving me crazy, I swear."

He caught one wrist and tugged it down. Pressing his lips to her temple, Ren murmured, "You're not going crazy, Aileas. When did you start feeling like they were watching you?"

They... How did you know about them?

She swallowed and made herself look into his eyes. She had to know—had to ask. "How did you know about that? I haven't told *anybody.*"

"The book," he said quietly. "I've come across the like before. The sort who've been watching you...they hunt the books. When did you first feel them, Ali? Tell me."

The book. He acted like he believed her—hell. He acted like he already *knew...*

And for some reason, Aileas wasn't even surprised.

Snuggling against him, she shivered as she recalled the first night when she'd woken up utterly *convinced* somebody had been outside her home, watching her. Watching...and waiting. She would have sworn she could almost feel the person *calling* to her.

Silently.

Summoning her.

And something about it had felt so alien.

She hadn't gone and that was when the whispers from the book had gotten worse. That was when she started seeing shadows out of the corner of her eye, feeling the weight of a stare on her back as she walked to her car after work, when she'd started to feel as though every step she took, every move she made was being watched, weighed...measured.

It seemed as though months, years had passed, but it was really only ten days. Ten painfully long days and she knew she couldn't keep going like this. Swallowing, she glanced at Ren and then away.

He cupped her cheek, guided her stare back to his. Keeping his hand on her face, his skin in direct contact, he said, "I don't think you're crazy, Aileas. I'm not pushing you out the door and you haven't surprised me yet. We had a deal. Keep talking, pet."

With his skin on hers, she should have been able to feel that much, sense that much, but she had her mental walls shored up, blocking him. Afraid to look, much less let him glimpse inside her.

But they'd made a bargain. She couldn't very well hold up her end of the bargain, or see if he was upholding his, if she kept hiding. Grimly, she lowered her shields as she prepared herself to say the rest of it.

"I sensed it first the day after the first nightmare. And that's not even the craziest thing, Ren. The book...I swear, it feels like it's alive. I swear it talks to me. I hear it. It tells me all sorts of crazy shit, and all I want to do is destroy the damn thing. I even tried tearing it apart, but the thing is made of steel." She said all of that without looking at him. But now, she shifted her gaze to his. "The book *talks*, Ren. It whispers. I *hear* it. In my head."

Now he's going to look at me as though I've lost it.

But all he did was say, "You can't destroy a book like that with your hands. It has to be burned."

A book like that.

The book...I've come across the like before. The sort who've been watching you...they hunt the books."

She couldn't decide if she was more *relieved* that he didn't seem to think she was crazy, or scared because it sounded like he knew what he was talking about. It sounded like he was familiar with that kind of book.

"A book like that," she echoed. Pushing against his arms, she climbed off his lap and rose, pacing the long expanse of hardwood floors. They were polished to a high, smooth shine and her tennis shoes were all but soundless on them. Shivering, she rubbed her hands up and down her arms. "How do know about the book?"

She turned around and watched as he reached down, stroked the black leather cuff at his wrist. There was a silver medallion, almost the size of a half-dollar, set in the leather. He stroked it with an absent-minded gesture, almost like he wasn't even aware of it.

There was a far-off look in his impossibly dark eyes.

"Ren?"

He looked at her then.

"How do know about it? Have you seen it before?"

His voice was deeper, rough as he murmured, "That book, no. But books like it...yes."

Aileas took a slow breath, remembered how yesterday he'd insisted he'd found her wandering through the woods. Saying she'd hit her head. That he hadn't found her by her car at all.

"And you know all about the one I have?" she said, lifting a brow.

"You no longer have it," he said gently.

Well, that was true. Because he punched out the back window of her car, shattering the glass like it was made of spun sugar.

Folding her arms over her chest, she hugged herself. "Why the mad-hatter routine? Why did you say you found me wandering around through the woods? And where is your friend, or your sister? Although, Ren, I know she's not your sister."

"Mad-hatter." He chuckled and rested his head on the back of the chair, staring up at the skylight. "As mad as a hatter. Oh, I like that."

Then he came out of the chair, that lean, graceful body of his uncoiling in one smooth, easy motion. "It's not exactly a routine, love. I'm not precisely what people would call *sane.* Although I'm not exactly in the running for a psychiatric hospital myself. As to why I told you a bit of a tale? Well, I was still trying to figure out how you'd landed in this mess—and you *are* in a mess, Ali, my dear. Make no mistake."

She blinked. A mess. Oh, that was putting it lightly. She had people trailing after her and she had no idea why. She had a book that seemed to talk to her, except now *Ren* had the book, it would appear. And Ren openly admitted he wasn't what people would call *sane,* and he was telling her crazy stories, and holy *shit,* she'd slept with him.

She wanted to again.

And again.

And again.

Something flashed in his eyes. They heated, although how eyes that dark could burn so hot...black fire, maybe. They heated her all the way through. Her mouth went dry and her heart started to pound in slow, heavy beats.

"So you decided to make me think I'd hit my head," she said, her voice sarcastic.

"It was the first thing that came to mind." He shrugged, his gaze focused on her mouth.

Her heart skipped a few beats. Shit, she couldn't think when he looked at her like that. Jerking her gaze away from his, she tried to find something else to stare at. The window. That seemed safe. Nothing sexy about the window, or the great outdoors. She moved over to lean against the wall and study the sprawling spread of mountains and trees.

And animals.

She blinked. They were still there. Reaching up, she rubbed her eyes, but when she lowered her hands, they were all still there. Rabbits. Dozens of them.

Birds, all sorts, hawks, owls, sparrows, starlings...all of them sitting in the branches of the trees.

She saw a few foxes, some raccoons.

And the big, black wolf-dog breed that had run in front of her car...when had that happened? Hours ago? Yesterday? She thought it was yesterday.

Spinning around, she glared at him and said, "I thought you said you didn't have a dog."

Ren glanced past her shoulder. A scowl tightened his features and he muttered, "So much for them staying out of sight."

At that moment, something came flying through the one of the partially closed doors along the far wall.

It took her brain nearly a minute to process it, even though she easily recognized what it was.

An owl.

One that was winging straight for Ren.

And Ren didn't look at all surprised.

With a resigned sigh, he lifted an arm—a completely bare arm—and the owl settled down.

Aileas gaped and then she dashed forward, prepared to see those talons pierce his tanned flesh, but then she stopped as Ren brought the owl against his naked chest, cuddling it like a baby. "You little fool," Ren muttered. "Didn't I tell you to stay put?"

The owl hooted, twisting his neck to stare up at Ren.

"I know, I know." He sighed again and scratched the owl's crest before launching him into the air.

Aileas watched, stunned, as the owl flapped over to a mounted perch that she hadn't noticed before, one a few feet away from the fireplace.

"You have a hybrid wolf/dog for a pet *and* an owl," she said. She shifted her gaze to the window, staring outside. "And the other critters out there? Are they yours too?"

Ren frowned. "Pan is more a friend than a pet," he said. "But yes, I'll lay claim to him. And Bo isn't a pet. He just likes it here."

"That's an *owl*," Aileas said, pointing at the raptor.

"I know what he is."

She rubbed at her aching head. Shit, she'd thought the insane part would come when she told him she had a book that whispered to her. An *evil* book. He'd taken that in stride.

But hell, he should. He was like some sexy, pirate version of Dr. Doolittle.

"What about the rest of them?" She walked to the other window, and oddly enough, she wasn't surprised when she saw more animals gathered out there. It was almost like they were having a commune or something. "Why are they are out there?"

She slid him a look over her shoulder. "And don't tell me you don't know. I won't buy it."

"They're here for me. Because of me," he said. His shoulders rose and fell on a sigh. "I've got a...knack for animals. Like Bo, they just like being around me. When I'm out of sorts, they pick up on it. They are out there because they think I might need them."

"For what?"

That same sad smile tugged at his lips. "A friend." He smoothed a hand back across his naked scalp and then reached down, touched his fingers to the black leather band at his wrist. "Often, they are the only friends I have."

The way he said it, so simply, it broke her heart. She felt tears clog her throat and she wanted to go to him, wrap her arms around him and do something, *anything* to ease the pain she saw in him, the pain she felt *from* him.

Swallowing, she hugged herself tighter.

Her world had gotten entirely too strange lately.

"What's going on, Ren? Who *are* you? How do you know about that damn book and how did you find me yesterday? It was like you *knew* I was coming. And where is that girl? Who are the men following me? I *know* you know."

Once more, he touched the leather cuff at his wrist and then looked away. Wearily, he sank down on the couch, his elbows braced on his knees. He covered his face with his hands and sighed.

"Do you believe in angels, Aileas?"

Chapter Nine

London, 1886

It had been ages since he had spoken to another. Seen another.

When the man appeared in the cellar, Thomas wondered if he had finally died. *Finally...*

"You're not dead, Thomas," the man said, and his voice was heavy with grief.

Very heavy—Thomas' chest ached with the echo of it, and he might have cried, except he hadn't had much water the past few days...they forgot to give it to him more and more often.

A blast of anger struck him, hard and fast, hazing his vision, tightening the muscles on his skinny frame, but he was so weak, when he launched himself at the intruder, he barely made it two feet before he collapsed.

Strong, kind hands caught him before he fell.

"Easy there, laddy. Easy. Forgive me, I'm making a mess of this," the man said, and this time, his voice was quiet and easy, no sign of grief or anger or misery.

Licking cracked and bloody lips, Thomas squinted and tried to see the man in the dark. "Who are you?"

"You may call me Will. And I'm here to help you."

Thomas shook his head. "You cannot help me. If I leave here, Fowler will tell all of London that I killed my sister and they'll hang me."

"I'll handle Fowler," the man promised. "Now come on. Let's get you out of here. Poor lad, can you walk?"

Pride had Thomas stiffening his spine. "Of course I can walk," he said. He wasn't certain he could walk, but he'd crawl before he would ask for help.

Will chuckled. "Yes, of course."

Then it struck Thomas. How had the man gotten down

here? The door hadn't opened since yesterday and only one of the servants had come down. Not this man with the deep, melodious voice.

Suspicious, Thomas tried once more to make out the man's face. "Who are you? Why are you trying to help me?"

Nobody had tried to help him in ages. Nobody. Not even his own mother.

They heard footsteps overhead.

Will muttered something unpleasant under his breath, and then a big, strong hand came around Thomas' arm. Panic hurtled through Thomas.

"Release me," he snapped, jerking away—or trying to.

"I'm not going to hurt you, lad, but we need to go. I'm not leaving you down here one more night." He paused and then, abruptly, a soft white light filled the cellar.

Flooded it. And it was coming from the man.

It was like *he* was light. Ren cringed, cowered away from it. It had been too long since his eyes had been exposed to light and it hurt. Blinking, he raised an arm to block out the light.

"What is this?" Thomas whispered. "What are *you?*"

The light dimmed, eased, until it wasn't so painfully bright to look upon. Slowly, Thomas lowered his arm and stared at Will's face. Will gazed back at him, his eyes a pale, silvery gray.

"Do you believe in angels, Thomas?"

Ren barely recognized his own reflection.

A day later, in a fine hotel, after several baths, and nearly twenty-four hours of sleep, he stood in front of a mirror and stared at his face.

He didn't know that face.

Reaching up, he smoothed a hand over his naked scalp. His hair had always been thin, but in the past two years, since he'd been trapped down in that cellar as his step-father's prisoner, all the hair had fallen out.

"How long do you plan to continue admiring your pretty reflection?"

Thomas looked up and met Will's eyes in the mirror. "I do not recognize myself."

"You spent two years in hell. You should expect to look different."

Two years.

It had been two years since Fowler had killed Rose. Thomas closed his eyes, grief and anger choking him. His sister lay dead in her grave and her killer lived in a fine house. Worse, their mother? She shared the monster's bed, called him her husband.

"Thomas."

He opened his eyes and looked at Will.

"The rage will consume you, if you let it."

In Thomas' opinion, that did not sound so bad. Rage, he thought, was better than the other options. Better than the fear and the shame. Better than the memories of what had first happened when Samuel Fowler had thrown him into that dark pit.

The darkness of those memories came rushing up on him, choking him. Literally choking him, a fist around his throat strangling him. It descended on him and time lost all meaning.

Ren blinked and came back to himself, aware that he'd spent far too much time lost in his memories. Well, better the memories than the darkness.

Aileas was staring at him as if he'd grown a second head and he realized his mind had wandered away from him at a very, very weird time.

Right about the time he'd asked her if she believed in angels.

He gave her a tight smile and said, "And to think you were worried I'd think you were the crazy one."

Then he looked away, focused on the leather band on his wrist.

The others, most of them at least, tended to wear their medallions around their neck. But he couldn't stand to have anything around his neck. Absently, he reached up and touched the sliver-thin scar, one that he'd gotten one of the times he'd let his darkness get the better of him. When he'd tried to exorcise his own demons.

"What are you going to tell me now?" She gave him a strained smile of her own and quipped, "Let me guess...*you* are an angel."

Ren just stared at her.

The smile on her face wobbled, then fell.

"We're called the Grimm," he said softly. "We're guardian angels...placed here by God to protect mortals from the demons who occasionally slip into this plain from their home in the netherplains."

She sagged back against the chair. The color drained out of her face and her brown eyes looked terribly dark against her skin in that moment. "*What?*"

Ren brushed his hand against the leather cuff on his wrist, waiting for...something. For Will to send out one of his trademark bursts of heat, warning him to shut up. Something.

But there was nothing.

"The book you had, it's called a demon tome. Basically, it contains spells that are used as gateways. Demons use the spells to forge a gateway between the netherplains and here, and whoever opens that gate becomes their host." He studied her through his lashes and said gently, "You have no idea how incredibly lucky, how incredibly blessed, how incredibly strong you must be to have resisted its call. It's a taint, a stain, an illness, but you resisted it."

"This isn't funny," Aileas snapped, her voice shaking.

"Nor should it be." He sighed and rubbed the etched markings on the medallion. "You've demons trailing after you, Ali. There is nothing remotely humorous about that."

She swiped the back of her hand over her mouth, then swallowed, and he knew the knot in her throat made it ache— his own ached in sympathy.

"This is a bunch of crap." Her brown eyes flashed at him, angry, scared...and hiding in the depths he saw the knowledge.

No matter what she said, he knew she already believed.

"What kind of crazy fuck are you, making up shit like this?" she demanded, her voice harsh and low. Angry—so angry.

Ren came up off the couch. He wanted to go to her, but he knew that wasn't what she wanted right now. He couldn't stand still though. He just couldn't. Blowing out a breath, he slid his hands inside his pockets and studied her. "I've been crazy more often than you could even begin to imagine," he said quietly.

"But I'm telling you the truth. And you know it."

"Like you told me the truth about me wandering around the woods. Or the dog. Or your sister...the girl." She firmed her jaw and demanded, "Where in the hell *is* she, anyway?"

"Mandy... Well, she's gotten a promotion, you could call it." There was no way he could tell her that he'd left Mandy behind to be slaughtered—the only way he could possibly have saved Aileas' neck. Aileas wouldn't have understood. Plus, it had been Mandy's choice. A choice she had to make, and one he had to respect.

"A promotion." A nervous giggle slipped free and Aileas clapped her hand over her mouth. "You're telling me that guardian angels get promotions? What, you go from silver wings to gold, then to platinum?"

Ren watched her, and the sympathy, the understanding she saw in his eyes made her want to punch him. She actually felt her hands curling into fists. She wanted to punch him, right square on that arrogant chin and then she wanted to do it again.

Then run.

He felt *sorry* for her. He *understood* why she felt so damned afraid, borderline hysterical.

She didn't *want* him feeling sorry for her, or understanding...crazy people who thought they were guardian angels should be too delusional for that kind of crazy crap.

She didn't *want* him to feel sorry.

She didn't want him to be telling the truth. She wanted him to be wrong, to be lying. Or even just insane.

Somewhere, deep inside, there was a quiet little voice that she just couldn't silence.

He isn't crazy.

You know *he isn't crazy.*

Remember how your brother changed? Something was wrong. You knew *something was wrong, and you thought it was drugs. But it wasn't drugs. It was...oh, shit. Oh, shit, no...no way...*

Swallowing the knot in her throat, swiping her sweaty palms down the front of her jeans, she said, "I want to leave now. *Right* now."

"You can't."

I can't, huh? She narrowed her eyes. "I'm leaving," she said quietly. Then she started toward the door.

In the microsecond it took her to blink, Ren was in front of her.

She never even saw him move.

One second, he was still off across the side of the room, and then he was between her and the door.

She never *saw* him move, and she never *heard* him move.

Coming to a dead stop, she gaped at him.

He watched her with sad, serious eyes. "Ali, you can't leave," he said softly.

"Don't call me *Ali*," she said, gritting her teeth. "And the hell I can't leave."

"It's not safe for you outside these walls." He gestured to the simple, elegant cabin, lifting one shoulder in a shrug. "It's just not."

"And what's so special about here?" she asked, curling her lip in a sneer.

"It's protected from demon-kind. It's set in a...blind, of sorts. The only way they'd find it would be if I literally led one to it, and I'm careful not to do that. They can't see this place, they can't sense it, and as long as you're in here, they can't sense you."

He took one step toward her.

Aileas backed away.

He went still. He barely seemed to breathe. She saw that look in his eyes—the one she'd seen before, the one that made her think she'd hurt him somehow. How? By backing away from the crazy man who thought he was a guardian angel? It hurt his feelings?

He isn't crazy, Aileas. You need to trust him.

No. Because the thought of trusting him was just too damn terrifying. Demons...after her. No. No fucking way.

Slowly, carefully, she backed away from him. From the corner of her eye, she could see the kitchen and that was her goal. There was another door there, one that opened out onto a balcony. There was also a big, shiny display of knives.

Not that she was actually going to try using one on him. But if she could get her hands on one, she'd feel better.

He wasn't trying to come after her. He stayed where he was by the front door. He didn't even blink when she grabbed one of those big, shiny knives from the big, shiny display. It flashed in the light as she inched closer to the door off the kitchen. "I'm leaving," she said softly, and she was pleased to hear that her voice wasn't shaking. She reached behind her, groping for the door. She managed to get the lock on the knob itself undone, but the rest of the locks, she couldn't do by touch alone. Shifting, keeping him in the line of her vision, she darted one quick look at the locks and then back at him.

"I've had *enough* of crazy shit, enough of weirdness. I've lost my brother, I don't need some psycho who thinks he's a—"

Ren was there.

Again, just that easy, just that quick.

One of his beautiful, long-fingered hands pressed against the door over her head, keeping her from opening it. "I'm sorry for your brother, Ali...Aileas. But running out and getting yourself hurt will not bring him back," Ren said quietly. "Stay here, until I know it's safe. Then you can go wherever you want. I'll take you there myself."

The calm, rational voice inside her head insisted she listen.

But the terrified screecher seemed to be in control and it ranted on, and on... *Oh, really. He will, huh? And when will that be? How will he know when it's safe? Does* God *tell him?*

Underneath the voice, she heard a sibilant, terribly familiar whisper, and although she *knew* where it was coming from, she couldn't block it out.

She had to get away.

She had to.

Swallowing, she glanced down at the knife she held. Clutching it in her sweaty, shaking fist, a red haze settling over her eyes, she swiped out.

The smell of blood flooded her head. She knew that

smell...she dealt with it damn near every day in her work. But she'd never actually intentionally hurt somebody.

Dazed, she lowered her hand and stared at what she'd done.

The knife started to slip from her fingers. Ren swore and caught it—bladed side down in his uninjured hand—but she didn't notice.

She was too acutely aware of what she'd done.

The red haze fogging her vision was gone like it had ever existed.

What had she done?

"Fuck, Ali, have a care, would you?" Ren muttered. "Do you want to cut yourself?"

But she didn't even hear. The blood roaring in her ears deafened her to everything else.

He was bleeding.

And she'd done that.

A vicious, crimson flood gushed from his arm, and after a few seconds of frozen terror, she leaped into action, grabbing a towel from the counter and pressing it to his arm. Babbled apologies sprang to her lips, but she bit them back. She'd damn near sliced a chunk of his arm—she could be *sorry* all she wanted. It wouldn't mean a whole hell of a lot right now, would it?

Inside, her stomach was a tangled, slippery knot of nerves, but she kept her voice cool, calm as she said, "Do you have a first-aid kit?"

A gentle hand brushed across hers. Blood smeared the back of it. She stared at the bright red smear. "I won't need it. It's all right, Ali. Let go."

Let go. She swallowed. She couldn't. She couldn't have severed anything important—it had been the middle of his forearm, the posterior side, but they'd have a long drive ahead of them to the nearest hospital and considering how much he'd already...lost...what...was...

Ren tugged the towel away from her despite her attempts otherwise. She fought him, but she might as well have fought a fucking grizzly for all the good it did.

Once he had the towel in his hand, he used it to start wiping up the blood. "Look," he said.

She tried to jerk the towel away. She needed to stop the blood. Needed...

He was holding his arm up.

There was hardly any bleeding at all.

And right before her eyes, as she watched, his flesh was knitting together. Bit by bit, smoothing out with every slow, shaking breath.

"Shit. Holy, holy shit," she whispered.

She would have backed away—hell, *run* away.

Except she couldn't move.

She didn't move, she didn't blink, she barely even breathed for the two minutes it took for the wound to completely smooth out and heal. When it was nothing but a scar on her memory, he went to wash his hands off, and his arm, taking care to get all the blood off.

When he turned back to look at her, she was still staring at the exact spot where he had been, still reliving those last few minutes, over and over.

He'd *healed*. Right before her very eyes.

It was like watching... Hell. She didn't even know how to describe it. She'd never seen anything like that before, except on movies.

As he moved to stand in front of her again, she swallowed and jerked her eyes away from him, barely able to look at him. She could still see the blood splattered on his chest—she'd *cut* him.

Why had she done that? *Why?*

"How did you do that?" she whispered. "How?"

"Goes with the territory." He sighed and skimmed a hand back over his naked scalp. "I was human once...just like you. When I was human, I could be hurt the same as any human. I could be hurt, wounded...I could take ill." A humorless smile twisted his lips and he added, "And I took ill. Often."

Then the smile faded. "I could die. I *did* die. Before my death, I made a choice. To become...this."

As he said that, he stroked the black cuff at his wrist.

That was when she saw the silvery disc, the one that had held her attention so acutely a number of times. Etched upswept wings. And right now, it was glowing a soft, silvery glow that reflected ever so lightly on his skin, although she doubted he noticed. He traced the disc with the tip of one finger, over and over, staring out the window with unseeing eyes.

"I became this—a Grimm. I hunt demons, protect people from those who'd try and claim their bodies. Either I succeed and the mortal goes free of the demonic influence. Or I...fail. Sometimes miserably. Either way, those who've been taken by demons, they die." He shot her a tired, frustrated look.

She licked her lips and looked down at her hands. She saw a few specks of blood and she froze. She'd cut him. *Hurt* him.

Nausea churned inside her gut and darkness edged in over her vision.

She swayed, staggered. But before she could fall, strong, gentle hands caught her.

"Aileas, stop."

Her teeth chattered.

Shock. Some still functioning part of her mind knew exactly what was happening. She was in shock.

But that small, sane, rational bit of her mind wasn't strong enough to keep her chaotic thoughts under control, wasn't enough to stem the rising flood of adrenaline coursing through her system. Shaking, she struggled against his hands. Why had she done that?

"*Enough!*"

His voice, hard and sharp, didn't quite penetrate the fog in her brain.

But his mouth, hungry and demanding, *that* made an impression.

One hand tangled in her hair, jerking her head back as he kissed her.

Kissed her like he could consume her...like he *would* consume her.

And she didn't mind at all.

She was breathless by the time he stopped, and her heart

was racing, but it was for entirely different reasons. Dazed, she stared at him. "What..." She licked her lips, could have moaned as she tasted him. "What was that for?"

"It seemed to be the right thing to do," he said, reaching up to trace the curve of her mouth. Then he eased back, took her arm and guided her over to the sink. She stood still and silent, watching him. It wasn't until he started to wash the splatters of blood from her hands that she realized what he was doing.

Embarrassed and still racked with guilt, she tugged on her hands and said, "Stop it."

"No."

"Why aren't you pissed off at me? I cut you," she said. Once more, she found herself staring at his arm. Once more, she found herself shaken by the smooth, unmarred perfection of his skin. Sleek, tawny gold, unscarred, unscathed.

If it wasn't for the blood she had on her hands, nobody would ever know she'd marked him.

I know, she thought, a knot settling in her throat. *I know...and that's enough.*

I know...and if all of this is for real, if he really is...if he's really an angel, *then I hurt him and all he's ever done is try to help me.*

He didn't answer her question, just rinsed the soapy water from her hands, even drying them off. But when he went to lace his fingers with hers, she snatched her hands back and moved away, shaking her head. "Why aren't you mad? How can't you be mad? I cut you. I hurt you."

Ren's mouth quirked up in a faint smile. "Love, I've hurt myself worse shaving."

She eyed his smooth, clean shaven face. "I doubt it."

He scowled. "All right then. I've hurt myself worse wrestling with my dogs, and that I can promise." He held out his arm, twisting it one way then other, so she could see the smooth, unbroken skin. "Do you see a mark on me? I'm not hurt. I heal fast, and I have had much worse injuries than a little slice on the arm."

"I guess fighting demons is hazardous." She tried to smile, but it fell flat. Hell. How insane had her life become? She was talking to a man who was almost too gorgeous, too perfect to be real...and he was a fricking *angel*. And he fought *demons*. And she even *believed* all of this insanity.

A far-off look entered his eyes. "I took worse injuries long before I became one of the Grimm," he murmured.

There it was again, that sadness in his eyes. That pain.

"Grim seems a weird thing to call guardian angels." Because he was there, because he was so close, she reached out and stroked a hand down his arm. "Shouldn't it be something cheery, happy?"

"My boss has a strange sense of humor. But it's not the *grim* you're thinking of. Think of the *Brothers* Grimm. The fairy tales. Up until a few hundred years ago, there wasn't much of a name for us. We just were."

Aileas stared at him. "The Brothers Grimm. As in the fairy tales. Why would you be named after the authors of a bunch of• fairy tales?"

"Well, the brothers weren't truly the authors. They just collected the tales and put them down on paper." Ren brushed her hair back from her face, trailed a finger across her brow, down the line of her nose.

There was something about the way he looked at her, like he wanted to commit her face to memory.

She certainly wanted to do just that with his. Not that it was necessary. There was no way she could ever forget a thing about him. Not a moment with him.

He'd leave soon, she realized.

And why in the hell did that hurt so bad?

She wanted to cry even thinking about it, and because she didn't understand it, she turned away and stared outside. "So why Grimm? There's got to be some weird significance."

"There is. Sooner or later, we do things, or things happen to us, either in our mortal lives or in our second lives that are noticed. It was...decided...that those things would get less notice if they were made more fantastical than they really were. A boy and girl following a trail of bread crumbs. A poor servant girl finding true love thanks to a fairy godmother and a glass slipper. A princess and her long hair locked in a tower."

Aileas snorted. "A bunch of kid's tales."

"Originally, they were anything but," Ren murmured. He

nuzzled her nape.

It sent a shiver down her spine, one she tried to ignore.

"But the point isn't the tales...it's what lay behind them." His hands stroked down her arms. "What is easier to brush off as a fairy tale, Ali? That a boy and girl followed a trail of breadcrumbs to a house made of gingerbread? Or that a girl was neglected and mistreated by a stepmother, a stepbrother, violently so...so much that she caught the attention of a woman who was...more than just a woman?"

Aileas stilled in his arms. Her heart knocked against her ribs as his question circled around through her head. The *words* made sense. In a distant, not quite *connected* sort of way.

But it took a full minute before she truly grasped it.

Then she knocked his arms aside and spun around, gaping at him.

"Are you *telling* me that Hansel and Gretel are real? That they are some kind of guardian angels and that their story was cooked up just to hide their real history?"

"Not at all."

"Oh." She took a deep breath, feeling slightly foolish...but a little bit better. A little less insane.

"His name was Hans, and he's rotting in hell if there's any justice in the world." Ren's mouth quirked in a smile as he added, "And she prefers the name Greta. But yes, she's real...and she's an angel. She was one of my first trainers."

Aileas covered her face with her hands.

Chapter Ten

Ren had to admit, she was taking it...rather well.

An hour later, she was still staring at him from the corner of her eye as if she expected him to point out a hidden camera, but in her heart, in her soul, she'd already accepted the truth.

Part of him knew it would have been easier if she had fought it.

It would make it easier when he disappeared from her life, as he knew he would have to do.

Angels, mortals...they didn't mix.

Aileas wasn't meant to be one of them.

There were all these crazy tales that the Grimms felt it when one of them were called to those they were intended to mentor, and that wasn't what he felt toward Aileas. No, what he wanted was to get her out of here. Far and away and out of this life, before it touched her life anymore.

It had already stolen her brother. It had left a darkness on her that he had to find some way to fix. He had to...had to take it off her before *they* sensed it, and found a way to exploit it. *Again.*

She wondered why she had lifted that knife to him, but he didn't.

He had felt that dark edge push her.

The book.

He needed to deal with it...and he couldn't wait much longer to do it.

"So which one are you?" she asked, interrupting his dark, brooding train of thoughts.

Crooking a grin at her, he said, "What makes you so certain I'm anybody of note? Not *all* of us are anybody special."

"You would be." A blush crept up her cheeks and she glanced away. "And besides, a bunch of guardian angels, how can *any* of you not be somebody special?" She drew her knees up and hugged them to her chest. "So...who are you?"

"Hmmm, that would be telling." There was nothing romantic, funny or remotely appealing behind his life. Nothing. Nothing but misery, that is. Bracing his elbows on his knees, he studied her face.

She was, without a doubt, one of the strongest mortals he'd ever known.

Blowing out a breath, he said, "I need to deal with the book and it's best I do it now. Before nightfall."

Her smooth, ivory complexion went even paler. "The book," she whispered. Her eyes seemed too dark against her skin and he could feel that fear. She licked her lips and her gaze skittered away, staring out the window, around the cabin before bouncing back to linger on his face. "Why before nightfall?"

"Demons are creatures of evil. While sunlight doesn't harm them, they fear the light. They hide from it. They cower from it. They'll return in force at night. We need to destroy it before that happens...they can't *find* this place, but they can apparently sense something about you. Or the book can. You'll be safer once the book is destroyed."

"Safer." She shook her head. "I don't know if I'll ever feel *safe* again."

Ren eased off the couch and sank to his knees in front of her. "You're safe now. Here." Brushing her hair back from her face, he touched his fingers to her chin and eased her face up until she met his gaze. "Safe with me, and I promise, while there's life in me, nothing will harm you."

Then he glanced past her, staring off into the wood. "And I'm not alone. There are others in the woods today. They'll return once this threat is done...once you're safe."

"Once I'm safe." She swallowed and shivered. "Are they after *me* or that damn book?"

"Likely both," Ren said. He lifted his shoulder and looked back at her. "I won't offer you false comfort or pretty lies, Ali. They want you, otherwise they wouldn't still be searching my territory for you. It's not worth it. They know it's madness to linger here—they know what I am. But they are willing to risk it, and it's not just for the sake of the book. There *are* other books."

Curling his hands around her ankles, he tugged her legs down. Then he pulled her down until she straddled his lap. "You resisted the book's call for a long while, even though it was close, very close. Not many mortals can do that. Most would have either dumped it or succumbed." Resting his hands on her thighs, he asked, "Why didn't you get rid of it?"

"It didn't seem right to just dump it somewhere. I was worried some kid might find it," she said. It didn't seem so foolish to voice that fear now. Now that she knew what it was. A nervous laugh escaped her. "I swear, I've spent the past couple of weeks thinking I was losing my mind. Right now I should be convinced. But I feel more sane now than I have in a long while."

Staring in his familiar, beautiful face, she laid a hand on his cheek and murmured, "Why is that?"

He turned his face into her hand and kissed it. She swayed closer and would have done more, but then, before she could blink, she was on her feet and he was swearing. "The book," he muttered, shaking his head. "Quit looking at me like that, Ali. We need to take care of the book."

Confused, she said, "Quit looking at you like what?"

"Like you can't decide if you're ready to eat me alive or have me eat you alive."

Aileas blinked. Actually, either option sounded kind of appealing. She was tempted to point that out to Ren, but he was already walking away.

It was eerie, Ren had to admit.

He had seen it happen a dozen times, and it still bothered him.

Standing behind Aileas, one arm wrapped around her shoulders, he pressed his lips to her temple and murmured to her as she stared in shock.

For the first thirty minutes, the book hadn't done much of anything, resisting the laws of physics, nature, everything. Ren had just piled more wood onto the fire and added more gasoline. Finally, there was a strange little *pop* and the book had made a weird gasping noise.

Then it started.

Screaming.

Aileas had jumped.

Now she just stared in shock. It had been nearly twenty minutes since she had made a sound, nearly that long since she had moved. Stroking a hand up and down her arm, he stared into the fire, watched as page by page curled and gave way to flame.

Another scream sounded through the air and Aileas shuddered.

"It's screaming," she whispered.

"They do that."

"It's a damn book. It's *inanimate*," she said. "It can't *scream*. But it is."

"Yes."

They did scream, like a thousand terrified children.

And it smoked, thick, black noxious smoke.

Ren was prepared for that, burning the thing outside in a cleared circle ringed with stone. The smoke churned up into the sky and he wasn't surprised when he sensed the approach of his friends sometime after the book had finally started to succumb to the flames.

He *was* a bit surprised that Aileas sensed them.

She stiffened in his arms, her sleek body tensing, the hands she had curled around his arm tightening until her nails bit into his flesh. Not a one of them had made a sound. She couldn't have heard them.

And although *he* felt them, their presence was muffled enough that Aileas shouldn't have.

She did though.

No other way to explain how she knew exactly where Greta and Rip were standing long before the smoke cleared enough to reveal their presence. No other way to explain how she knew that Elle and Michael would approach from behind, or the others who came after.

It was eerie...almost as eerie as the way the book screamed its demise. Stroking a hand down her back, he pressed his lips to her brow and murmured, "Ali."

"Who..." She barely forced the word out past her teeth before her voice died on her.

"Just friends, Aileas," he said. "Just friends."

Friends.

They didn't feel...*here.*

Aileas didn't know how else to explain it, except that they didn't feel like they were entirely *part* of this world.

Terror gripped her, tried to control her, but she forced it aside. Although she already knew *what* they were, she wasn't content with that. She had to know who they were—not just *what* but *who*, because until she asked, until she *knew*, she couldn't make them real in her head.

Staring at the brunette woman before her, she found her voice. She didn't even have to ask. The waves of compassion, something about the way she watched Ren, they filled in some of those blanks in Aileas' head.

Gretel.

No. *Greta.*

The woman who had trained him.

She didn't look much older than twenty-two or twenty-three, her hair a dark, warm brown, twisted up and worn in a complicated knot. Her eyes were deep blue, warm and soft. The man at her shoulder looked like he'd stood there her entire life—a unit. That's what they looked like—a unit.

Unsure of what to say, unsure of what she *wanted* to say, Aileas opened her mouth and said the first thing that came to mind.

"When my mom read the story *Hansel and Gretel* to me, I never once pictured Gretel looking anything like you. I always had this rosy-cheeked little blonde girl in my head."

Greta cocked her head. A slow, amused smile curled her lips and then she glanced at Ren. "You're going to get your ass kicked, my friend...telling secrets."

Ren's hand curled over the back of Aileas' nape, rested there. She felt the strength there, the warmth. "What fun are secrets, if you don't share them from time to time?" he asked.

"Hmmm. Well, then. Have your fun." Greta looked back at

Aileas. "Is the book yours?"

Aileas curled her lip. "Hell, no. Not my kind of reading material."

"Good." Then Greta rocked back on the back of her heels and focused on the fire.

Feeling the weight of somebody's gaze, Aileas looked up and found herself the object of a blonde woman's attention.

The blonde was...beautiful. Angelically so. Seductively so. Almost impossibly so. When their gazes met, a smile bowed up the other's pretty mouth. "Hello," the woman said, offering a friendly smile. "I'm Elle. Ren and I are old friends."

There was the faintest hint of an accent there...something sexy, subtle...French maybe. And although there was nothing about the way Elle looked at Ren, nothing about the way she said it, Aileas knew as well as she knew her own name that these two had been more than friends.

A *lot* more.

Jealousy wanted to curl inside her, wanted to fester.

But Aileas wouldn't let it take hold, not here. Not now.

There were too many of *them* around.

If Ren could feel what she was thinking, it was possible one of these newcomers could as well, and Aileas wasn't interested in broadcasting her thoughts, her feelings, her insecurities for all asunder.

So instead of letting jealousy take hold, she pushed it aside. She could think about that, focus on it later. "Aileas," she said.

Elle gestured to the man at her back. "This is my husband, Michael."

Another matched set. Did they all come in pairs? Aileas found her gaze wandering toward Ren, wondering about the women in his life. Where was his mate? The one who made him look like these four...a matched set. Complete. Whole. Had it been the woman she'd first seen with him? Mandy?

But even as she thought it, she pushed it aside. No. That woman hadn't been his match—his other half.

He had one though, Aileas knew, and just the thought was enough to churn up despair inside her.

Because she couldn't focus on that, on the jealousy or the pain, she pushed it aside.

Couldn't think about that, none of it. Instead, she focused on the book and asked, "So what is this? A book burning party?"

Ren could feel her pain, her distress, but he didn't know what to do about it—didn't understand what had caused it. Taking the time to understand it would be too distracting, and he couldn't get distracted right now.

Staring into the flames, he nuzzled Aileas' hair. "A party...why not? And we'll have some unwanted guests. That's why I wanted this done during the day."

In his arms, Ali tensed.

Alarm shimmered through his mind.

Closing his eyes, he opened his mind, tasted the wind on the back of his tongue.

One of his birds—the hawk—glimpsed something that didn't belong in the woods. Moving in fast, so fast.

Miles away.

But closing ground fast.

Before his mind had time to acclimate to that one, there were more whispers. All around. Nine demons in all, coming from all directions. Wrapping his arms around Aileas, he swept her into his arms. "Rip."

Without saying a word, the other man reached inside his coat. As he moved to take Ren's place at the fire, he pulled out the bladed staff he'd designed. Greta took position opposite him. As she pulled her own staff out, she said, "Get her inside, Ren. And stay with her in case one of the bastards try to get in your home."

Aileas shoved against his chest, blood rushing to her cheeks.

"Damn it, put me down," she said, squirming, blushing.

"No. I need you in the house. Trouble is coming and you're too vulnerable."

Should have moved the damn book farther away.

But he hadn't wanted to leave her alone for more than a

few minutes, and destroying a book tended to take upwards of an hour. A few minutes just wasn't enough.

At least here he had his friends able to protect her.

He had her inside the house in a matter of minutes. Settling her on the couch, he focused again.

Closer. Much closer. Damn monstrosities.

"You'll stay inside," he said quietly, reaching up to brush her hair back from her face. "No matter what. I plan on staying here, but no matter what happens, you don't leave. Understand?"

"No matter what happens?" She reached up and closed her fingers around his wrist. "What do you think is going to happen?"

"I think they'll all die." He rubbed his thumb over her lower lip. "But just to be safe, I want your word. You'll stay in the house."

Now his hand curled around the back of her neck and he squeezed. "Your word."

A sigh huffed out of her and then she whispered, "You have it."

What good did it do to *not* promise him? she wondered. Seriously.

Demons.

Could she really do a damn thing against a demon?

They aren't real. You're going crazy.

That sly little voice forced its way into her head, creating little worms to feed and fester away inside her.

Demons. Come on. Go outside and see. People, they are just people. Angels? Those friends of his are just friends. Nothing special.

Aileas closed her eyes and pressed her hands against her eye sockets, trying to block that voice out of her head.

You have to get away from this guy. He's bad for you. You've gotten worse since you've been around him. If you weren't going crazy before, you're certainly going crazy now.

"Ali?"

Dazed, she lifted her head and stared at him.

He stroked a hand down her cheek. "What's wrong?"

"Wrong?"

He pinched her chin lightly and said, "Yes. Something's wrong. I hear it, feel it. There's a voice muttering to you—I can feel it in the back of my head, like a forgotten song. But I don't know what it's saying to you. I just know something is wrong."

"It wants me to leave," she said quietly, rubbing hands up and down her arms. "Wants me out of this house. Now. Right now."

Outside, they heard something whistle through the air. Followed by a roar...then a crash.

Aileas jumped.

Ren pulled her into his arms. "Stay with me," he whispered. He pressed her head against his chest, cradled her close.

She rubbed her cheek against him, listened to the slow, heavy beat of his heart and tried to ignore that oily, nasty voice.

Come out, Aileas. Come out...

The voice was getting louder.

Louder, louder.

Taunting her.

Beckoning...

And then she heard a voice.

Not *inside* her head.

No. This time, it came from outside the cabin.

"Ali!"

She tensed in Ren's arms and then shoved away from him so hard she almost fell backward.

Her brother—that was her brother's voice.

Ren caught her arm. "Whoever you think that is, you're wrong."

She tried to dislodge him, staring past him out the window. And what she saw outside made her blood run cold.

Aileas hadn't lived a sheltered life—not exactly. But bloody, real violence, the sort of thing that happened between the pages of a book or on the silver screen? She had no experience with it, until this very moment.

The shock of it was enough to jar her out of her daze and she stood there, slack-jawed, with the blood roaring in her ears and her heart slamming against her rib cage.

"Oh, shit," she breathed out.

They moved so fast, her eyes could hardly keep up with them.

Blood flew. Weapons flashed.

Bodies fell only to leap back into the fray with single-minded intent.

In the midst of it all, there was only one soul *not* caught up in the fighting.

He stood out on the very outskirts of the clearing, and Aileas' heart skipped a beat.

He was staring straight at her.

She felt it.

He opened his mouth and again, she heard her brother's voice as he said, "Ali. Come here...come talk to me."

Her brother's voice. But not his face, and not his body.

Not him.

"Who is he to you?" Ren asked quietly.

"My brother," she said. Tears welled in her eyes and burned their way free, rolling down her cheeks in hot, stinging tracks. "He sounds like my brother. What is he? Is he...is he one of these demons?"

"Yes."

Ren didn't like the way the *orin* watched Aileas, as though she was already a tasty little treat spread out before him.

Didn't like it at all.

Backing away, Ren glanced around, tried to get a headcount, see which of his friends he could see, where they were.

Aileas—needed to do something about Aileas.

Just then, he felt something dark and powerful shudder, rip through the earth.

Powerful. Something big, something bad.

And *close*.

Aileas screamed.

Ren went to turn.

That was when he saw the *orin* make his move.

Shifting, keeping Aileas pressed close, he turned to face the other problem that had just arrived.

Bocans—aw, fuck.

The dull gold scales caught his eye, warned him and he moved, just in time. A huge, clawed hand swiped through the air, nearly taking his head off.

He heard glass shatter.

And again...Aileas.

According to Ren, this thing had once been human, but Aileas wasn't entirely sure she believed that.

Oh, the package looked human. Right up until you saw the eyes.

But the eyes?

Nothing human. Nothing sane. Just cold, hungry and empty...

"Hello, Aileas," it murmured.

She swallowed, backing away one step at a time, the fireplace at her left, the living room at her right.

It cocked its head. "Why don't you want to talk to me? Don't you know me?"

She felt something push at her mind. The face of the thing tried to shift—no, it was like a mask tried to *settle* over the thing's face, but it just wouldn't.

It was trying to make her think it was her brother.

She didn't know *why*, but Aileas knew better.

She'd buried her brother.

And somehow, something like this creature was responsible.

"You're not my brother," she said softly.

From the corner of her eye, she could see Ren, see the flash of wood and steel in his hands.

There was a crash, followed by a vicious swear.

"Don't worry about him, sweetie. He's going to be busy for a while," the thing said. "Look at me...let me see your eyes."

Behind her, she heard a hoarse shout.

The thing in front of her chuckled. "Oh, dear. Your poor little angel just got his wings clipped..."

Something sick, painful hit her in the stomach. She staggered.

The thing in front of her smiled.

One second later, she was staggering over some horrible knowledge—something she couldn't let herself think about. Then she had the metal poker from the fireplace in her hand.

As the thing lunged for her, she lifted it and plunged.

The demon howled and jerked back, the poker buried in its eye.

Greta appeared at its back, a vicious, hot smile on her face. She looked at Aileas over the thing's shoulder and said, "Well done, kid. I knew I'd like you."

As Greta buried a blade in the demon's heart, Aileas turned, her eyes seeking out Ren.

When she saw him, fallen, broken and still, the very light went out of her world.

Chapter Eleven

He hovered in a place of white...nothingness.

The light, it came from everywhere and nowhere.

Will was there, and no one else.

"Will?"

"Hello, Thomas."

Ren looked around and then down at himself.

The last thing he could remember was the clawed hand of the *bocan*, coming down at him. He hadn't been able to move in time—splitting his attention between the *orin* and the *bocan*—a damn big demon. Who had brought that bastard in?

"The *orin* did," Will said, answering Ren's unspoken question. "He wanted your lady—a soul as strong hers, it would keep him amused for quite some time, and he wanted you busy with something else. It worked."

Ren grimaced and touched his chest. Under his hand, it was whole. But back on earth, back in the mortal world, somehow, he doubted that was the case.

The Grimm could survive most injuries, but not all. If the heart was destroyed, the heart, the brain...

That first, fiery pain had lasted but a second and then everything had gone dark.

"I'm dead, aren't I?" he asked, his voice quiet, accepting. It was over. He was done. And he had failed...again. "I'm dead and that thing got his hands on Ali."

"Oh, your Ali is a tough one. Strong. Stronger than your sister, stronger than your mother," Will said. He moved through the wispy white fog wrapping around their ankles and rested a hand on Ren's shoulder. "I think it's time you accept one simple truth, Thom. What happened to your sister, your mother...it isn't your fault."

Ren closed his eyes.

That was a truth he couldn't accept.

He should have protected them—

"You were a boy, trying to do an adult's job. Your mother should have done the protecting. If anybody failed, it was her. Not you."

Ren looked around them, looked at the sheer, utter nothingness. "Isn't this an odd time to be discussing this? It's over. It's done."

"Is it?" Will murmured. He reached up, touched his fingers to Ren's temple. "You play the part of the madman so well, but there were times when you did slip a little too close to the line...how well do you remember them? Do you remember the *first* time?"

Ren jerked away as he felt Will's push at his mind, at his memories. "What does it matter if I pretend to be a bit more insane than I am? It's not like I ever harmed a soul for it." Grief twisted his heart and he rubbed the heel of his hand over his chest. Even here, in this place past death he could feel the guilt. "Aileas. Please tell me the *orin* didn't take her body. Please tell me that."

"Her soul is too strong for him." Will stared at Ren, his silver eyes glowing. "You need to remember, Thom, remember what pushed you to that madness. You need to remember, so you can let go of the guilt."

"*No.*" Ren went to spin away. But he found he couldn't move.

Then he couldn't see.

He was lost in darkness, falling back. Back...back...

London, 1889

It was Rose.

Thom couldn't believe it.

It was *Rose.*

He went to leap out of the carriage, to catch his sister in his arms and embrace her, but a hand on his arm stopped him.

"Thom, wait," Greta said, her voice quiet and soft.

She was staring out the window, her eyes on the young woman walking down the street, but the look in her eyes was one that turned Thom's joy to worry...then fear.

"Greta, that is Rose. The sister I told you about. The one I thought had died."

When she looked back at him, there was such sorrow, such sadness in her eyes.

"I am so sorry, Thom, but that isn't your sister."

"*No!*" Aileas scrambled for Ren's side, slipping through the blood, uncaring about the dead thing at her back.

Or the...thing twitching and jerking a few feet away. Her eyes couldn't even process what *that* was, but one thing was certain. *It* had never been human.

Her heel slipped in the blood.

Ren's blood and she damned near fell on her ass, but she caught her balance, steadied and then stumbled her way to his side.

No.

She pressed her hands to her mouth, but they didn't quite muffle the sob. *No...*

Slowly, she started to rock, staring at his face.

Only his face though, because she couldn't stare anywhere else. If she did... Reaching up, she touched one cheek, already cool. His eyes, dark, so dark, stared ahead.

"Ren," she whispered.

A pristine pair of white boots appeared in her field of vision. Numb, she lifted her gaze and found herself staring at a stranger.

"Hello, Aileas."

The stranger held out a hand.

She just shook her head and looked back at Ren. She touched his left shoulder and stroked a hand down his arm, closed her hand around his. Lifting his fingers to her lips, she kissed them.

Fate, she realized, was a bitter, ugly bitch.

Finally, there was a man in her life that she could really care about, really get attached to, and there were obstacles—oh, were there obstacles. One. He was an angel.

Two...now he was dead.

A sob was trapped in her throat, desperate to break free.

"How can you die?" she whispered. "Angels aren't supposed to die, are they?"

It had been easier, Thom realized, when he had thought Rose was dead.

Now, staring into those mad, hungry eyes, he closed his fingers around her fine-boned wrists and struggled to keep her from touching him. "That is quite enough," he snarled.

"Oh, don't be such a bore," she said, smiling at him.

He shoved her back. She tripped and went down as he went for the door.

But before he reached it, his mother—or what had *used* to be his mother—was there blocking him.

"Oh, you couldn't possibly leave us yet," she whispered.

She wrapped something around his neck, sharp—strong— *too* strong. She squeezed, and squeezed, and as she choked the life out of him, both she and the thing that had been Rose, they laughed.

Small hands touched him, bare skin to bare skin, and he felt the sickness, the darkness, and the evil that lived inside the human shell. It snapped something inside him.

No...this was no longer his sister.

Three years had passed since he'd been lifted out of that cellar, and he was no longer the skinny, sickly boy he'd been. Strong and healthy and pushed too far, he reached out and grabbed the delicate, slender woman...a woman who fought with the strength of a demon.

A woman who now *housed* a demon.

Snarling, infuriated, mourning the sister who was now forever lost to him, Thom snapped the thing's neck, even as the demon behind him wailed and once more started to choke him.

When he came back to himself, his first coherent thought was...*let her.*

Of course, it was more than a century too late, and that demon was already dead.

Groaning, he opened his eyes and glared at Will. "Did I

have to have that memory back?"

"You blame yourself. For the death of your sister, but if anybody is to blame, it's your mother. You warned her about the man she was going to marry and she did it anyway. When she married him, she placed your sister in the hands of evil— that's not your fault. Stop carrying that burden, Ren."

Shooting Will a wry grin, Ren tucked his hands in his pockets and said, "Isn't this an odd time for a pep talk? Right outside the pearly gates?"

"Is that really where you want to go?"

Will turned and lifted a hand.

The fog cleared and Ren found himself staring into his cabin.

His seriously destroyed cabin.

Aileas was there. Kneeling beside him.

"Ahh, bloody hell," Ren muttered, staring at the ruin of his body. "Get her out of there, Will. And take that memory away. She doesn't need to remember that."

"I've no right to alter the memory of mortals," Will said.

"Don't hand me the company line," Ren snarled. "You can take that memory, I know you can. Get her out of there and take that from her. She doesn't need to remember me dead and gutted. She'd be best if she didn't remember me at all."

"Is that what you want?" Will looked at him. "Wouldn't you rather have your life with her?"

Ren gritted his teeth. "I'm dead," he snarled. "Look at me. I'm nothing but meat there."

"What do you want, Thom?" Will continued to stare at him. "Your life? With her?"

"She's not to be one of us. I'd have felt it."

Will shook his head. "That's not your only choice, lad. You know this."

Something inside Ren's heart, in his gut started to burn. He wanted to look back at Aileas—wanted to reach out and touch her. But he feared to...feared to hope. Feared to want.

"What are you asking me?" he rasped.

"I'm asking you...*what do you want?*"

"Her. I want *her*."

119

Slowly, Will's mouth curled into a smile.

And then...the light exploded.

"Come, Aileas," the man said again, holding out his hand. "There isn't much time for me to do this."

Greta moved to kneel next to her. "Trust him," she said quietly.

Aileas shook her head, unable to do that, unable to think, unable to do anything but stare at Ren's face.

The man crouched down across from her, just on the other side of Ren's ruined body.

"Do you want him?" he asked quietly, drawing her eyes to him.

Aileas found herself staring into his eyes. Strange silver eyes. Eyes that glowed.

"I hardly know him," she said, forcing out the words she *should* say.

"That isn't what I asked. Do you want him?" he asked again.

"Yes..."

He held out a hand. "Then come."

Slowly, uncertain what he was about, she placed her hand in his.

As she did, he laid the other on Ren's shoulder.

There was light.

There was rushing wind.

And then she remembered *nothing...*

Greta wiped her watering eyes as she stood up.

Rip waited for her, staring at the spot where Ren had lain, bleeding.

The floor was nearly black with his blood. Too much of it. Far too much of it.

"Did I just see that?" Rip asked softly.

"Yes." Then she scowled and said, "At least I think you did. I think."

"Good." He nodded. Thoughtfully, he reached up and stroked his chin. Then he asked, "Okay, explain to me what I just saw."

"Now *that* I can't say."

She glanced up as Elle and Michael came inside—through the window. The very much destroyed window. They looked as mystified, as confused as she felt. Lifting her hands, she said, "Don't ask me. I don't have a clue."

Then she looked at the dead body of the *bocan*, the human corpse—all that remained of the *orin*. Once the demon hosts died, the host bodies died as well, which meant there were now six or seven dead bodies to deal with, as well as the *bocan*.

With a sigh, she said, "Let's get to work on clean-up."

Chapter Twelve

He could smell her hair, Ren realized.

A figment of his imagination, most likely, and something twisted in his heart. Grief.

He'd promised to protect her and he'd failed.

Then pain tore through his chest and he groaned, curling inward against the pain.

That hurt even more.

The pain, more than anything else, had him opening his eyes.

And that was when he realized he was in his cabin.

His cabin.

Not in some fogged, misty white nowhere land.

And Aileas was sleeping, curled up against him, one hand resting on his chest.

"Ali..."

She sighed in her sleep, but didn't wake.

Easing upright, he studied the heavy white bandage swathing his chest. He didn't remember that—well, he remembered taking a wound, but what the bocan had done should have cut him open clear to his spine, not left him with an oversized Band-Aid.

"Wondering why you aren't dead?"

Following the sound of that familiar voice, he saw Will sitting in a chair near the window. The boarded-up window.

That was when he grew aware of the faint sounds of hammering, sawing. Laughter and talking.

"What's going on?"

"Your friends are fixing your cabin," Will said. "It will be a while before you're up to it. You won't heal the way you used to, you know."

Frowning, Ren tried to follow that, but he was still trying to figure out why he was *here*. Passing a hand over his eyes, he eased back down in the bed. He felt so weak—hadn't felt this weak since he'd been...*mortal*.

Hell.

"You took my wings," he said, looking at Will.

"No—you gave them up," Will corrected. "But...I knew you would. It was time for you. And maybe I cheated a bit—I can use my gifts to undo the damage done when you become a Grimm. Why not use them to undo the damage done to give you one more chance at life?"

Then Will stood. "Don't make me regret it, Thom."

Before Ren could even process that, Will was gone.

Somehow, Ren knew he wouldn't be seeing the man again. Not in this life.

Closing his eyes, he murmured, "Thank you."

Turning his face into Aileas' hair, he fell back asleep.

"No, no, no..."

"Wake up," Ren said.

Ali whimpered in her sleep.

Although the pain in his chest made him half-sick, he sat up and pulled her into his lap. "Ali, wake up," he said again, louder. He tapped her cheek lightly, and then harder, but it didn't do any good.

She struggled in his arms, harder, harder, and then she screamed.

Ren swore. "Damn it, Ali, wake *up*!"

Her eyes flew open, glazed and blind, staring at him, but he knew she wasn't seeing him.

"You're dead," she said, her voice harsh, ragged and high. "I saw you. You're dead...it killed you, but you're not supposed to die..."

Capturing her face in his hands, he dipped his head and pressed his mouth to hers. "I'm not dead, Ali. I'm here."

Her mouth trembled under his.

Then a half-sob escaped her. "Ren?"

"Shhh," he murmured. "I'm here. I'm right here."

She jerked away, her eyes wide and unseeing. "But I saw you. You were dead. You were..." She ran her eyes over him, staring at the heavy bandage on his chest. "You were dead."

"Somebody cheated, bent the rules a little for me," he murmured, plucking at the bandage. "I...ah...but I think I'm going to have to hang around and live the normal life for a while. As in...for good."

Ali didn't seem to notice as she rolled to her knees, inspecting the bandage. "This isn't real, can't be happening," she muttered. "I *saw* you. Wait..." She paused and covered her face with her hands. "There was a guy. White-haired guy, but not old. Just...well, he had white hair, white clothes. Silver eyes. He felt *strange*."

"That's Will." He caught one of her hands and lifted it to his lips, pressed a kiss to the back.

"He was in the cabin, asking me what I wanted. Then he gave me his hand, and he touched you and there was this blast of light and we were someplace...*else*. I can remember feeling his hand on mine and he was telling me to hold on to you, to keep talking, not to let you go." A soft sob escaped her. "Then...I don't know. I don't remember."

She scrubbed the tears from her face and stared at him. "How can you be *here*?"

"A miracle?" He reached out and traced his finger over the curve of her lip. "I wasn't ready to leave this world yet. I could have, but..."

She caught his wrist. "But what?"

"I'd just discovered the most amazing woman, and I wanted to know more about her."

She blushed. "That's insane. You hardly know me."

"It's not insane," Ren said, shrugging. He caught her hand in his, held it as he eased back on the bed. He was so damn tired. "And if anybody would be insane, it would be me. I felt drawn to you the first time I saw you. What's insane is ignoring it. Can you tell me you don't feel it too?"

"No." She stared down at him, stroked his cheek. "No, I can't tell you that. But this is still insane. I don't even know your name...is Ren your first name? Your last?"

He grimaced. "It's part of my last name."

Then he sighed and closed his eyes. "I was born Thomas Renfield, but I haven't gone by that name in a very, very long time. I'm not overly fond of it."

"Why not? It's not like they named you something like *Milton* or some super-geek name."

"Milton." Ren laughed and opened his eyes, smiled up at her. "It's not the name, so much though. It's the life that was attached to that name. It was a miserable one, truth be told. Not many happy memories there."

He grimaced. Might as well get it all out, let her know the whole of it. "Do you read much? Watch movies?"

"Yeah. I guess."

"You asked me who I'm supposed to be...or I *was* would be more accurate." A grimace twisted his lips. "What does the name *Renfield* mean to you?"

"Renfield—he was the crazy guy in Dracula."

"Yes." Ren stared at her.

Her eyes went wide. "Holy shit." Then she clapped her hand over her mouth and blushed a painful shade of red.

He snorted. "Ali, I've had a long time to adjust to the stories that attached themselves to that name. Trust me, I've heard it all, but why don't I make it easy for you? No, I never attached myself to some blood-drinking monster, and no, I don't recall eating spiders or birds. But there was a time when I ate a number of unsavory things—if a bird or spider had been placed before me and I could catch it, I might well have eaten it." He stared at the ceiling, remembering the years he'd spent trapped in a cellar.

He slid her a look and managed a tight smile. "I do have more than a passing acquaintance with insanity though. For a while, insanity and I were close friends. *Very* close. And there were times through the past century or so where that darkness pushed too close."

Certain he'd look into her eyes and see disgust, or fear, or pity, he braced himself.

But she just laid a hand on his cheek. "I think quite a few of us have had a brush or two like that. You just came closer than some, maybe. But I still don't get how you and the nut from that book..." She winced. "Shit, I'm sorry."

Ren caught her wrist and tugged her down, nuzzled her neck. "Don't be. It started after one of my 'brushes' with insanity. Apparently the author of the book saw me having one of my...moments. I don't remember it, but Will was there and he... Well, by the time he was done explaining that moment, he'd painted a nice, crazy picture."

"Now that seriously sucks. You spent the past hundred years dealing with that because your friend's got a weird sense of humor?"

Ren laughed. "After you've been around as long as he has, a weird sense of humor keeps you sane. Maybe I should have cultivated a stranger sense of humor myself."

He slid an arm around her, eased her closer. "You realize...I'm not leaving."

"You need to heal up."

"Yes, and it's going to take a while." Pressing his brow to hers, he said, "My wings are gone, Ali. I'm not one of them anymore. I'm mortal again. I'm human. I'm going to grow old. I'm going to die. But before I do that, I've got a life to live...and I want to do it with you."

Tears glinted in her eyes. A watery laugh escaped her. "This really is insane. We don't know each other. Not at all."

"Yes, we do." He rubbed his mouth against hers. "We know what we need to know...that's how we recognized each other the moment we saw each other. I've been waiting my whole life to find you, Ali. And I think you've been waiting for me."

She smiled against his lips. "Maybe you really are crazy. And maybe I am too. Because I think you just might be right."

Tarnished Knight

Dedication

Mandy...you still have to wait. As you can see, you're not ready yet.

Lynn, I never would have thought to try Rapunzel. But then I got to nosing around and discovered the older version and wheels started to turn.

Ann in CA, thanks for the help. I appreciate it!

Prologue

She looked...broken.

Will stared at her face and tried to remind himself that in stasis, her body healed, her mind slept, and she knew nothing of the painful memories. It had been only weeks...

A warm, comforting presence brushed against his mind.

He wanted to shut it out, but he knew he could not.

"I don't want to leave her alone," he said quietly.

There was an acknowledgement...and understanding.

He hadn't been able to leave Mandy's side since he'd brought her here.

He couldn't leave her now.

But—

The knowledge came to him, filled his mind and he knew the job that awaited, who was meant to go to the job and what lay ahead.

What awaited Perci.

Only Perci.

Abruptly, he scowled.

"You mean to separate them? But they belong together," he said. They needed only to heal to see that.

Even as he said it, he wondered why he asked. He always questioned...and he was always wrong.

There was no answer this time. Just a patient silence.

"Very well."

Shifting his gaze, he said, "Who is to tell them though? If I'm to remain here...?"

Chapter One

"All of it?"

Luc smirked as he listened to the hair stylist's horror.

He'd heard the dismay a hundred times, it seemed. More. Every time Perci did this.

"Yep. All of it."

"But...I don't get it. Oh, wait, maybe this is for *Locks of Love* or something? Sweetie, you know, it's nice you wanting to help those kids with cancer, but most of that's nothing but a scam. I heard they don't even get all the hair. There's better ways to help them, you know."

At his side, Krell stiffened.

Luc rested a hand on the dog's head, and without a blink he melded their minds and stared through the dog's eyes. It was his only way to see...unless Perci let him use her eyes, and she wouldn't.

Not right now.

She never let him inside when she hurt, and now, she hurt.

Through Krell's eyes, he could see that her face had gone tight with grief.

Her hands gripped the armrests of the chair.

Swearing under his breath, Luc reached down and grabbed Krell's harness. He didn't need it though—he used it more to make those around him comfortable.

He might be blind, but he'd developed a phenomenal sense of awareness living like that for three hundred years.

I am one of with the force.

Besides, he also had Krell's vision. He stopped just a few inches from the chair, reached out and rested a hand on the counter where the stylist kept her tools. There was a pair of scissors there, shears, whatever they called them. "So it's a haircut you want, *chere*?" he said.

The stylist gasped with horror as he took the scissors. And she wasn't quite swift enough to stop him as he spun the chair around, found the thick, heavy cable of Perci's hair.

"Rapunzel, let down your hair..." he teased as he began to cut through the golden braid.

He was halfway through when the stylist finally emerged from her frozen state.

"Sir, you can't do that! You...you're blind!"

"Well, you weren't doing it," he pointed out. Politely, he held out the scissors. "She asked for you to cut it off, and you stand here babbling about it instead of doing it, although I do believe that's your job. If you don't want *me* doing it, perhaps you would like to finish it up?"

They left thirty minutes later.

Slipping his arm around her waist, he pressed his lips to Perci's brow. "She did not intend to make you sad, *chere*."

"I know." She sighed and leaned into him. "I think you almost gave her a heart attack, baby. You really can't go picking up sharp objects around all these people who don't get that you're not going to stumble into them."

He would have replied, but at just that moment, the pendant he wore around his neck heated.

Perci stiffened, then sighed.

"Well, it looks like we're working tonight," she murmured. "Damn it, I wanted to go out, have a drink or something."

Of course she wanted to go out. Anything to avoid having a quiet night alone with him.

She hated those.

She avoided them as often as possible.

"Perhaps tomorrow." As he said it, he felt a heavy, painful ache in his heart, one he didn't entirely understand. Brushing it aside, he reached up and touched his hand to her nape. Touch wasn't needed for him to see through her eyes, but knowing her emotions were raw, he wanted to warn her before he did so.

Although after so many years together, she likely knew. She turned her head and together, they glanced through the metal exit doors tucked off the side of the mall's main walkway.

It was empty.

"Cameras," Perci said.

"Yes. Well, if it's that important, he can handle them. He'll know they are there."

"Yes."

They pushed through the doors and headed outside. Krell walked at their side, his nails clicking on the ground. Luc bent down and lifted the dog in his arms as he felt the tightening in the air. The dog didn't care for this method of transportation. Gently, he pressed on the dog's throat until he went lax.

"Sorry, my friend," he whispered. "It will be easier if you just sleep through this."

A moment later, he saw the brilliant flash of light through Perci's eyes.

And then they were passing through it.

The silent and swift travel was a means available only to Will. He could let anybody use it though. Luc didn't need much time to figure out why they had come to Will, instead of Will coming to them.

It was the girl.

There were a hundred rumors floating among the Grimm about this girl...and Will.

Their leader, all but brought to his knees by a mortal girl who liked to dye her hair purple, one who teased and mocked him.

Except she was no longer mortal.

Mandy was now one of the Grimm—a guardian angel, and her passage from her old life must have been brutal.

Very brutal, Luc realized. It had been a few weeks since her mortal death and she still slept, her body in stasis as she healed. He could not see, but his other senses were remarkably acute, and he could smell the unmistakable scent of raw, healing flesh. A *lot* of it.

The image of her fogged and he knelt down, placed Krell's sleeping form on the ground before he rose and wrapped an arm around Perci's shoulders.

It hurt for Perci to look at the girl, at what had been done to her. "She heals, *cher*," he whispered.

"Yes." She nodded and blinked away the tears. "We all heal...more or less."

Then she reached up and touched the corner of one sightless eye. "Right?"

Catching her wrist, he pressed a kiss to her hand. He had healed better than she had. Perhaps he couldn't see, but he had adjusted to that. Her broken heart though...it had never healed. Not over what had been done to her, or him, or to their children.

He'd failed her...failed to protect her, failed to help her heal...failed her so miserably.

I hate it when he looks at me like that. Even though he can't see me right now. That only happens when he's looking at me through Krell's eyes or if I'm looking in a mirror.

He doesn't have to *see* me to really see me.

Not Luc.

He sees clearer than anybody.

He sees me, he loves me...and I no longer love him.

It's not that I don't *want* to. If I could force myself to do it, I would have done it ages ago. Centuries. But I can't make my heart feel what just isn't there. The cold lump of muscle and flesh inside my chest is mostly worthless anyway.

What little love I *am* capable of, what little love I *do* feel, I give to Luc, but it isn't enough.

I know I'm not giving him what he needs. I'm not in love with him.

He died for me, he came back for me and even though I know he needs me, I can't feel much more than a distant sort of love for him. I don't love anybody since our babies died.

"Perci."

I looked away from Luc and saw Will. He was in a chair by the woman's bed. Mandy, I thought. Her name was Mandy.

My shields buckled and shuddered under the pain I felt coming off her, even in stasis. *Steady...steady...*

Although the thought of feeling *that* much pain was enough to make my stomach clench, I eased myself closer to the bed. If it was this bad for me, I couldn't think of how bad it had been for her. If Will needed me to ease things for her, speed her healing, I could do that.

"Do you need my help?" I asked, lifting a hand. My fingers curled into a fist, then spread out, hovering over her battered, broken body. Just the thought of taking on that agony had me shuddering.

Luc rested a hand on my spine, steadying me.

But Will reached up, closed a hand around my wrist and squeezed lightly. "No, Perci," he said softly, never taking his eyes from Mandy's face. "She cannot heal fast."

I looked at him.

His face was emotionless, his silver eyes flat.

But something about his words made me ache.

Looking back at the woman, I studied her injuries deeper. The bandages and dressings and blankets in the way made no difference—they wouldn't, not to a healer. We can *feel* the damage. I sank ever so slightly inside her and then stumbled back, staggering into Luc's long, lean form.

He caught me, steadied me.

"Perci?" He hugged me gently.

Shaking my head, I whispered, "Holy shit."

I've seen bad things in my time. Very bad things. In three hundred years, you realize there are things that people can do to the human body that defy description. And that's just what the *humans* do—that's not including the demons.

But I wasn't sure I'd ever seen anybody living with this much damage. I know I'd never *felt* this much. Not even when I'd healed Luc…

She did still live—she healed. She would eventually wake from the healing sleep of stasis and she'd be one of us—was already one of us really, because no human could live with those injuries.

Although why would she *want* to be one of us…when we hadn't been able to do a better job caring for her when she was still mortal?

"Man, what did they do to her?" I whispered before I could stop myself.

"You don't want to know what they did to her," Will murmured.

A spasm tightened Will's face. I realized he looked...older. Not old, at least not physically. We don't age, at least not unless we decide we're done with the guardian bit, and I don't think Will is ever going to be done. It's all he knows.

Then again, maybe not. Judging by how he looks at this girl...this *kid*...because she couldn't be much more than that, even by mortal standards.

I hadn't ever seen his face so heavy with grief.

It was a nice face too. Pretty, almost too pretty.

But he had sad, sad eyes.

He looked away from Mandy's face, focused on mine. Those silvery eyes were emotionless now, flat and hard. "I have a job...for you, Perci. Just you."

"Just me?" I blinked, then shook my head. I didn't *do* jobs on my own. I hadn't, not even once. I couldn't. Shit...Luc...he needed me. Damn it, Luc *needed* me.

And even as I stood there gaping at Will, thinking it, even as that little voice was circling through my head, part of me thought... *Luc needs you?*

Damn straight he needed me. Without me he spent his days totally lost in darkness. He *needed* me. *Me.*

"No." Focusing my eyes on Will, I shook my head. "No. Can't happen."

Will lifted a brow. "It's not up for discussion. This assignment falls to you, and you alone."

"But Luc needs me."

"Perci," Luc said, his voice soft and level.

Turning, I stared at him. "No. We don't get separated. Ever."

Not in three hundred years. We just don't. Even thinking about it was enough to leave me shaking.

"Perci, I think I can take care of myself." His eyes, beautiful green eyes, sought out my face, and although I knew he didn't see me, it looked like he did. Felt like he did.

Three hundred years ago, he had been one of the finest marksmen in France. A skilled swordsman. My husband. My *life.*

I might not love him anymore, but I owed him.

And damn it, even after all these years, I sometimes forget how easily he can sense my moods, my thoughts.

I can feel a person's physical pain, but his gifts run deeper than that...especially with me.

His face went tight, hard.

"Will, if you would, open your pathway." Luc knelt down and took Krell in his arms, not sparing me even a glance.

"Damn it, Luc, whatever this job is, there's no reason we can't both go."

"There must be," Luc said, his voice soft...incredibly reasonable, incredibly calm.

And sad.

So sad, my throat felt thick with tears. "Luc..."

But Will was already opening the path.

A moment later, Luc was gone.

Damn it!

No.

Damn *me*. I'd done it again—ripped out his heart. *Again.*

Turning around, I glared at Will. "Damn it, he needs me."

"No, he doesn't." Will stood, staring at me. "And you don't need or want him. How long will you make him suffer like this?"

I gaped at him. "Make him *suffer*? Damn it, he wants me with him. He *wants* me. He *loves* me."

"Yes...but he wants you to love him, and you'll never love him again. Not the way you once did."

"That isn't fair."

"And is it fair to him for you to hurt him as you do, Perci? Is it fair for him to grieve, to reach for you and have you turn your back on him? Fair of you to do anything and everything to avoid spending any time alone with him?"

I flinched. Pain clawed at me. It was nothing but truth...and it hurt. "That's none of your business, damn it."

"No. None of my business. But Luc doesn't *need* you, and clinging to him, for fear of life, to keep from living, it's not fair to either of you. You use him as a shield. He might use your eyes so he can still glimpse this world, but you use him to hide from it. That is over—no more hiding, Perci." He lifted a hand and another silver circle of light flashed into existence. "Life is living, Perci. Even for us. Go live it."

I didn't step into the circle. I wanted to stand here, fight with him, argue. Resist whatever he was trying to push me into.

But then he did *push* me. Maybe not with his hands, but I felt the push all the same.

I started to fall, and I just kept falling for moments on end. When it stopped, I crashed to my knees on hard, rough pavement, hard enough to split the skin. It hurt and I swore, even as warmth rushed through, healing the minor injuries.

Rising to my feet, I looked all around, trying to figure out what in the hell was going on.

And there, right in front of me, was a man surrounded by three of the demonic.

Taunting them.

"I will never have her back, will I?" Luc asked quietly when he found himself back in the cabin.

"No."

He nodded.

"I'm sorry."

Surprise rippled through him. He wished he could see Will's face, but Krell was still sleeping, and he wouldn't have brought him through that passageway, not unless he had no choice.

"You're sorry," Luc murmured. "Why are you sorry?"

"You love her still."

Sadly, Luc smiled. "Yes. I love her still. Three hundred years—do you think I could stop loving her as easy as that?" Then he reached up and touched his dead eyes. "She is a part of me, a part of my life, my past. Yes. I will always love her."

He turned away, feeling so raw, so exposed. "I wanted so much to heal her, to give her peace for what was taken from us. For what was *done* to us, for what I let happen to her. I couldn't protect her from that, I couldn't protect our children, and I couldn't give her peace. How much more completely could I fail her, Will?"

"You didn't fail her, Luc. She wouldn't *let* herself heal. You can't fault yourself for that," Will said quietly.

Humorlessly, Luc smiled. "Can't I?"

Pain, guilt gnawed at him. "Will..." He paused and then blew the breath out. "Is she going to be happier now? Is she going to find whatever it is that I could never give her?"

"I think she will find what she needs," Will said, choosing his words carefully. "But this is no fault of yours. Perci's pain— she kept it close, Luc. You know that. Part of her wouldn't *let* it go. She wouldn't let you help her."

"Yes. I know this." Bitter anger tried to rise inside him, but he wouldn't let it.

The anger would bubble and burn and boil out, but not here.

He'd give into it when he was alone...and lost in his own darkness. This time, forever.

Selfish, selfish bastard...

"It's not selfish to be angry over losing your window into the world," Will said quietly. "And you're fooling yourself if you think that's the only reason you're angry."

"Send me back, Will." The anger grew and grew. He had to get out before it exploded. Before it killed him.

Chapter Two

This was one bad-ass idea that's going to kill me, Jack Wallace thought.

But he didn't regret it.

"Oh, come on, you fucking pussy," he said, panting as one of them tried to sneak around him. He dropped and spun, taking the bastard's feet out from under him. "Can't three of you handle me? I'm human, crying out loud."

He knew what these things were, and if that fucking Will didn't show up and help out the way he'd promised, the way he'd always done in the past—

A flash of red-gold caught his eye.

It was a girl, reed-slender, long and lean, her hair cropped close to her scalp. She didn't belong here—that heart-shaped face, those big brown eyes. She didn't belong here and she'd be lucky if she didn't end up dead or worse—and oh, man, was there worse than dead.

The image of worse stained his mind, and the savage pleasure he'd felt as he lost himself in the fight faded.

Swearing, Jack reached inside his jacket and pulled out the Desert Eagle he'd kept tucked inside his coat. It was modified, silenced, deadly as hell.

It would take down the demon-possessed, mostly by putting a hole the size of Kansas through their sternums, and that was why he didn't like using it. It left too noticeable a trail. But if he didn't...do...something...

Holy...

Shit.

He lowered the Eagle to his side and stared dumbly around him.

The girl—no—woman.

As young as she looked, she wasn't a girl.

She wasn't a girl, and she wasn't human either, he realized.

If he'd taken more than a split second to look at her earlier, he would have seen it. It all but glowed...*all* over her. And for the briefest moment, she looked damned familiar. She stood there, with one hand on a cocked hip, her head tilted to the side and a smirk on her lips.

And three demons at her feet.

Jack had only taken down one of them. And it wasn't even dead yet—or at least, the demon inside it wasn't giving up. Jack could feel it pushing at him. Pushing against him psychically, and as he grimaced and prepared himself for that mental battle, the woman came sauntering up and smirked at him. "Amateur," she said, her voice vaguely accented.

Then she crouched down and used a blade to hurry along the demon's demise.

Abruptly, the pushing and shoving and crowding Jack had felt against his mental shields stopped.

He barely noticed though.

A silver chain had slipped free from her white shirt.

It held a silver disc...*wings.*

Mesmerized, Jack stared at the pendant.

As she straightened up, she reached inside her pocket and withdrew a snowy white handkerchief and used it to wipe the blood from the knife.

"A word of advice if you're going to play with things like this? When you actually try to kill them, make sure you don't just *try*. Do it. If that thing had gotten its hooks inside you... Well, by the time you figured it out, it would be too late."

She waggled her knife so that the blade caught the light and reflected it. "Then I'd also be sticking this knife inside *you*."

With that, she tucked the knife away, turned on her heel and sauntered away.

He might have said something—told himself he needed to. But he couldn't think. At least not just yet. His brain was still trying to process what he had just seen—that silver necklace...a silver disc.

Upswept wings...

He'd seen that before.

On the neck of his mother.
Before she died.

What the hell...

"Just keep walking," I muttered. I kept telling myself that, over and over, and somehow I managed to keep walking.

One foot after the other, and fast, because if I stopped or even slowed, I knew I'd look back, and I wasn't about to let myself get curious over what I'd just seen.

And what *did* I just see?

Who...man, I wonder what his name is...

"No. Don't think about that. Or him. And it's a *what*, don't think about him as a who."

Just a *what*, I told myself. An anomaly, just an anomaly. "You saw some demons. They are dead now. End of. Doesn't matter how they got dead, as long as they *are* dead."

And throughout that entire mental pep talk, I kept walking.

Fast. Very fast.

Before I could give in to the urge to look back.

And I desperately wanted to look back and see him. Curiosity wasn't something I'd felt much of, not in a good long while. But I wanted to look back, wanted to see him again. Badly.

He wasn't a pretty man...no polished, perfect prince. About as far from Luc as he could be. Broad and rough, that craggy face looked like it had been carved from golden granite or something. His eyes had stared into mine with something that closely resembled the shock I'd felt, although man, I hoped I hid it better.

I probably had. Several hundred years of practice had better prove useful for that much at least.

His eyes...

I swallowed. My knees got a little weak thinking about those eyes. They were the color of the mist in the early morning, almost too soft, too gentle for that hard face, but as he'd stared at me, they'd darkened. Darkened to smoke...

Part of me wondered if maybe that wasn't something I couldn't get lost in. And even as I thought that, I wanted to kick myself. It was wrong to think that.

Luc. I needed to think of Luc. I needed to finish this damn job so I could get back to him.

He was no longer my husband.

No, I'd seen to that well enough. It had broken something inside us both when I forced that issue, and I'd hated myself for knowing I'd broken Luc's heart. We stayed together though, and I told myself that it didn't matter if we were married or not.

I told myself it was enough because he needed me. I needed him.

We were a pair, the two of us, whether we were married or not.

But it didn't matter if I *was* married—Luc was still there, still a part of my life and thinking about a sexy *mortal* stranger? We can just place that in a column marked "Things I don't need to do".

Although one thing I *did* need to do. I needed to figure out just *why* a mortal had been fighting a couple of *orin* in an alley.

How in the *hell* had he managed to hold his own?

Well, other than the obvious—being damn strong. And fast. Shit, he was fast. Almost too fast for me to believe he was human, but there was no way he wasn't human.

He knew how to fight too. Pretty damn obvious he knew he was facing something not exactly normal. And that gun—shit. Most of the Grimm didn't like guns—too messy and mortals tend to get in more trouble with those things.

But I didn't have to like them to be able to admire the *serious* firepower that thing would possess. It had been a miniature cannon, and if he had needed to use it, it would have destroyed any of the demonic fool enough to get caught in his range.

He'd done too good a job holding his own against them, especially up until I'd distracted him. How had he been able to do that? And who was he?

He was mortal. I could feel it.

But still, there was also something...*more*.

Dawn broke with him sitting on the deck of the small

house, staring out over the Chesapeake Bay and nursing a beer.

Jack held a picture of his mother, not that he needed to see it to remember what her medallion looked liked.

He knew far too well.

He couldn't exactly compare it to the one he'd seen tonight, of course. He'd like to, but he hadn't seen a piece like that since her death.

Cancer had killed his mother shortly before his thirteenth birthday and he'd been at her side. Him and a dude by the name of Will.

He hadn't ever known his dad.

When he had been a kid, a part of him had kind of hoped, sometimes even pretended it had been Will. He had already known it wasn't true.

Still, even if he hadn't been his father, Will had been there. Always.

The guy had come and gone all too often, but whenever Jack had needed somebody around, he had always been able to count on Will.

That was better than nobody, he supposed. And other than Will, after his mom had died, *nobody* was about all he'd had.

And other than Will and his mother, he'd never seen another living soul with one of those pieces either.

Not until tonight.

Will hadn't ever told him the meaning of the piece, but Jack knew what it was. He'd always known it. Even just touching it was enough to tell him. The lightest touch was like sticking his finger in a light socket—that odd, sizzling jolt.

She was one of them.

She wasn't as old as Will, but that didn't change what she was.

There really wasn't much question about it, although he was still sitting here, feeling stunned, shocked and downright... Hell. Jack didn't know *how* he felt. Confused. Curious.

His hand started to tighten around the picture's frame. The metal dented under his hand and carefully, he sat it down.

"Careful, Jack," he muttered. "Careful."

Pissed off.

Shit. *Pissed off* didn't touch it.

Standing up, he started to pace the porch. He shoved his hands through his hair, linked them behind his neck, staring off into the lightening skies without truly seeing it.

Yeah. He was pissed off.

He'd been pissed off at the world in general for the past twenty years of his life. Maybe even before that. Sometimes Jack felt like he'd been born with a grudge.

He knew he'd been born with a mission.

Killing things.

All those things he *shouldn't* know about, but did.

The things his mother had fought and killed before she'd decided to give up that life. She hadn't told him about any of it, but then again, she hadn't needed to.

He'd just...known.

Jack hadn't ever *not* known those things. He hated it, because he knew the weird knowledge he carried had broken his mother's heart. She had wanted away from whatever life she'd left behind. And she'd gotten away from it, all right.

But bits and pieces of it followed her...through her son.

Bits and pieces of memory.

Battles.

A knowledge he shouldn't have.

He had looked at the things earlier and known they were no longer human.

Orin. Soul stealers. The closest thing to vampires that existed, but there was nothing about them that could be romanticized. Demonic parasites. Whatever had once been human inside them was long gone, and the mortal body wasn't anything more than a vehicle.

Jack couldn't even explain *how* he knew, but he did know, and he fought with the ease born of practice, something that made no sense. Even as he hacked away with a bowie knife, part of him felt like he'd done it before a thousand times—but with a longer blade.

For as long as he could remember, he'd dreamt of killing monsters. Demons.

And he'd known the different sort of demons too. He could recall them from vivid, vivid dreams. But the dreams never terrified him. Even when he awoke at night and found his mother sitting by his bed, watching him with concerned, sad eyes, he hadn't worried.

To Jack, it seemed normal to dream of battling demons. So many demons.

The time had come when he didn't just battle them in his dreams, but in reality. He'd killed the first one when he was fifteen, and it had felt so easy...so natural...like a habit. It hadn't felt like the first time. It wasn't exactly something he'd *planned* on, but it was what he was meant to do—what he was built for. What he was *destined* for.

The battle.

Always the battle.

Each day.

Each night.

Nothing mattered but the demons, ending as many of them as he could, before they got to another human, before they hurt another human, before they killed.

Some of them didn't always kill the human right away. Some of them just sort of *pushed* the human aside, but kept them in there. An unwilling passenger along for the ride. A very gruesome ride.

There were others, but the ones Jack hated the most were the ones like he'd been fighting earlier. The kinds that could push inside and feed on the soul until there was nothing left...nothing but a husk.

Those husks though, they could be pretty dangerous. The demons controlling them could stay in them for quite a while— Jack didn't know how long. He'd be damned if he turned out that way.

Absently, he muttered, "If I end up like that, princess, just do me a favor, make it quick."

"Oh, don't worry. I will."

He drew his Desert Eagle, spun and aimed, all in one smooth, practiced motion.

Most people would have been scared shitless to have the piece of equipment pointed at their forehead.

Red? She just looked amused, one strawberry-blonde brow lifted, a slight smirk on that pretty, lush mouth. She focused her gaze on the Desert Eagle and then looked back at him. Her smirk widened into an all-out grin and she tucked her hands into her back pockets. Rocking back on her heels, she said, "You know, I could take that away from you so fast, it would make you cry."

"Try it." Jack braced himself. He might not be as fast as they were. But he had years of *trying* to be…and all of them, the demons and the Grimm, they all underestimated him.

But she just shrugged one smooth, soft, white shoulder. "It wouldn't be that much fun. Like taking candy from a baby."

That last part was tossed back over one of those smooth white shoulders as she sauntered over to one of his chaise lounges and flung her lean, sexy body down on it.

As she stretched out, Jack realized he couldn't quite take his eyes from those legs of hers. They stretched on forever, it seemed.

She crossed them at the ankle and smiled at him. Although it wasn't exactly a smile. It was that very appealing smirk.

He wanted to kiss the look off her face.

And if she kept staring at him, he just might start panting.

Or drooling.

Or both.

Scrubbing a hand down his face, he took a few seconds and then put his gun away since he probably wasn't going to use it. He'd much rather fuck her than shoot her.

He thought.

That was right up until he saw that she'd snagged his beer and was lifting it to that pretty, rosebud mouth of hers.

"Do you mind?" he snapped, storming over to her and grabbing it.

She lifted a brow and smiled. "You're not a very good host."

"You're not exactly a guest. You weren't invited—actually, that makes you a trespasser."

"Hmm. Good point." She came to her feet, all long legs and sleek curves. Shooting him a slow smile, she said, "I'll get my own."

Staring at her back, he decided he'd just stay right where he was instead of arguing with her. Definitely the wiser option just now. It would give him a few seconds to figure out what the hell she might be doing here, how she'd gotten here, and what in the hell he should do about it.

Chapter Three

What in the hell am I doing?

I stared into the fridge for a few seconds longer than it really took to grab a bottle of beer. A beer I really didn't want, but damn it, I needed something to drink.

For some reason, just looking at him was enough to make my tongue stick to the roof of my mouth, make my throat dry. Just looking at him made my heart race, made my belly clench and my knees weak.

Logically, I knew what all of this was.

Logically.

But it had been...ages...since I'd felt this way.

Not since before...

Not since Luc.

Back when we had still...been whole.

Shit. Luc.

Swearing, I grabbed a bottle of Bud and straightened up, twisting it open and lifting it to my lips. I drained half of it, but it didn't do anything to ease the burning in my veins...or the ache in my heart.

What in the hell was I doing here?

Feeling a pair of eyes on me, I turned my head and saw him standing there in the open doorway.

The sun was rising behind him, coming up over the bay, casting him into shadow, doing all sorts of lovely, lovely things to that body of his. He had one massive shoulder propped against the doorframe. He held the bottle of beer loosely in his hand. A big hand.

Damn it, I didn't like big men.

Never had.

The sight of a big man was enough to bring back memories I'd rather never think about.

But this guy...

Not now, Perci, I told myself.

Lifting the beer to my lips, I gave him my best, wide-eyed, innocent look. "So..." I took a drink and then smiled at him over the bottle.

"How in the hell did you find my house?"

I shrugged. "Wasn't hard. Just kind of followed my gut."

He narrowed those amazing, beautiful eyes. They all but glowed against the warm gold of his skin. Those eyes... Man, I think I could get lost in them. I hadn't felt like this with a man in far, far too long. Guilt swelled inside me and I knew I should put the bottle down and leave. Knew I should figure out what all Will wanted done here so I could get back to Luc.

Luc...

But I couldn't walk away from this. Couldn't walk away from this mortal just yet.

Standing here made me feel more alive than I had in years. Decades. Centuries.

Abruptly, I found myself remembering what Will had said just before he'd pushed me into this man's way.

Life is living, Perci. Even for us. Go live it.

Will. Oh, shit. It dawned on me then. *I'm in major trouble.*

"Just followed your gut. What, were you born with some sort of genetic GPS?" he asked sarcastically. "Try again, princess."

I flinched. From the darkness of the past, a whisper of memory rushed up to torment me. *My lovely princess, locked away in your tower.* But I shoved it away. No. I wouldn't let this happen now. Not now. Refusing to let him see the pain of memory, I looked back at him and gave him a sharp-edged smile.

"Do yourself a favor, my friend. Don't call me that."

He shoved off the wall and sauntered to me. For a man his size, hell, for a *human*, he moved far too silently, far too easily, far too at ease in his skin. He dipped his head until we were eye to eye, then he murmured, "Or what, princess?"

His mouth twisted in a smirk as he reached past me and snagged a bottle of beer. I could feel my hand curling into a fist and I was a little amazed at just how much I wanted to hit him. How much I was tempted to do it, just to see the shock on his face when I sent him flying back across the room. I refused, and just stood there, counting silently as he sauntered across the room and leaned against the counter opposite me.

"So, let's try this again. How did you find me?" he asked, watching me with that same smirk.

I closed the refrigerator and leaned against the other counter. "I already did. What's your name?"

"Jack. Yours?"

"Perci." Then I scowled and looked down at the beer I held. Why had I told him that?

"Perci..." he murmured. Something flickered in the depths of his beautiful eyes, there, then gone again, so fast. Too fast for me to quite understand what it was. He shook his head and then looked at me again. "How did you find my place, Perci?"

"I already told you." I rolled my eyes. "Why don't you tell about what I saw earlier?"

Without batting an eyelash, he said, "What, is there something wrong with your eyesight, princess?"

Anger—irrational and incomprehensible—rolled through me. Slamming my beer down, I stormed across the floor and glared at him. "Don't call me that," I said, forcing the words out through clenched teeth.

That arrogant smirk on his face as he took another swig of his beer was like glass scraping across raw skin.

"Yeah, yeah, so you've said. Look, I'm tired. If you're not going to be straight with me, then do me a favor and get out, okay, honey?"

"Honey?" I gaped at him. And what...was he calling me a liar? Planting my hands on my hips, I glared. "I already told you how I found you. You think I somehow managed to plant a bug up your ass in the two seconds we were in the alley together?"

"Hmm. The idea occurred to me. Although if you feel the need to do anything to my ass, you're welcome to...just no bugs." Then he winked at me. "Unless you ask me really nice. Who knows, maybe I'd like it."

Heat rushed up my neck, stained my cheeks. Holy hell, I was blushing.

He reached out, brushed the tip of his finger over my lip.

Inside my chest, my heart started to race.

Oh, hell.

"All of a sudden, you're not quite so mouthy, Perci," he murmured, his voice rougher, lower.

And he was closer. When had he gotten closer?

Blood pounded in my ears.

Roared.

He was so close...I could feel his body heat. I could smell him. Then he was touching me.

One big hand was cupping my chin, angling my face back so that I was meeting his gaze...that smoky, deep gaze.

"What's the matter, princess? Cat got your tongue?" He reached up and toyed with my pendant, and part of me wanted to smack that big hand of his away. But the other part...as long as he kept touching me, what did I care?

"I've got a name," I said. I licked my lips and almost groaned when his gaze dropped to my mouth.

Then I did groan, because he dipped his head and pressed his mouth to mine.

Shit.

No. This wasn't good. Not good at all.

His tongue stroked over my lower lip and I opened for him. Those big hands of his gripped my waist and lifted me, hauling me against him, hard and tight and close. One forearm rested just under my ass while his free hand stroked under the hemline of my shirt and stroked my back. The heat of him threatened to scald me. Mark me.

No. This wasn't good...it was so beyond good it was frightening.

And I knew I needed to get the hell away from him.

But I couldn't.

Her mouth...

Jack shuddered as her mouth opened under his. She tasted like cinnamon and cream and honey and heaven and damn it, he didn't think he'd get enough of that taste. Then she tore her mouth away from his and he growled, reached up and

151

fisted his hand in her short, silken hair. "Kiss me," he muttered against her cheek.

"This is insane," she whispered.

"Yeah. Don't care. Kiss me."

A sigh shuddered out of her. "I can't be doing this." Her shoulders rose and fell and Jack found himself staring at those sleek, pale curves. Soft...

Without realizing it, he found himself lowering his head and pressing his mouth to one shoulder, left all but bare by the skinny strap of her tank. Soft...smooth. *Hmmm.*

He touched his tongue to her skin. She stiffened, then shuddered.

Turning around, he walked blindly until he could put her down on the counter by the refrigerator. Lifting his head, he stared into her dark eyes, watched her face as he slid his hand under the hem of her shirt. Simple, basic cotton—nothing fancy, and yet it would be a pleasure to peel away from her.

An image flashed through his mind.

Her...her hair long and luxurious. Her lean body had been softer then, clad in a lush gown of velvet.

A man was with her, and he was peeling that velvet away from her body. Slowly. Teasingly. And watching her with a look of such love and awe. They knelt together on a blanket.

He could see them—*had* seen them. Watched...wanted. *Loved.*

It hit him in the gut like a punch and he should have pulled away.

Would have pulled away.

But then Perci rested her hands on his forearms, stroked up. The image shattered, fell away under her touch. Need and hunger swamped him. She cupped his face in her hands and tugged his mouth to hers.

"I thought you said this was insane," he muttered against her lips. *Pull away, Jack. Something strange is going on here, man.*

"It is. I'll figure it out later." She caught his hands and guided them to her breasts. "Touch me...damn it, please touch me. I... Shit, I feel alive when you're touching me."

There was something so broken, so raw in her voice.

He couldn't not touch her. Couldn't not cup her face in his hands, lift it to his and brush his lips over hers. "I think I like the taste of you," he muttered. "The feel of you."

He wanted to make love to her...gentle, slow. Needed it.

But she didn't want gentle. Greedy, hungry, she skimmed her hands down his sides, grabbed the hem of his shirt and jerked it up and over his head. As she bared his chest, she leaned forward and nipped at his nipple with sharp teeth. "I don't want slow, and I don't want soft and sweet words. Fuck me," she said, tipping her head back and staring at him.

She scraped her nails over the denim-covered ridge of his cock and Jack shuddered. Reaching down, he closed his hand around her wrist. "Is there any reason to rush?" he muttered against her mouth.

She cupped him with her other hand and squeezed.

Groaning, he caught that hand as well and then pinned them behind her back. He lifted his head to stare down into her glittering, hungry eyes. "What's the rush, princess?"

She snarled at him. "Don't call me that."

"Fuck, but I think it turns me on when you glare at me," he muttered, dipping his head and nipping her lower lip. Then he licked it with his tongue and kissed a trail down along her chin, her neck, until he could bite her gently through her bra. "I want to see you naked."

"Then let go of my hands and I'll get naked."

He smiled at the command in her voice. "And what if I'd rather be the one to get you naked?" He let go of her hands, but before she could take care of her shirt, he did it by reaching up and grabbing the neckline. He smiled down into her eyes and watched the surprise flicker as he tore the thin cotton apart.

Her breath caught in her throat and she glanced down, stared at the torn tank top before looking back up at him. "You forgot something." Then a smirk twisted her mouth. "Although I bet you can't tear the bra quite so easy. They make them pretty sturdy."

That smirk...damn but it turned him on, and he was already so fucking hot, he hurt. "I can think of a way to get it off." Holding her gaze, he reached up and grabbed one of the blades he had on the refrigerator.

He kept sharp, shiny objects in a variety of places all over his house. It had saved his ass a time or two.

But this time, it proved to be worth it for a different reason.

As he pulled the blade down and slipped the tip of it under her bra, he watched her eyes widen, watched as her lashes fluttered.

"You scared?" he teased.

Not that he really thought she would be, and he wasn't surprised when her brown eyes opened and she smiled at him. "Of you? No way in hell."

Keeping the knife still, he watched her. "Should I stop?" All it would take was the slightest bit of pressure, just the slightest bit.

"If you stop, how are you going to finish getting me naked?"

He gave the slightest flick of his wrist and watched as the blade cut through the lace and silk. Her eyes went dark, and as he reached up and pushed the straps off her shoulders, she smiled at him.

Holy hell.

Just one look from her was enough to make him weak in the knees.

He laid the knife down and she glanced at it, flicked him a look from under her lashes. "What, you're not going to cut my pants off too?"

"Don't tempt me," he muttered. He reached up, fisted his hand in the waistband of her jeans and tugged her forward. She slid off, keeping her palms resting on the counter as he unbuttoned her jeans and started to slide them down. His mouth went dry as he realized something. "You're not wearing any panties."

"No. Is that a problem?"

"Shit, no." But if he'd realized she was naked under that denim, he might have lost his mind even sooner.

She was naked thirty seconds later.

Jack just about went to his knees—might have done just that so he could press his mouth to the curls that covered her sex, but she was still watching him with that taunting smile.

He wanted, needed, to see just how much more he could push her.

Grasping her waist, he turned them around and rested his hips against the counter. "Your turn," he said, his voice hoarse.

She grinned at him and then glanced at the knife. "And are you going to trust me if I decide to start cutting your clothes off?"

Jack knew she wouldn't need it. But he shrugged. "You didn't seem worried when you saw me with it. I think it's safe."

"Oh, you shouldn't be so trusting, Jack," she murmured, reaching for the knife and trailing the tip of it across his belly.

The muscles quivered in response, but he just smiled. She wasn't about to do anything stupid with that blade and he knew it—of course, she didn't realize he knew what she was.

"Why not, darlin'? I don't think you're going to do anything too bad with it, but whatever you're going to do? Hurry it up. I'm dying here."

Then he dropped his gaze and stared at the pale, sweet curves of her breasts. "Slowly and painfully dying."

A flush settled on her cheeks and she set the knife down, reached for the button on his jeans. "You look pretty healthy to me."

As she lowered the zipper to his jeans, her breath caught in her throat and she shot him a glance.

"Okay," I muttered. "Very healthy."

My belly cramped as I thought about taking him inside me.

Hard. Rough. Fast.

That was what I wanted—what I needed.

He could give me that, and damn it, he would. I pushed his jeans and the snug-fitting boxers he wore out of the way, just past the hard, taut muscle of his ass. Then I bent over and caught the head of his cock in my mouth, listened as he grunted, first in shock, then in pleasure, as I started to suck on him. His hand stroked down my back, rested on the flare of my hip, kneading the flesh lightly.

Salty, sweaty and hard...

I sucked and licked and nipped his flesh until he started to rock against my mouth and then I straightened and stared at him. Because I'd already figured out that it drove him crazy, I smirked at him.

He reached out and hauled me to him, his mouth slanting against mine. He growled against my lips. "You're trying to drive me nuts," he muttered. "I know it."

I rubbed against him, wished I was taller. I could feel his length at my belly and I wanted him inside me. I rocked against him, desperate. Screw this. I braced my hands on his shoulders and jumped, using my knees to grip his hips and that—oh, hell yes...

I reached down and gripped him, held him steady.

"Damn it, stop," he muttered, banding one arm around me and pressing tight. But it couldn't stop me. I wouldn't let it.

Then I found myself on my feet, my head spinning at how fast it happened, how fast he *moved*.

"Slow down," he muttered against my ear. He stroked a hand down my side. "Would you slow down? I've barely had a chance to touch you, to taste you..."

"I just want you to fuck me," I snarled.

"You can't always have your way, princess." Then he tried to kiss me.

I bit him. Hard. "I told you not to call me that." I glared at him.

Something glittered in his eyes. A weird mix of rage and heat and hunger...and it made me burn so much hotter.

Lifting my chin, I said, "Are you going to fuck me or not?"

"Oh, you bet your darling little ass I am...*princess*," he purred. Then, before I could blink, he had me bent over the counter.

I caught my breath. It was all I had time for, and then he was pressing against me, pushing inside me...and oh, *shit*—he was big, thick. Heavy. Stretching me.

With one hand resting low on my spine, he held me still as he fed me one slow, inexorable inch after another. I keened and shifted my hips, reaching down to brace my elbows on the counter, thinking to lift up, anything to ease the pressure.

He stilled, then reached up, caught one wrist, then the

other. "You wanted to get fucked," he muttered in my ear. "Fine. You're getting fucked, and right now, it's my way."

I shoved back against him and jerked on my wrists. "Let me go."

"No way." He tightened his grip and started to withdraw, then pressed against me again, harder. Deeper. Faster.

My breath caught.

He did it again. Again. And that was when I realized he was still being cautious, that I still hadn't taken all of him. Swearing, I twisted my hips against him, tried to take him deeper. Desperate for it. Desperate for him—all of him.

But as I pushed back, he retreated as well.

"Damn it, what are you waiting for?" I snarled.

"I don't want to hurt you."

Hell, maybe that was what I *wanted*—maybe I even needed it.

I tugged against his hold and shot him a look over my shoulder the best I could. "I can handle anything you think you can give me," I whispered. Then I clenched down, using my muscles to milk his cock. It had been years since I'd deliberately set out to drive a man wild...but I still knew how. Milking him with my pussy, smirking at him—

"Brat," he muttered. "Stop it."

I didn't. I could almost hear it when his patience snapped. He growled low in his throat and started to slam into me, harder. Faster. I tried to get my hands under me, tried to brace myself, but he caught my wrists again, leaned over me. I could feel him...*all* of him. Pressed hard and tight and firm against me while his cock dug into me, stroking deep, deep, so fucking deep. I cried out, squeezed my eyes shut as hot, brilliant pleasure stormed through me.

It was heaven...and it was hell, because in the back of my mind, I knew I shouldn't feel this, shouldn't want more of this, shouldn't crave more of this...of *him*.

Tears burned my eyes and I begged, "More, damn it. Please. Oh, please..."

His breath was hot on my ear. My neck. He bit my shoulder and muttered, "Yeah, princess. I'll give you more. Say my name."

"Jack," I whispered.

I didn't even care that he'd called me princess. He could call me whatever in the hell he wanted as long as he kept touching me.

And then he let go of me. Stopped. He pulled away and I could have cried.

"What...what are you doing?" Damn it, I was *going to* cry. Either that or I was going to attack him and beat him bloody if he didn't touch me, come back to me...something...

But then he lifted me in his arms and took me to the floor. "I need more than that," he whispered, stretching me out.

That plain linoleum floor could have been a bed of roses for all the care he gave me. I could have dressed in silk and velvet and lace, the way his eyes gleamed as he stared down at me. He lay between my thighs and when he pressed his mouth to my sex, I cried out.

No. I couldn't...no.

Hard, driving sex was one thing...but the tenderness, that was something else.

"Damn it, stop," I begged him.

"Not on your life." He licked my clit. "Not on mine."

I brought my knees up, fisted my hands in his hair. *Pull away*, I told myself. I could do that, could make myself do it.

Except I couldn't. As he pressed his tongue against me, inside me, all I could manage was to lie there...and take it...and enjoy. When he made me come, I cried out. And when he came back up over me, I clutched him close, needed to feel his weight.

But even as he brought me to climax again, even as he came, I knew it wasn't enough.

I hadn't felt this alive in far, far too long.

And it was going to hurt far, far too much to lose it again.

I had no right.

None.

Chapter Four

Will wasn't surprised when somebody else joined him at the cabin.

And he wasn't surprised at who it was either.

Glancing up, he met Sina's blue gaze. He wasn't surprised at the censure he saw there either.

Her gifts were those of sights.

She saw things...many things. Things of the past, of the future...and of the present.

No doubt she'd somehow picked up on something connected to Perci.

No. Judging by the anger he felt in her, it wasn't Perci.

It was Luc.

"Hello, Sina," he said softly.

Her blue eyes, blue as sapphires, narrowed on his face. "Don't you just sit there and use that tone with me."

She sounded like she'd been born and raised in the southern United States.

But she was older than that. Much older. She was one of his older recruits, and normally she wouldn't have spoken to him with that censure in her tone, because she knew, better than most, that he had no control over the things that happened.

But Sina... Well, she had a blind spot when it came to Luc. She always had.

"And what tone should I use?" he asked blandly. "Should I sing soprano? I'm not sure I can."

"Maybe if I helped, it could be arranged."

Will just stared at her. "Sina, I had no control over this."

"Oh, don't give me that."

He just sighed. He was so tired of this. He hadn't realized *how* tired until recently. But now, as he watched over Mandy, watched her body struggle to heal from what had been done to it, he realized how tired he was. How fucking lonely.

How empty he was.

The white fall of his hair hid his face. "Sina, I was told who to send, and where."

"And you couldn't send him *with* her? Do you know what he is doing right now?"

He lifted his head and stared into her blue eyes. "Yes. He's hurting. And for the first time in several hundred years, he's accepted one crucial fact—she can't *love* him anymore. Which means he'll eventually move on."

For the longest time, she just glared at him.

"Will..."

He shook his head.

"Sina, Perci *can't* love Luc the way she needs to. The way *he* deserves. Hell, the way *she* deserves. She's too damaged inside. And that's through no fault of hers...or his." He closed his eyes. "Neither of them deserved this, you know. They should have had the choice, a long, somewhat happy life with each other. But that crazy bitch..."

Sina made a strange, somewhat strangled sound low in her throat.

Yes, that crazy bitch—she was something of a legend. One who had made Luc and Perci's lives sheer hell. One who had killed innocents. One who had done the very worst things imaginable.

And they should have been able to trust her.

"There is no hope for them?" Sina asked, rubbing the heel of her hand over her heart. "He loves her so much."

He, Will thought. Sina made no reference to Perci, although Perci was the one who had yet to heal. Luc had more or less dealt with the lot life had dealt him. Perci never had.

But it was Luc that Sina was concerned about.

"Oh, there is hope for them," Will said quietly, tearing his gaze from Mandy's slumbering form and looking at Sina. "But not together. If they were meant to be *together*, would they be pulled apart?"

Sina just stared at him.

He saw the heartbreak in the depths of her eyes though.

She'd accepted that Luc loved Perci. Now she must accept that Luc would find another.

In the back of his mind, he started to wonder...

Sina had always watched the Frenchman.

Always, it seemed.

In the back of Will's mind, he began to wonder.

But he couldn't dwell on that for long, not with Sina here. Her gift was strong and even though he shielded, it wasn't always possible *to* shield against precognition.

As though his thoughts had brought it on, he saw Sina's dark eyes cloud, the blue turning milky and opaque. "We will be needed soon," she whispered, her voice husky and rough. Her gaze shifted to Mandy, although he knew she didn't see the other woman right now. "Call for your brother, Will. He shall have to watch over her, as I know you won't leave her alone."

"No." Will stiffened. He couldn't leave her—couldn't.

Sina shook her head. "You will have to...or Perci dies. As will he. He was just returned to us. Is he to die again? Because you cannot leave your woman's side?"

Then, Sina's eyes cleared, and she sighed.

"We often do things we wish not to do. And this is a small thing," she said, shaking her head. "Do you not trust him to care for her?"

Will closed his eyes. It wasn't a matter of trust...it was a matter of leaving her.

"Very well. I will call him."

Chapter Five

They were called the Grimm.

They had a name...*now*. But they hadn't always.

It wasn't until the stories started to circulate and they realized that there were dangers that awaited them if they caught too much notice...*that* was when they decided they needed to hide themselves.

And what better way to do it than fanciful tales?

It took time.

A great deal of time, more than mortals would understand. Several hundred years went into the concocting what would become the most clever ruse known to man. Or rather...the most clever ruse man would *never* know.

And the man known as Jacques had helped create that story.

"If they believe it is but a story, a fancy, they will not look beyond it," he said, watching as the man known as William paced the hard-packed, earthen floor.

"It is ridiculous," William said, shaking his head. "And far too dangerous."

"Is it not more dangerous to let people see and hear things they should never know? People talk. Word will spread. We must take precaution. But if we are going to do this, we must begin now. It will take time for this to take root. A great deal of time."

William sighed and rubbed his eyes. Then he stopped and looked past Jacques to another...another brother-in-arms.

"It seems to be the wisest choice."

"Yes."

William nodded. "The wisest choice."

Time drifted away. For the very oldest among them, time sometimes lost all meaning, and by the time the eighteenth century rolled around, many of the tales were already being spread.

Help came in the form of Sina—one of their seers.

Sometimes she glimpsed who would come to them and she started the tales early...a lifetime early. They hadn't been wrong when they had decided it would take time for the stories to take root.

There were still problems, yes, but for the most part, already men were quick to explain away what they didn't choose to believe.

"And nobody questions what happened to Giselle?" William asked, scrutinizing Jacques closely.

"No. She was of little importance, I fear."

William nodded. "What of the prince?"

"He searches for her still. I do not know if he will accept her disappearance."

"Sina warned me of this," William murmured. "I shall handle it. I believe I need to have a word with him."

"With the prince? Is that wise?"

"Wise or not, it is what I am to do." He looked at Jacques. "We will speak of it more when you return. For now, there is an assignment for you. Another two mortals—they will be like us in time. You will act as their guard for now. War comes, and they must be guarded."

Jacques nodded.

He would, of course, do as he was asked. He would protect those who were yet unable. He wouldn't fail.

Only that was exactly what he did.

Jacques did not fail.

He did not know the meaning of the word. He upheld his duty. His honor. His word.

Right up until the moment he laid eyes upon Persinette.

Had it just been a lovely package, he might have been able to ignore it. He was just a man—yes, an immortal one, but just a man. But the lovely package was only the beginning.

She was so lovely, but her soul was as pure and lovely as her body. So strong and true. Her heart never wavered and her soul was strong. She stood steady in the face of adversity and even when she was frightened, she never let it show.

As war ravaged their country, she never faltered, never hesitated. She provided for those under her care and when soldiers would have tried to claim her lands, she held them back.

Nothing made her pause. Nothing made her blink.

He suspected he'd loved her from the very first. But she had been wedded to another long before he even knew her name. Wedded...and so very in love.

Her name was Persinette, and in time she'd become one of them, as would her husband.

If Jacques was a wise man, he would distance himself.

Loving her, loving a wedded woman, was only opening himself up for heartbreak, and he'd gone hundreds of years without that. He'd happily forgo that experience.

But in the end, he couldn't stop himself from loving her. And in the end, he couldn't save her either. All he could do was love her. And he lost her anyway.

Not that she ever knew...

Twisting, tearing away from the sheets, Jack rolled out of the bed and landed on his hands and knees.

No. He didn't have nightmares about demons and monsters...but the nightmare he'd just had was far, far worse.

Perci.

Fuck, had he just slept with one of them? He'd known it even as he was taking her, but damned if he could resist.

Yes, he had. He could smell her on his skin. Almost feel the silken brush of her lips gliding over him. Even though she was gone. Long gone.

Squeezing his eyes closed, he settled back and pressed the heels of his hands against his eye sockets, hoping it might block out the visions there.

Shit.

Shit.

Shit.

Why had he dreamed that? And why did it seem like he had

dreamed it before?

Why did it seem more like a memory than dream?

Even as he tried to scrub the memory away, it came on stronger and stronger, and before he even knew what was happening, he was falling back...back through time, back through space.

Into another life.

His name was Jacques.

In this life.

He stood at the side of a young maiden by the name of Persinette. Her dark eyes filled with tears she wouldn't let fall as she watched her husband ride away with his men.

"He will return to you," Jacques murmured.

"I know." She gave him a tight smile. "It is not as though he leaves me alone, is it?"

No. She hadn't been left alone. She stayed in the large home of his mother, many servants to care for her, and a protector at her side.

A protector who was more than human, because both Persinette and Luc were special.

Jacques was there to watch over them until her time came.

Until Luc's time came.

He was there to guard them...and while Luc was away, he was there to protect Persinette.

He was not there to fall in love with her.

No man would come near her and no harm would befall her. Not while he was near. Perhaps war might ravage much of the countryside, but it wouldn't harm Persinette.

Not while he breathed.

Even as he made himself that promise, he felt a blinding, hideous pain tear through him...and all was dark.

Jack was choking. Hardly able to breathe, lopping around like a landed fish—

A pair of feet came into view, followed by a familiar face.

Will reached out and poked him in the chest. "It's over and done now, old friend. You can breathe again, you know."

Choking, still feeling like a landed fish, he smacked at the hand and struggled to sit up. He shot Will a glare. "What in the fuck are you doing here?"

Wheezing, trying to breathe past the hideous, blinding pain, he rolled over to push himself to his hands and knees. His body didn't want to cooperate and his head ached. His heart raced. His throat felt raw, like butchered, minced meat.

It took him almost two minutes just to get up, and then all he could do was sit on the edge of the bed and wonder if he was going to puke.

He felt like he had the flu, a hangover and an adrenaline rush all at once. He also felt like somebody had pounded on his ass for the last six months straight.

And at the same time, he was reliving the very last moments of that dream.

Seeing Perci's face...it *was* her face. In another time. But it felt so fucking real...

Abruptly, he remembered Will was there and he looked up, glared at him. "What are you doing here?"

"This very moment? I'm waiting for you to calm down," he said, that familiar smirk on his face. It widened to an outright grin as he studied Jack's face. "You look like you were having an interesting dream there, Jack."

"Interesting?" Jack swiped the back of his hand over his mouth. "Interesting doesn't touch it."

"Hmmm." Will leaned against the wall and studied the bedroom, the tangled mess of the sheets.

Although Jack couldn't really see any signs of Perci's presence, he had the weirdest feeling Will saw something.

Shit, Will seemed to see *everything*.

"An interesting night, altogether," Will murmured.

Jack curled his lip. "Yeah, interesting. Whatever happened to '*If you have a need of me, I'll know, and I'll be there*'? Whatever happened to that? Because I had a need last night and almost ended up gutted. Where the hell were you?"

"I made certain you had the help you needed." Will shrugged negligently. "Perci is quite capable, isn't she?"

Capable? Yeah. Jack just stared at Will for a long moment,

trying to figure out what the hell was going on inside the man's head. Then he sighed and rubbed the back of his neck.

He could smell Perci on his skin, he realized. He needed to shower, but he almost hated to do it, because he didn't want to wash her scent away. But he needed to shower to see if he could wash the cobwebs out of his head, the nasty dregs of that dream.

Absently, he reached up and rubbed his throat. It still hurt. Still felt raw.

"What the fuck..." he muttered.

Feeling the weight of Will's gaze, he looked up.

"The mind forgets," Will said quietly. "But the body doesn't."

A chill raced down his spine as he stared into strange, glowing silver eyes.

"The body doesn't forget what?" he whispered.

"Dying."

I hadn't slept.

Dry-eyed, tired and desperate for the mental escape of sleep, I lay on the bed in my hotel room.

The lights were off, the curtains were drawn but despite the dim light, I saw fine. Not that there was much to see in the bland, impersonal room. It was a nice hotel—I had a thing for comfort. Although right now, I figured I should be somewhere lying on a bed of nails.

What in the hell had I done?

And then my memory started to fill in the details...

I'd slept with a total stranger. Well, actually, I hadn't slept. I'd had the best sex of my entire life with a complete and total stranger. And not just once, but several times over. It wasn't until sleep had claimed him that I'd been able to tear myself away.

He'd fucked me six different ways to Sunday and my body had been a sweet, sweet ache when I slid out of his house after he'd drifted off to sleep. Thankfully, he was mortal and he *did* need to sleep, although extricating myself from those big arms of his had been a task. One I hadn't really wanted to do, but I couldn't just stay there.

Never mind the fact that I *wanted* to do just that.

I could have happily stayed with him the rest of the day, and probably that night, and the next, and the next—

"Stop it," I muttered, covering my face with my hands.

Job. I had a job to do, and then I needed to get back to Luc.

Luc—think about Luc.

But as I tried to pull that face to mind, another face kept superimposing itself. Misty gray eyes instead of clear and vivid green. A roughly hewn face instead of Luc's angelic, almost poetic beauty.

Groaning, I rolled over to my belly and buried my face in the pillow, but then I had the vivid, sensory memory of Jack covering my body with his, that hard, muscled length crushing into me. He hadn't been careful, or cautious and I'd loved it.

Just thinking about it, about him, made me burn for more.

A lot more.

I stiffened as the air tightened. Grabbing one of the blankets, I wrapped it around myself and sat up only seconds before Will arrived. I blinked at the brilliant flash of light. As it faded, I had only one clear thought in my mind.

Thank God he's alone.

Immediately guilt flooded me. I should be dying to have Luc back with me. But just then, I couldn't have handled it. I could barely handle looking at my own reflection.

And before me stood the source of my problems. If he hadn't separated us...

"What in the hell do you want?" I demanded.

"And hello to you too."

I curled my lip at him. "What do you want? Just out with it so you can get back to babysitting your new angel."

Something flashed through his eyes. If I hadn't known better, I might have thought it was pain...grief.

But this was Will.

"Perci, you're being quite the bitch today," Will said mildly.

"Will, you're being quite the ass. What in the hell do you want?"

For a long moment, he just watched me, his pale silver eyes

shrewd, measuring. Then, as though he'd found some answer only he could see, he nodded. "You're on assignment—the mortal you fought with last night. He's to be one of us, and you're to watch over him."

"I...what?" I gaped at him.

"You heard me well enough."

Silver light flashed.

I lunged for him and caught his arm before he could step through the light. "Oh, hell, no. You're not dumping that surprise on me and just disappearing. How long am I to watch over him?"

"For however long he needs it," Will said, lifting one shoulder in a lazy shrug.

"No. Oh, hell, no. Have you forgotten I've already *got* a partner?"

"You're being reassigned."

"You can't do that." My hand curled into a fist and I wanted to hit something—no. Not something. Will. I wanted to hit Will. "Damn it, what about Luc?"

"Luc isn't your concern."

"And who in the hell is going to be his eyes?" I shook my head. "You can't do this to him. He *needs* me."

"He'll have a new partner...and I imagine it will be one who will be well-suited to his needs," Will said. He glanced at my hand where I still clutched his arm, and then back at my face. "And no, he doesn't *need* you. Stop telling yourself that. It's been your crutch for far too long, Perci."

"It's the truth," I growled.

"No. It's *your* truth, and you refuse to see anything else." Will sighed, and then he waved a hand. The light collapsed in on itself and he reached out and caught my arm.

I stiffened, but reluctantly followed as he led me to the bed.

"Persinette, you have never let yourself heal from what was done to you, to him, to your children."

I flinched. Heal? How could I heal...? Swallowing, I shook my head and whispered, "I don't want to talk about this."

Will gazed at me, his silver eyes gentle and warm. "Nor would I. And we don't have to. But it's time you and Luc let go of the past—it's *past* time you let go. You can't heal, you won't love him...and worse, you blame him."

"No, I don't." I jerked away from him and stormed across the room. My voice shook as I said it again. "I don't."

"You do. Just as you blame yourself."

"It wasn't *our* fault it was done. I *know* that."

Will lifted a brow. "Yes, and logic always goes so well with heartbreak and grief. Of *course*, you *know* it isn't his fault. Just as you know it isn't your fault. Nonetheless, you blame Luc for the deaths of your children. For what was done to you, to him. Just as you blame yourself. That is why you were never able to love him as you once did."

Each word was a brutal, bitter dagger in my heart.

He was *wrong*.

"No." I shook my head. Tears burned my eyes. He *had* to be wrong.

"Look inside your heart, Perci. Am I truly wrong?"

I turned away and covered my face with my hands. Cold air danced along my skin and I realized I'd dropped the sheet, but I didn't—couldn't care.

Then something warm came around my shoulders—the robe from the bathroom. Will wrapped a comforting arm around me. "There is too much grief, too much pain trapped inside you, Perci. I feel it any time I am near you. Luc feels it every day. It's a festering wound—a poisoned one—and it's tearing you apart. It's destroying Luc."

I could handle the pain tearing *me* apart. Hell, I lived with it.

But as I realized what Will was saying, and just how glaringly obvious it was, I started to shake. No, I hadn't been in love with Luc for centuries. But I *did* love him. And I'd been torturing him.

"Oh, God, what am I doing?" I whispered. "What *have* I been doing?"

The truth was there, lurking...waiting for me to see it, to acknowledge it.

Will wasn't wrong.

Deep inside, I had blamed Luc. I had blamed myself. I

could live with blaming myself, hating myself. But blaming him, letting him feel that...no. I couldn't stomach that.

And all this time, Luc *knew*.

"Oh, God..."

My legs gave out and I would have fallen if Will hadn't been there. He caught me, but I barely noticed. Sick inside, full of so much self-hatred, I wanted to scream. I wanted to rant. I wanted to hurt myself.

Badly.

"You will not," Will said, his voice flat and hard.

"Leave me alone," I rasped.

"No." His hands braceleted my wrists when I would have pulled away, and although I'm strong, nobody can move Will when he doesn't want to be moved. "You will not harm yourself, and if you think I've told you this so you will place *more* blame, *more* guilt on yourself, then you're a fool. Perci...you are not a fool."

I jerked against his hold. "Damn it, let me go and leave me alone."

"No. I've let this go and I've left the two of you alone, hoping you would work it out on your own for far too long. But if you haven't dealt with it in the past three centuries, it's rather clear you will not work it out on your own. So I'm stepping in."

Stepping in? I glared at him and tried once more to pull away from him. When that didn't work, I kicked him. But he was prepared for that, and the second time I tried to kick him, he narrowed his eyes. "Either act like an adult and be still, or I'll make you."

"Bite me, Will," I snarled. I kicked him again—I wanted him to retaliate. Hell, I *needed* it. Poison inside me? Damn straight, there was poison. Poison and I needed to spew it out somehow. Oh, hell, Luc...

Tears burned my eyes. I shoved my weight against Will and this time, he retaliated.

But not physically.

Of all of us, he's the strongest. He has gifts I know nothing about, gifts I want to know nothing about. Someone once told me that if it's a talent one of the Grimm has, then Will has it as well...just in case nobody else is able to help train.

This was one of the gifts I knew nothing about, and as his mind slammed into mine and froze me, physically, I wished I'd listened when he said he would *make* me be still.

As I struggled to force my body to respond to my commands, Will stepped back. He adjusted the robe I wore, tying it shut at my waist—such a gentleman—and then crossed his arms over his chest and watched me narrowly.

"Do you think this is *easy* for me, Perci? Do you think I want to come down and intervene in everybody's lives?" he asked.

I could speak, I realize. "Why the hell not? You're constantly doing it."

"No—not constantly, and think on this—if I didn't hate seeing you so miserably unhappy, I wouldn't bother."

Well, that was one way to take the wind out of my sails. "Damn it, Will..."

He sighed and looked down. White hair fell down, shielding his face.

I could move again.

But I didn't try to attack him. Wrapping my arms around myself, I moved to the window, opened the curtains and stared outside. The hotel was perched on the edge of the beach and I stared out over the sparkling water, but I wasn't seeing the water, the sunbathers, or anything else.

All I could see was Luc.

A hundred times, a thousand times.

"How many times have I broken his heart?" I whispered.

"I don't know."

Closing my eyes, I pressed my brow against the sun-warmed glass. I was freezing, I realized. Freezing. "Why didn't you tell me?"

"I don't know. I should have. I'm sorry."

"Sorry..." Tears clogged my throat. I turned around and looked at him. "I've been ripping his heart to shreds for three hundred years and I've been too fucking blind, too self-centered, too caught up in my own pain to even care. How can I face him? How can I make this up to him?"

"Perci, you don't *need* to." Will came to me then, reached

up and cupped my cheek. "All he ever wanted, more than anything, was to see you happy. You can't have that until you forgive yourself. Do that...and you'll be able to look at him again without so much anger and rage in your heart. That's what he needs from you."

"He wants me to love him again and I can't." I licked my lips and shook my head. I tried to picture myself loving Luc, being with him. And despite the raging grief in my heart, despite the pain, I found myself thinking of the mortal...of Jack.

Blood rushed to my cheeks and I banished the thought of him from my mind.

Luc. I needed to think of Luc now.

"I *have* blamed him, you know. You're right. And he's not to blame. I...I have to acknowledge that and let it go. Forgive him. I can do that, and I *will*, but even after I do that, I still can't give him what he wants. He wants me to love again, for us to be what we were."

"Nothing is ever as it was—life is about change. For you...*and* for him."

I looked up, saw a weird glimmer in Will's eyes. "Will?"

He smiled.

Something fluttered in my heart. Maybe it was hope. For Luc.

"Is there...is he...?"

"Luc will move on, Perci. Once he knows you're happy. Once he knows you will be fine."

The hope that had begun to bloom died.

"Happy?" I shook my head. "I don't *deserve* to be happy."

"Yes." He pinched my chin. "You do. And you will be."

He pressed a kiss to my brow. "I think we tore open that badly healed wound...let the poison come out now, Persinette. And remember what I told you the other day. Life is for living— go live. And find your trainee before he gets into too much trouble."

Chapter Six

Dying.

He couldn't get drunk enough to wipe those words from his mind.

The mind forgets. But the body doesn't.

The body doesn't forget what?

Dying.

"Fuck," he muttered.

He needed to forget those words, forget them, or wipe them from his mind.

Try as he might, he couldn't quite manage to convince himself that Will had been pulling his leg.

But since he couldn't forget, and since he couldn't make himself believe Will was fucking with him, Jack was determined to get drunk. Shit-faced drunk.

Sitting at the far end of the bar, he tossed back another shot of tequila, grimaced and then reached for the bottle. The bartender was watching him warily, but Jack ignored him. He had plenty of cash to buy more booze, and at some point he'd either pass out or drop dead of alcohol poisoning—either way, problem solved. He wouldn't have to figure out just what Will had been getting at.

He wouldn't have to *think* about it. He'd been trying pretty damn hard all day *not* to think about it.

A shadow fell across him, but he ignored it. The scent of woman rose above the stink of the bar. Perfumed flesh...a little too much perfume. Jack preferred his women to smell a little more natural. That much perfume gave him a headache anyway. As she leaned in and laid a hand next to his, Jack reached for the bottle again.

"Hey there, sugar."

Jack flicked a glance at her. Big blonde hair. Big blue eyes.

Big boobs. And something inside her eyes he didn't like. It nipped and clawed to get out.

Demon. *Succubae.*

Too fucking bad. She wasn't here looking to body-swap, she just wanted to fuck. He wasn't interested. "Go away," he said, pouring himself another shot.

Instead of going away, she sidled closer, pressing her generous chest against his arm. "You want some company?"

Jack sighed. Absently, he flexed his ankle, his forearm, checking for his knives. He'd left the Desert Eagle in the car, but he didn't go unarmed if he could avoid it. He really wasn't in the mood for a fight though. Especially not here, and not with a *succubae.* Any other soul that looked at her would see just a blue-eyed blonde out looking for action, and the last thing he wanted was to get noticed.

He tossed back the tequila, eyed the level in the bottle. If he just guzzled it, would it be enough to put him under? She couldn't do jack with him if he was passed out. But that wasn't likely, because he still felt way too sober. Setting the shot glass down, he looked at the demon-possessed. "I'm not interested, lady."

"You don't seem to be finding whatever you want at the bottom of that bottle." She trailed a blood-red finger down his hand.

What the hell... Jerking away, he glared at her as he slid off the stool. "Can you not take a hint?"

The hunger in her eyes burned hotter. Brighter.

She advanced a step, lifted a hand and pressed it to his chest. "You just look lonely. I know I'm lonely..."

"Lonely?"

Jack had been so focused on the blonde, he hadn't realized the redhead was here watching them. But at the sound of Perci's voice, he went still. Lifting up his head, he stared past the blonde into big, brown eyes. Sad eyes, he thought, and his heart wrenched.

She looked terribly, terribly sad...and so tired. Her eyes met his for the briefest moment, then she looked at the blonde.

"He's not lonely. Get lost," Perci said, her voice flat, hard.

Did she already know? Could she sense it? *Them?*

"Precious, you don't want to be here," Perci said softly, shaking her head. "It's a bad, bad idea..."

Oh, yes. She knew.

"Honey, if you can't keep your man at home, that's not my fault," the blonde said, smirking.

Those warm brown eyes could flash as cold as ice, Jack realized. He watched as she smiled at the woman, watched as she reached up, ran a finger down the silver chain of her necklace. The medallion wasn't visible. It disappeared under her shirt, nestled in her cleavage, and although he hadn't been the least bit interested by the blonde's offer, all he wanted to do was go to Perci and nuzzle around the neckline of her shirt, nuzzle the pale, soft flesh and taste her. Again. And again. And again.

His cock started to throb.

Like a fucking shark, the *succubae* sensed his hunger, but she didn't realize she wasn't the target. She pressed her tits against his arm and smiled up at him. "You maybe wanna come outside with me?"

"No. I maybe don't wanna," he bit off, moving away.

She was like a damn two-armed octopus though. Following him, clutching at him and rubbing against him. All he had to do was look in her eyes and see the demon peering out at him to lose interest, but then he'd see Perci again. That was all it took.

And fuck, she was smirking now, watching him with a glint of amusement in her eyes, one that had managed to chase the shadows from her eyes.

"You think this is funny?" he growled at her as the blonde slid her hand down the front of his crotch.

She cocked a brow at him. "It has certain amusing aspects," she drawled.

Then she reached over and grabbed the blonde's hair.

Hard.

The blonde screeched and whirled, lifting a hand. She came down with a force that would have shattered bone if Perci had been human.

Perci just blocked it easily, and then she used her grip on the *succubae* to hurl her to the floor.

There was knowledge in the demon's eyes as she looked up

at Perci. Perci stroked a finger down the chain and tugged it free.

The *succubae* hissed, leaped to her feet and took off out the door quick as a blink.

Perci shot him a look. "I'll be back. You be here when I am."

Then she was gone.

"What the..."

He might have tried to go after them, but he wouldn't be able to catch up and he knew it.

Plus, he realized a few too many people had been watching them, and there was a look of uneasiness in their eyes.

Too uneasy. They'd seen something their minds weren't wanting to process—didn't *want* to process. Although it was just two women with unusual strength and then the blonde moving with a speed that just a little too much, it still wasn't...normal.

People didn't like the unexplained. All he had to do was give them an explanation. They'd let it go.

"The redhead's my girlfriend," he said, the lie coming with just a little too much ease. "The blonde is her cousin—used to be big into running, almost made it into the Olympics, but had a drug problem. They'll work it out."

It was far-fetched as hell, but people would rather believe the improbable than the truth, Jack had realized. Even when the improbable was a little far-fetched itself.

Within another thirty seconds, the small crowd was no longer paying him much attention. And he was sitting back on his stool, contemplating the bottle of tequila once more.

If I'd been asked a few hours earlier, I would have said a kill would do me good.

But right now, I was tired. So fucking tired. By the time I'd dealt with the *succubae* and the human's body, all I really wanted to do was sleep.

Except that I had to go back to the bar and find Jack.

The mortal Will expected me to train. The mortal I'd slept with. The mortal who made me feel strangely alive. The mortal who seemed to know far, far too much about things he shouldn't.

He hadn't said as much, but he'd known there was something not right about me...something different. And he had known there was something weird about the blonde earlier—I'd seen it in his eyes.

I wasn't ready to face him, to deal with him. I felt too drained. I wanted to curl up someplace and sleep for weeks. Months, even. Idly, I wondered if Will had ever had one of us request stasis. Right now, it would suit me just fine.

Except I'd already let some part of me exist in limbo for too long and look at the damage I'd done.

Shit, Luc...

Tears burned my eyes, and I wanted so desperately to go see him. To find him. To tell him how sorry I was.

I needed to get myself together first though, because Will had been right. Luc needed to see that I'd be okay first. But how could I make myself okay...?

As I drew closer to the bar, I heard the rumble of noise. Too much noise. I paused and closed my eyes, filtering through it all. Fight.

Hell.

I didn't even have to see it to know Jack was involved. Somehow.

Picking up my pace, I made it inside just in time to see one of the guys in the bar take a cue stick and swing toward Jack's back. I winced in sympathy as it broke, watched as he staggered a little, then shifted around and aimed a kick at Cue Stick Boy's knee. The guy went down hard, and judging by the sound of bone crunching, he wouldn't be getting up soon, and not without crutches and a cast for a good long while.

Good. Hitting at somebody's back?

Dismissing him, I looked around the bar. Hell. It was *trashed*.

Besides Cue Stick, three more lay around in various stages of injury. I glanced at Jack, watched as he drove a fist into somebody's gut and then followed it up with an elbow. And another one bit the dust.

Damn.

The guy was a one-man wrecking crew. Shit, what did he need *me* for? To make him more dangerous than he already was? It was a damn good thing he was on the side of the angels, that was for sure.

I glanced behind the bar, saw the bartender standing there with a gun. He looked worried and pissed and I couldn't blame him. Then I saw the phone in his other hand. Hell. Cops. He'd called the cops.

Sighing, I bent down and grabbed one of the cue sticks. They were lying scattered all over the place and a quick look at the back of the bar revealed why. The pool table lay on its side. Took some strength for that—somehow I suspected Jack was involved.

Three brave souls decided the best way to get at Jack was to rush him as one.

Smart plan.

Bad timing.

I took one of them out with the cue stick, using just enough force to make sure he went down and would wake up with a headache. Jack dealt with one of them and the third was as easy as tripping when he stumbled and glanced around to look for his buddy.

There weren't many people left willing to give Jack a go.

I could see why.

As he turned around and caught sight of me, that one look was enough to make my heart do a crazed little dance in my chest. If I'd still been mortal, if I'd still been that blushing maiden who had fallen in love with Luc, I think I might have fainted dead away at the sight of him.

He looked like hell on earth...like a warrior bent on destruction.

He also looked so damned hot, even smeared with blood, I just wanted to jump him.

Man. I was sick. Twisted and sick.

Hoping none of it showed, I jerked my head to the back door. "We need to be gone. Now. The cops are coming."

He curled his lip. "Figures."

"Did you drive?"

"Yeah." He started toward me and then winced and pressed a hand to his side. I knew that look, felt the echo of pain whisper through him. Grimly, I lowered my shields and that whisper of pain became a scream as I read the injuries on his body.

Oh, a lot of injuries. The worst were the ribs. Nothing fatal, but it was hurting him like a bitch. Somebody had busted a rib or two. I'd have to deal with that later.

I just hoped he'd prove as tough as he looked. Right now, we needed to move.

I reached into my hip pocket and pulled out the cash. As I counted off some bills, I said, "I sure hope you didn't start this."

"Yeah, princess. That's my idea of fun—picking a fight with a bunch of drunk morons."

On my way out the door, I threw the bills at the bartender. "For the damage. If you can avoid giving too clear a description of my friend here, I'll even see to it that more money is delivered within the next few weeks."

The bartender glanced at the cash, then at me. "He didn't start it. No reason to get too detailed, I reckon."

The money was tucked away before we even made the door.

We'd just pulled out of the parking lot in his beat-up old truck when the first of the flashing lights appeared in the rearview mirror. A little too close for comfort.

Shooting Jack a narrow look, I muttered, "You're going to be trouble."

"I've always been trouble." A ghost of a smile danced around his lips. But his eyes were closed, lines of pain fanning out from the corners.

We hit a bump and he grimaced. "We might need to find an ED. I've got some ribs busted—need to make sure they aren't poking into anything."

"They aren't." I'd feel it if they were. It would be a different pain.

He shot me a sidelong glance. "You got X-ray vision?"

"Something like that." As I drove, I drummed my fingers on the steering wheel. I needed a drink. It was going to be a long, long night. And a painful one. For both of us. But I didn't think about what was coming. I was better off not doing that. If I thought about it too much, it was going to put me in a bad, bad place.

The illness within him was enough to make Persinette's belly clench, even from here.

She could not risk going near him.

She already knew he could not be saved.

Looking at Jacques, she said, "I cannot help him. Would you please..."

She had no need to say another word to him. He gestured to several of her men. As they escorted her away, he went to speak to her mother-in-law, Cosette.

She had come to Persinette, begging, pleading. "I cannot bury another man I love...I cannot."

Persinette's heart broke for her, truly. She was not Luc's mother, although she had raised him, loved him as a mother would. Luc's mother had died shortly after she had given birth to him and just a few months later, Cosette had come into his life.

Sadly Luc had lost his father when he was but ten, and Cosette was all he had. She had remarried but her husband had taken ill, and now he lay dying.

Cosette had looked to Persinette.

Many people looked to Persinette. They did not understand why she was able to help so many, and Persinette would not enlighten them. Let them think it was the teas and the tonics— they need not know the truth. But Cosette was one of the few who did know. Persinette could heal. She couldn't heal all ills, though.

Cosette's husband would not be healed, and if Persinette tried it would kill her. It would kill her and the baby she carried. Pressing a hand to the swell of her stomach, she glanced back over her shoulder as Cosette started to sob. One of her ladies wrapped an arm around her and gave Persinette a censuring look. Persinette closed her eyes. There was nothing she could do for the man. She had to live with that.

As Jacques strode toward her, she carefully wiped the grief from her features. This brooding, protective man saw too much, read her too easily, and she wouldn't have him see this pain.

But he saw it, nonetheless.

He rested a big hand on her shoulder. "There is nothing you can do for him, milady. If you tried, you would endanger yourself and the child you carry."

"I know." She sighed and looked back once more at Cosette. "She has never asked anything of me though. I only wish to help—"

"She should not have asked this—not now. Not of a woman with child." A grim look crossed his face. "Your husband wouldn't be pleased to know his mother has asked this of you."

She reached out and caught his arm. "You will not tell him. When he returns, it will be hard enough to learn that his mother has been forced to bury another husband. He will be dead in days. He cannot be saved. There is no reason to trouble Luc with this."

"He is your husband. He would want to know—he *should* know." Jacques studied her face, his gray eyes dark and unreadable.

"You cannot tell him..."

She would have tried to make him promise, but just then, a harsh, brutal pain gripped her belly and she cried out. Darkness swamped her. The last thing she knew was his hands catching her.

Something had her pissed off, Jack decided.

Or upset her...something. The drive to his place was made in complete silence. And considering it was a good forty-minute drive, that was a lot of silence. He didn't mind it, but he rather liked listening to her talk, even if she was a smart-ass guardian angel. Even if he didn't know why she was here...or why she wouldn't take him to the damn ED, because shit, he was *hurting.*

Well, she'd dump him on his ass and then he'd just haul himself to the local county ED, make sure nothing was broken. He had some Vicodin in the medicine cabinet and if he popped a few of those, he'd get some sleep. He healed fast, and in a few days he'd be feeling okay.

Still, he wished she'd say something.

But she didn't. She just stared straight ahead as she drove.

She barely blinked, hardly even seemed to breathe.

When she pulled up in front of his place, he stayed where he was as she slid out.

"You coming?" she asked, lifting a red-gold brow at him.

"I'll wait here a few." He kept his eyes closed, tried not to breathe too deep. No way in hell was he climbing out of the truck, then back in once she disappeared.

Perci sighed. "Would you get out of the damn truck so I can take a look at you?"

"Unless you're a doctor, you taking a look at me isn't going to do much good." He cracked one eye open and slanted a look at her. "I need to go get an X-Ray, and I'd rather do it now because I'm already hurting like a bitch."

"Get the fuck out of the truck or I'll haul you out." She gave him a sharp-edged smile and added, "And somehow, I think you know I *can*."

"Damn it." He glared at her and started to shift, only to freeze as pain lanced through him. Sweat broke out all over him and he gritted his teeth, fought to breathe through it. After the wave passed, he gritted out, "Look, unlike *you*, I get hurt, and I don't heal the way you do."

"You know, I'm really curious just how you know these things." Then she came over and touched a finger to his lower lip. Pain flared and he remembered somebody had punched him in the mouth. That pain had seemed minor compared to his ribs though. He'd forgotten about it until she'd touched him. "Look at me. Don't blink. Don't close your eyes, not even for a second, Jack."

Then she pressed down. He grimaced and he might have knocked her hand away, but before he could, he saw it happen. He watched as her mouth—her perfect, bow-shaped mouth bloomed with an ugly bruise, a cut splitting her lower lip.

Although he hadn't looked in the mirror, he suspected that was a lot how his mouth looked. As the bruising on *her* face spread, the pain in his own faded.

He was still gaping at her as she reached up and touched her fingers to his blackened eye.

And as she took that injury away, took it onto *herself*, the injury on her lower lip was knitting together, fading away bit by bit.

"You don't need a doctor," she said. "I can take care of your side. But I'm not doing it out here."

"No."

I narrowed my eyes at him as he refused to get out of the truck.

He was in so much pain, I was almost ill with it. I wouldn't block it out though, because if I did, I wouldn't be able to tell if the pain was anything serious. I didn't think it *was*, but he had quite a few injuries on him.

I sighed and pushed my hand through my hair, debated on my choices.

I really did *not* want to do this out here. Once I took the injuries on his ribs, I was going to be in much worse shape than him. I'd heal quicker, but the price of that was I'd be damn near incapacitated for a short period of time and I'd rather not collapse out here.

Not that he'd leave me unconscious on the ground though...

Well, hell.

"Are you going to haul your butt inside or not?" I asked him, folding my arms across my chest.

"No." He glared at me, his face unmarked, his eyes furious and glinting at me. Oh, he was pissed. This was lovely. He was mad because I had healed him. This was just plain lovely.

Fine. He was going to be even more pissed off in a minute.

Sidling closer, careful not to let him see what I was up to, I said, "So what are you going to do? Just deal with the busted ribs and the pain?"

"I've had worse."

Yeah, I suspected he had. He watched me warily. Like he knew I was up to something.

Smart guy. Just as he went to shift away from me, I moved, flowing into the front seat of the truck and curling up on the small space in the floorboard. I slammed my hands onto either side of him so he couldn't evade me that way. "Sorry. I can't let you suffer," I said.

He started cussing and jerked away.

As I laid my hands on him, I did the same thing—cussing in English, then switching to French when I ran out of creative ways to swear. I kept right on cursing until the pain stole my breath away.

Vicious and brutal...that was the only way to describe this kind of pain. It sucks the breath right out of you and every single microsecond is agonizing. I tasted blood in the back of my throat, and even though his broken ribs hadn't pierced his lungs, I suspected I wouldn't be so lucky. Black dots danced in front of my eyes and I knew consciousness wasn't going to hold out much longer. I pressed the flats of my hands against his sides, searched for the pain inside. But it was gone.

All gone.

Thank God.

I collapsed in a heap and he caught me. I glimpsed his rigid, angry face through my lashes and my last clear thought was... *Have we done this before?*

She weighed nothing.

Jack carried her into his house and tried not to think about how fragile she felt, how delicate.

As he lay her on his bed, he sat down beside her and touched the pulse in her neck, although he wasn't sure why.

It wasn't like she could die, right?

But she'd coughed up blood. She'd collapsed. She was unconscious, and damn it, why the hell had she done that? It wasn't like he hadn't dealt with busted ribs before.

The pulse under his touch was strong, steady, although slower than he would have expected. He sighed and shifted around, buried his face in his hands, and even as he did it, he marveled that he could do it without pain. Not even ten minutes ago, he'd been all but ready to beg for her to just leave him the hell alone just so he could do something about his fucking ribs, and now he was fine.

Driven by curiosity, he stood and moved to the mirror over his bureau, staring at his face. He should have looked like a human punching bag.

But there wasn't even a damn mark on him.

He grabbed the hem of his bloodied and stained T-shirt and pulled it off. His ribs should have been black and blue, but there was nothing.

In the mirror, he looked at Perci's reflection, watched as she shifted, watched her face tighten with pain. He clenched his jaw and turned around, strode across the floor.

She'd taken his injuries, his fucking busted ribs. Sitting down on the side of the bed, he caught her shirt and eased it up. And felt like he'd been sucker-punched all over again. Because her ribs looked easily twice as bad as his *should* have looked.

"It's...passing."

Shifting his gaze up, he realized she'd woken up and was staring at him, her brown eyes clouded with pain.

"If you hadn't fucking *done* that, there wouldn't be anything to pass."

"I still would have been hurting, as long as I was anywhere near you." She grimaced. "I heal. I can't be around somebody in physical pain without feeling something, and it's worse with somebody I know, somebody I've...ah...well..."

"Fucked?"

She wrinkled her nose. "I was thinking *connected with*. If there's some sort of connection, it's a lot worse."

"Then you should have just gotten the hell away from me." He stared at the bruises, willing them to fade. But it didn't seem like they were. Impatient, he grabbed the knife from his boot and sliced her shirt open.

Perci glared at him. "Damn it, what are you doing?"

"You said you heal fast. You *should* heal fast and I'm not seeing it happen."

"It's only been a few minutes." Then she closed her eyes and took a slow, clearly cautious breath. "I can breathe easier, and it's not hurting as much. The bruises will be the last thing to go. But it's getting better."

Gently, he touched one finger to a bruise. It was an ugly stain on her pale, pale skin and just the sight of it was like an obscenity. "You shouldn't have done this," he muttered. "It was my fight, my fault. You shouldn't have had to deal with the pain."

"I was given a gift to use it." She stared at him with unconcerned eyes, liked she wasn't bothered by the fact that her entire torso was a dark rainbow. "And hey, I've had worse."

"You honestly feel the pain of everybody around you?"

She shrugged. "Not all the time. I can shield against it and I don't help everybody. I can't. Even my energy isn't endless. I've figured that out." She closed her eyes. "And the gift has...changed over time. But this was easy."

"You call this easy?"

"Compared to some of the people I've had to heal? Yes."

He was staring so hard at the bruises it took him a few moments to realize they were actually lessening. Fading away.

It was a slow, gradual thing, and he counted the minutes away as he watched her body slowly absorb the bruises she'd taken from him.

Fifteen minutes after she'd opened her eyes, she squinted at him and demanded, "Are you going to sit there until every last bruise is gone?"

"Yes." He curled his hand over her hip, rubbed one bruise with his thumb. "They never should have gone to you to begin with."

"Oh, for crying out loud..." She went to sit up, but then she froze.

Her brown eyes were only inches away from him, her mouth so very, very close.

"I don't like seeing marks on you," Jack muttered.

Perci's lashes lowered over her eyes. "Unfortunately, I get marked up a lot. But I heal fast. Deal with it."

"Hmmm." He dipped his head and skimmed his lips down her neck. "Why did you leave so fast?"

"I..." She shuddered. "I needed to think."

"Thinking can be very overrated."

"Yeah. But it needed to be done."

"Okay." He brushed the ruin of her shirt aside and nipped the soft curve of her shoulder. "Did it help you figure anything out?"

"No. Not a damn thing." She tilted her head to the side, baring her neck.

Jack took the hint and nuzzled her neck again, scraping the flesh with his teeth and smiling as she shivered. "I like the feel of you, Perci. I like the taste of you."

"Hmmm. The feeling is mutual." She stroked a hand up his side and then whispered, "Jack, can I ask you something?"

"Anything." Damn, he'd give her anything...

"I could use a shower."

Hell. Not quite what he'd been hoping for.

Dipping his head, he caught her lower lip between his teeth and tugged. Then he stood up and caught her in his arms. She snorted. "I can walk."

"Yeah. This works too though. And I figure you owe me for taking ten years of my life when you passed out on me."

She lifted a brow. "If you'd listened and come inside the house, I would have explained that I'd be in bad shape when I was done."

"Bad shape and passing out are two different things. *I* was in bad shape. You passed out." He shouldered the door open and sat her down on the counter before flicking the light on. "Shower or bath?"

She eyed the bath, a wistful little sigh escaping her. "Shower, although a soak sounds lovely."

"There's no reason you can't have one."

"Actually, yeah, there is. We need to talk."

He knelt down in front of her and went to work on the laces of her boots. "Talk about what?"

"All sorts of things. And I can handle my boots."

"So can I." He dropped one on the floor. "See?"

As he straightened in front of me, I found myself staring at his chest. I really should look away from his chest—really. I knew this. But I was having the hardest damn time.

As a matter of fact, instead of looking *away*, I found myself leaning closer and pressing my mouth against him. Just above his heart.

His breath hissed out of him and his hand came up, cradled the back of my head.

"We're not going to talk, and you're not going to shower if

you keep things like this up," he muttered. "At least not for a good long while."

I looked at him from under my lashes. "You could always join me in the shower."

He skimmed a hand down my side. "You're not up for that."

"Aren't I?" I took a deep breath and there was no pain, no tightness. Leaning back, I glanced down at my torso. All but a few yellowish, green shadows were gone and I barely even felt the discomfort from those. "I feel fine. A little stiff, but that's what the shower is for."

Heat, hunger, they burned in his eyes and turned that misty gray to smoke. He laid his hands on my thighs and I could feel the warmth of him through the denim. I wanted to feel it on my bare skin—wanted to feel *him* on my bare skin.

I shouldn't do this...

The whisper of guilt tried to rouse in the back of my mind, but this time, instead of ignoring it and shoving it aside—I faced it. Actually, there was no real reason why I shouldn't, was there? After all, we already had.

There is Luc, that voice whispered. *You still need to face Luc.*

But Luc already knew. Luc had known for years, and I'd been cruelly, foolishly clinging to him and letting him keep his illusions. But we were no longer married, and although I loved him, I wasn't in love with him. More...he knew it.

Yes, I needed to tell him that, but it wasn't enough to keep me from taking pleasure with this man, was it?

Although... I sighed and closed my eyes. Damn my brain anyway. Damn my heart.

Jack reached up and cupped my face. He pressed a kiss to my brow. "So you're not up for it."

Yeah. Let him think that. It was easier, right?

As he pulled away, I gave him a strained smile. "You know, I think maybe a bath wouldn't be a bad idea, after all."

Baths took longer, right?

Chapter Seven

Luc loved the mountains.

Although Perci wasn't here with him, he could still enjoy the beauty and enjoy them he would. Alaska didn't feel the same though. Not without Perci.

Nothing would ever feel the same without Perci.

He walked the paths of the house they had built three decades earlier and tried to find peace. It wasn't here.

He tried to find comfort. It wasn't here.

He wondered if perhaps he had given her up too easily, but after three hundred years, was it really *easy*? It wasn't like he hadn't waited for her to heal, for her to come back to him.

It just wasn't meant to be.

It was edging closer to dusk when he returned home, not that he could tell by sight. He hadn't used Krell's eyes once since Perci had been taken from him. For some reason, it was easier to just live in the darkness right now, although he didn't know why.

He knew it was night by the change in the air, the feel of it, the smell of it.

When he felt the air draw tight, he was tempted to use the dog's sight though. After all, it would make it easier to get his hands around Will's throat if he could see the bastard.

"Hello, Luc."

His heart stuttered.

It was Perci. And the ache that had resided in her heart for three hundred years...

"Perci," he said, amazed that his voice sounded so normal. So calm. He reached down and rested a hand on Krell's head. The dog didn't stiffen, didn't blink as he merged their minds and gazed at Perci.

He hissed out a breath at the sight of her. Bruises faded on her narrow torso and her shirt was missing. "You're in a state."

"Yeah. Healed somebody and it was bad." She glanced down and grimaced as she eyed the fading bruises.

That didn't explain the loss of her shirt though. Keeping his connection with Krell, he released the dog and crossed the ground to her, studying her face. Something had changed on her...*within* her. Something major, something momentous...and in such a short time.

There was grief in her eyes.

And there was a strange sort of peace as well. That pain that knotted her heart, it was easing. He had waited years, centuries for this...dare he hope?

Perci kicked at the ground and he realized she was missing a boot.

Just one.

Perplexed, he looked at her face. "Perci, where is your other boot?"

She scowled and glanced down. "Shoot." Shoving a hand through her hair, she said, "I was in a rush. I needed to get this done while it was on my mind and I just got a hold of Will, made him send me here. I wasn't thinking clearly."

Get it done.

No. He didn't dare hope. That was something he shouldn't have even considered. Didn't he know better than that by now?

"Get what done?" he asked. Although he hadn't thought it was possible to hurt more, the crack in his heart widened and started to spill something vile and bitter through him. He wanted to back away—perhaps go into the house, away from her. Could she make him listen if he wasn't here?

"I need to tell you I'm sorry."

Caught off-guard, Luc stilled. "You are sorry." He curled a hand into a fist, wished he could reach for her. Inside her mind, she was a dark tangle of misery, and although it had eased, the pain was there. He wanted to take that from her, but he couldn't. She had never allowed him to help ease that pain. "Why are you sorry?"

"For blaming you...all this time. For never letting go of you, even when both of us knew it was over."

Over. Luc closed his sightless eyes against the burn of tears. She'd finally said it. He wanted to make her take the words back. But he couldn't undo what was happening inside her. And he couldn't make her love him again.

"Perhaps I wasn't ready to admit it was over," he whispered quietly. "I wasn't ready to let you go either."

She sighed and it was a sad, desolate sound. "We were only married for fifteen years. And nearly half of that, you were gone from me. Why is it so hard to let go of something that existed so long ago?"

For him, it was only yesterday. But he didn't tell her that. She needed this. He would let her have it. He still loved her, after all. How could he do otherwise?

Crossing to her, he laid a hand on her cheek. Memory slammed into him...yes, for him, it was only yesterday. He remembered the day they wed, the day she pledged herself to him. He had touched her just so and promised always to love her...and he had meant it. Although theirs had been an arranged marriage, as had so many, it had also been one of love. A gift, he'd always thought.

Until the day the gift had become a nightmare.

"We were happy," he said quietly. "And although we've lived many, many years, Persinette, it was the only time we were truly happy. Is it any wonder we cannot let those memories go?"

She took a deep breath and it caught in her throat. "I've been so unfair to you, Luc. You were never to blame, and if I hadn't spent the past three centuries hating myself, blaming myself, blaming *you*, maybe you could have moved on, found something...found *somebody*. You deserve to be happy."

Pressing his thumb to her lips, he said, "Enough. I have spent this time exactly where I wanted to be. Yes, I had hopes you would in time heal...and return to me. But in my heart of hearts, I knew I fooled myself. And that fault is mine. Not yours."

"Luc—"

"Shhh." He kissed her softly. "You are my heart, Perci, and I have hoped, have prayed, that in time you would come to love me again. But that is not meant to be. But it was my choice to wait, to hope...my choice. Not yours. Because I knew it wouldn't happen, even if I didn't want to admit it."

"If I could have made it happen, I would have. I do love you. I just can't love you like I did when we married. Before..."

"Shhh."

She was crying now. Crying, and every tear tore a dagger into his already broken heart. Brushing the tears aside, he said gently, "If we could control the heart, what good would we be? The heart isn't meant to be controlled, love. And you know it. Now stop hating yourself. Let it go, Perci. Perhaps we have both clung to the past for far too long."

She rested her head on his shoulder. One harsh sob escaped her.

He stroked a hand up her back and closed his eyes. For years, he had prayed one simple prayer... *Bring her back to me.*

But he realized, he had prayed for the wrong thing.

Now he opened his sightless eyes and stared at the heavens he could no longer see. *Give her peace. Let her be happy again.*

If it was without him, then fine—he'd swallow that nasty, bitter pill.

Because he just couldn't handle thinking about her out there...and without him there to watch over her.

"It was never our fault, Perci," he murmured. He kissed her brow. "Never."

The air grew tight.

He knew what it meant and he wanted to cling to her, press her close.

Instead, he caught her chin in his hand. "One kiss, Perci?"

He tasted her tears as she pressed her mouth to his.

"I'm going to make myself okay, Luc. I wanted to tell you that."

Although it was the very last thing he wanted to do, he let her go. "I'll hold you to that."

"But you need to promise me something."

She was backing away from him, and because he couldn't stand to watch her leave him for the very last time, he severed his connection with Krell. Lost in the darkness, he forced a smile. "And what would you have me promise you?"

"Will told me that life is for living...even for us. If I'm

supposed to go and live, then so are you. We both held on too long. Go and live, Luc. There's something, somebody out there for you. *Find* her."

And then she was gone.

Luc closed his eyes. "I found her three hundred years ago," he said quietly.

Krell pressed himself against his leg and whined. Luc shook his head, unable to find comfort in his friend's presence. "Just give her peace...and I'll make myself accept this," he muttered. "Somehow."

Chapter Eight

The water was cooling by the time I sank my aching bones into it.

I felt old. Yeah, I *am* old, but I usually don't feel that way.

Shit, that had been hard. I'm not tuned into emotional pain, thank God, but I didn't have to be for me to feel his agony.

I'd just broken Luc's heart.

Again.

For probably the thousandth time. I worried the medallion absently. He'd be better for this though. He'd have to be. I was like the albatross around his neck and once he realized that...

The door flew open. Jack stood there, his eyes narrowed and furious.

"What in the hell..." he growled.

I lifted a brow.

"I could say the same thing."

"Where have you been?"

I glanced at the water. "Taking a bath?"

"Don't lie to me." His lip peeled back from his teeth, and although my heart was still aching from what I'd just done, I felt a ridiculous little quiver too. "I came in here fifteen minutes ago to check on you and you weren't *here*."

Oops.

I just stared at him. He glared back at me.

Huffing out a sigh, I said, "Well, I'm here now, aren't I?"

He stalked over to the tub and bent over, bracing his hands on either side. "Is there any particular reason you've decided to plant your cute little ass in my life? Is there?"

"Actually...yes." My heart banged against my ribs so hard, it was a miracle neither of us actually *heard* it. "And we can talk about that. *After* my bath. Now if you don't mind..."

For the longest time, he didn't move. I didn't dare breathe until he straightened up and pulled away. When he did leave, I sagged and sank into the water until it covered my head.

Shit.

This had been one hellaciously exhausting day. Yeah, so what if I'd felt more alive than I had in centuries? Even just now with Luc, when I'd been shredding his heart—yeah, it had hurt—but I'd let myself feel. I hadn't let myself feel in so long...

Right now I wasn't entirely sure this was a good thing.

Jack stormed into the kitchen and only one thing kept him from plowing his fist into the solid granite counter top.

It was the knowledge that if he did it, he'd end up bashing the hell out of his hand, and then what? If Perci did felt the physical pain of those around her, what in the hell would he do if he actually busted his hand?

He was pissed enough right now to do that, but shit, he couldn't risk actually causing her pain.

Where in the hell had she been?

"Have a care with her, would you, Jack?"

He spun around, snarling as Will stepped through the doorway.

Will.

Jack knew him by no other name. As far as he knew, the man *had* no other name. In all the years he'd known him, Will hadn't aged a day, hadn't changed a bit. He was Jack's height—topping off at six foot two, but where Jack was broadly built, Will was lean. He was pale, his hair silvery-white, although it wasn't from age. No, the guy's face was unlined and smooth.

He wasn't a young man though. Jack knew that just by looking in those silver-gray eyes.

Will had seen things. He'd seen civilizations rise, fall. He'd seen life and death and things Jack didn't even want to think about. Not that Will had ever told him. Jack just knew.

Normally, he wouldn't have minded seeing the man in his home, even though he did have a problem knocking. Will just tended to appear. Wherever, whenever he wanted.

But right now, he wasn't in the mood.

Closing one hand into a fist, he snarled, "Get the hell out."

Will cocked a brow. "Have a care with her," he repeated, his voice soft. Mild.

But the warning was clear.

Jack curled his lip. "It's not like I'm going to go whaling on her. Even if I was inclined to beat women, she's one of yours. She could kick my ass and we both know it."

"I didn't mean physically." Will sighed.

He looked...tired.

Jack frowned and shoved off the counter, crossing his arms over his chest as he studied the other man's face.

But any questions he might have asked fell to the wayside as Will focused his strange, unearthly eyes on Jack's face. "Perci doesn't need gentle *physical* handling, and you're quite right, she'd hand your ass to you on a platter if you had a mind to get rough with her. Not that you would. Perci is just...fragile right now, Jack." He looked away, staring off into the distance.

In an absent voice, he said, "I pushed her too hard, I think."

"What are you talking about?"

Will looked back at him. "Some wounds, they are buried so deep...they heal wrong. You know that? Perci's wounds healed very, very wrong. She finally faced some of that, but I should have forced her to do it long before now. Long before..."

Will went quiet.

"Before what?"

But Will wouldn't say, and as he shifted his silver gaze to the doorway, Jack figured out why.

Perci was coming.

"Have a care with her," Will murmured again, his voice almost soundless.

Jack snarled but kept the question behind his teeth, ready for Will to disappear, the way he liked to do.

But as Perci appeared in the doorway, Will lingered.

She didn't look surprised to see him, although her mouth went tight.

"Damn it, haven't I had to handle *enough* in the past few days?" she muttered.

As Jack tried to figure out how to address that cryptic question, Will moved to join her. "Yes."

Tension jerked Jack's spine straight as a poker as Will came to a stop at her side. He rested a hand on her shoulder and Jack couldn't help but notice...they looked...well...nice together.

Not exactly like a matched set, but Will had that easy elegance about him, and Perci looked like she'd been born to well silks and satins and lace. Jack felt more at home in his jeans. He'd take a beer over a glass of wine any day. He was out of place with her and he knew it.

And what the hell did that matter? They didn't know each other. He had no idea why she was in his life. Once she'd taken care of whatever she felt she needed to take care of, she'd be gone and he'd probably never see her again. Just thinking that left a bad, bad ache in his heart. An old, old wound...one that had never healed...

Perci edged away from Will and Jack wanted to grab her, pull her against him. He didn't want the other man touching her. At all. Not at all.

She shot Jack a shuttered look, and it was a punch in the gut to see the grief there. That pain.

Have a care with her.

Perci is just...fragile right now.

Fragile?

She looked shattered. Heartbroken.

Her brown eyes stared into his and despite the anger that still burned in his gut, he found himself reaching up, skimming his fingers down her cheek. "What's the matter, princess?" he murmured. "You didn't look quite so sad earlier."

She reached up, but instead of knocking his hand away the way he'd expected, she just sighed, wrapped her fingers around his wrist and squeezed. "Nothing's wrong, Jack. Nothing more than normal, at least." Then, with some hint of her normal attitude, she cocked a brow and added, "Stop calling me princess."

She let go, moved to the table and settled down in the chair with easy, boneless grace. Her gaze moved to Will and she stared at him for a long moment before looking back at Jack.

"You know this guy, I take it?"

"Ah...yeah." Jack shot Will a glance, but the man had his inscrutable mask in place and Jack had no idea what he was up to.

"Hmm. Figures." She rubbed her hands over her face. "Will, is there a reason you're gracing us with your presence or did you just miss the pleasure of my company?"

She smirked with the last bit and Will gave her a ghost of a smile.

"Well, you're being so charming, Persinette," he murmured. "How can I resist?"

She snorted and then sighed. "Stop worrying. I'm fine. Or I will be. Go on. You've got other...issues on your mind."

"Issues," Will mused. "Yes. Issues."

Will still had that strange look in his eyes and although he said nothing, Jack felt the weight of his words slamming through him all over again.

Have a care.

What in the hell?

In the blink between moments, Will disappeared.

He barely noticed, but Perci gazed at the spot where Will had been, like she could almost see the echo of his passage.

Could she, he wondered?

Maybe she could have, except she wasn't exactly too focused on the here and now.

Her eyes looked so damned sad.

Abruptly, the anger he'd felt drained away.

Hauling the chair out, he spun it around and sat. He brought his arms up and rested his chin on the back, staring at her. The delicate lines of her face didn't look any different than they had earlier. But there was a grief on her...pain. "You look miserable," he said quietly.

"You're a real sweet-talker." She gave him a whisper of a smile, but her heart wasn't in it. "Anybody ever tell you that?"

"What has you so sad?"

I looked away. I couldn't talk about this with him. And damn it, where was that vaunted self-control of mine? I should be able to look at him without him seeing all the misery and pain, without him knowing a damn thing I felt. I was good at hiding what I felt. Years of practice.

Years that proved useless with him.

Determined to distract him, I looked back at him. "How do you know Will?"

"He knew my mother. And you haven't answered me."

I blinked. "He knew your *mother*?" I repeated. Leaning forward, I peered at his face. "What do you mean he knew your mother?"

He reached out and when he touched me, I felt the shock of it clear down to my toes. I would have leaned into that touch, happily, maybe even invited a deeper, more intimate touch. But he was more interested in toying with the silver chain wrapped around my neck.

"I've seen this before," he said quietly.

"Seen...what? My necklace?"

"Not yours. One like it."

My heart started to race. Somewhere deep inside I could feel things coiling tight, cold. My hands were sweating. "Will wears one."

Jack's gaze swept up to meet mine.

"Yeah. He does. But it wasn't his." He rubbed his thumb over the etched wings, and I saw grief in the soft, misty gray of his eyes.

"Who was it, Jack?"

"My mother," he murmured. "She wore one just like this. Until the day she died."

I jerked away so hard the chair clattered to the floor and the chain broke. He was left holding my pendant and I snatched it away from him. "You lying son of a bitch. If she had one *just* like this, then she wouldn't be dead."

I didn't say it out loud, but *we* didn't procreate either. He *couldn't* have one of us for a mother.

"Liar. You're fucking lying," I said, shaking my head at him.

He lifted a brow. "You sure about that?"

"Yeah, I'm sure." I shoved a hand through my hair. What in the hell was I doing here? Had Will stuck me with some screwed-up head case that I was going to have to "guide" before he could be one of us? Why was he handing me this story?

Maybe it's not a story...he seems to know too much.

I shot him a look. "Just like this?"

"Exactly."

"There's only one way she could have gotten one *just* like this. One way."

He shrugged. "Then I guess that's how she got it. I never asked. She always had it. I never saw her without it."

"How old were you when she died?"

His lashes flickered. "Almost thirteen," he said, his voice gruff.

I ached for him. It must have been almost twenty years, but the heart never forgot those we loved. "Thirteen..." I shook my head. Okay, there was another slim possibility. Maybe she'd taken him in when he was young—maybe *she* had been the one set intended to train him, and then she'd gotten in a fight she couldn't win.

We *can* die—it's just not that easy to kill us. Maybe she just let him think she was his mom, although that didn't settle well...

"Are you sure she was your mother?"

A grim smile twisted his lips. "Oh, yeah. She was my mother. Birth-mother, don't go trying to find another explanation out of it."

He sounded certain of it—*too* certain. And I *believed* him.

"Doesn't make sense," I muttered. None of it.

"Why not?"

I looked down at my pendant. "These...mean something."

He smirked at me. "I know what they mean, princess."

"Do you?"

He stood and kicked a leg over the chair. I had the bizarre image of a man dismounting a horse—a man wearing tarnished armor, wielding a sword. Then the image changed and the armor became chain mail. I rubbed my eyes and the image altered yet again and I saw him in the garb I would have seen in the time when I had lived as a human.

My knees buckled and I had to slam a hand against the

wall to keep from falling.

The face...it seemed all wrong. But something about his eyes...the way he moved, even the body...

A shiver raced down my spine.

I passed a hand over my eyes and then looked at Jack. "What do you know about the pendants, Jack? About...?"

"About the Grimm?" he asked, his voice mocking. "Enough. Everything."

The Grimm—

My heart knocked against my ribs. How did he know?

His mother...?

"Did your mother tell you about us?"

"Shit, no. My mother never broke her vows and there are all sorts of promises they make you give—they don't end when you give up your wings, do they, Perci?" he asked softly.

Give up your wings...

"She gave up her wings."

"Yes. She met my dad and fell in love with him—got knocked up with me. Somewhere along the way, my dad disappeared. I don't know what happened, but I never knew him and it hurt her too much to talk about it, so I didn't ask. I don't know how long she had before she got pregnant with me, but I don't think it was long. And she died before I was thirteen. She could have had eternity...and she died in so much fucking pain, she barely knew her own name." Jack's voice was so thick with bitterness it hurt to even listen to him.

"I'm so sorry," I murmured.

"Yeah." He closed his eyes. "Will was coming around before then. He'd always been coming around."

"Is he the one who told you about us?"

"No." Jack opened his eyes and stared at me. "Nobody told me, princess. I've always known. Always."

Then he stood and shoved the chair toward the table, violence barely restrained.

Always.

As he left the kitchen, his words echoed in my head.

Always.

Chapter Nine

So much for trying to help her get over the pain she felt, Jack thought.

Fragile.

Shit.

That woman wasn't fragile. She might look a bit more...well, *human*, than normal, but she wasn't fragile. Still, the pain he'd glimpsed in her eyes tore at him. He wanted to soothe...stroke, take it away.

Liar.

Shit, what had he expected, that she'd believed him? And why in the hell was he so angry? Jack didn't know, but he was beyond furious. Beyond pissed and he unloaded on the heavy bag with unrestrained rage. He'd been pounding away for damn near an hour and his arms felt like lead, but he couldn't stop.

Liar.

Yeah, probably seemed easier to think he was lying than to consider he might be telling the truth, he supposed.

Abruptly, he realized he wasn't alone.

Without looking at her, he said, "Do us both a favor and just get the hell out of my house, princess."

"One of these days, you'll get the point when I tell you not to call me that," she said, sighing. But the heat was missing from her voice. "And I'm not leaving. In case you haven't figured it out, I'm here for a reason."

"Yeah? You mean other than pissing me off?" He landed one last punch on the bag and then turned to stare at her. Sweat dripped into his eyes, stinging them. He stalked over to the edge of the workout area he had installed in his garage, grabbed the towel and wiped his face off.

Perci remained quiet. He shot her a glance and immediately wished he hadn't. The look in those dark brown eyes was enough to lay him low.

Fuck...that hunger just might stop his heart.

He choked back a groan and looked away, throwing the towel down. Bracing his hands on the unpainted concrete wall, he bowed his head and closed his eyes. *Don't look at her. She can't read emotion—just pain, and seriously, having your dick tied into a knot isn't* real *pain. Is it?*

He heard the heavy bag's chain rustle and he looked back, saw her standing next to it, watched as she stroked one hand down the worn leather.

He wanted to see that hand stroking something else.

Fuck, fuck, fuck.

She needed to get the hell out of here.

"You and me both know you would knock that thing clear off the chain in one punch," he said. He smirked at her. "And although I really don't need to coddle my ego, I'd just as soon not watch a woman bust the bag. So let's just not."

Perci smiled at him. Then, quicker than he could even track, she moved. That long, slender body moved up in the air, she kicked—jumping back kick, he thought, but damn she was fast. The bag went flying...and stayed on the chain. She caught it on the first backswing and smiled at him. "I know how to pull it. We learn that early on. Control. It's important."

"Considering you could probably break me in half? Yeah. Important." He tried another tactic. "I need a shower. So if you're not going to get the hell out, can we chat when I'm done, princess?"

Her lashes flickered over dark eyes and he sauntered over to her, reached up. He trailed one finger along her jaw line, watched as her eyes closed, as a breath shuddered out of her. "Unless you want to join me. Want to wash my back, princess?"

Her lashes lifted and she stared at him, her gaze hot, heavy...and so fucking hungry.

Backfire.

His mind started to screech a warning as she closed the scant distance between them. "Sure, slick. I'll wash your back...after." Then she reached up, curled a hand around the back of his neck and pulled his head down to hers.

As their mouths met, Jack realized this hadn't quite been

the outcome he'd been pushing for.

She slid her hands up his sweaty sides and he tore his mouth away.

"Stop it," he muttered. "I need a damn shower and not that long ago, *you* invited me into the shower and then decided maybe we shouldn't. If you weren't up for it then, you aren't up for it now."

Perci leaned in and licked him, stroking her tongue along the line of his neck like a little cat, and he shuddered. "I think I know if I'm feeling up for it or not. Come on, Jack. I think I can handle you." She pushed up on her toes and murmured in his ear, "Unless you're that convinced you can't handle me."

She bit his earlobe and then eased back down, her breasts rubbing over his chest.

Jack caught her arms and forced her back.

"Stop it," he snarled. "Unless you really want me on you, right here, right now...just stop it."

"Right here, right now?"

I stared at him, my mouth going dry.

Unless you really want me on you, right here, right now.

Damn it, I couldn't even *explain* how badly I wanted that.

He glared at me, those misty gray eyes glinting and hot and hungry. Dark red flags of color rode on his cheekbones and his mouth was a sexy snarl that had me wanting to bite him.

I think that was exactly what I was going to do too. This ache for him wasn't going to go away. No matter what I did, and no matter what I said.

Life is living, Perci. Even for us. Go live it.

That was what Will had said to me, right before he sent me to this man who wouldn't stay out of my thoughts. If I was supposed to start living, then damn it, why not start with him? I grabbed the hem of my shirt, pulled it off and let it fall to my feet.

Jack's eyes locked on my mostly naked chest and I think almost stopped breathing.

"What in the hell are you doing?" he rasped.

I reached behind me and undid the clasp of my bra.

"Making it easy for you," I said with a smile. "If you're going to be on me, right here, right now, can't we get the clothes out of the way?"

He froze.

As I reached for the zipper of my jeans, he stared at my fingers like he was mesmerized. I pushed them down and stepped out of them, but as I reached for panties, he swore and stepped forward, gripping my wrists in a tight, uncompromising grip.

"What in the hell are you doing?" he repeated.

I smiled. "Isn't it obvious?"

"Why?"

Oh, now that was harder to answer...even though I *knew* the answer. I didn't understand it, but I *knew* it. Quietly, I said, "Let go of my hands."

For a few seconds, Jack just stared at me, and then he let go slowly. I rested my hands on his waist and stared at how it looked. I was still so pale. I could stay out in the sun for days on end and I wouldn't tan. Fortunately, I didn't burn either.

But I was so pale...his skin looked unbelievably dark by comparison, deep, swarthy and glistening with a fine sheen of sweat.

Stroking my hands upward, I mused, "Do you know, the first time I looked at you, I think that was the first time I actually *felt* anything in years?"

My hands were on his chest now, and I felt the way his heart banged against my hand, felt his reaction. I didn't look at him though. Not at his face.

We may not react to physical injuries the way mortals do...but our hearts, they are still all too human, and I don't know how I'd handle it if he pulled away. I knew he wanted me, but wanting is easy...and it doesn't necessarily mean much of anything.

"I can fight anything you put in front of me, and not feel a damn thing," I continued. "It doesn't matter if I'm winning, if I'm losing, if I've got a hole in my gut the size of the Grand Canyon...I don't feel it. It doesn't matter if I'm this close to true death...and we *can* die. Just takes a whole hell of a lot to make it happen. But as close as I can come to death, I've been that close and it doesn't touch me. Not emotionally. Physical pain passes so fast. I almost welcome it, because at least I *feel* something. It's the only time I've felt...in years."

His heart was racing now. So fast...so strong and so fast. I slid my hands higher and curled them over his shoulders.

Finally, I made myself look into his eyes.

"But then I saw you and I finally felt something else. And it sure as hell wasn't pain."

That misty gray gaze burned. I caught the barest flicker of something...that familiar hunger, but also something else. It went deeper, burned hotter, brighter.

But there was no time to process it.

His hands curved around my waist and he pulled me close. The heat of his body all but scorched me. My feet left the ground as he lifted me up. One hand cradled the back of my head and his mouth was close...so damn close.

"Be sure, Perci," he whispered against my lips. "You damned sure you want this?"

I nibbled his lower lip. "What do you think?"

"And are you going to disappear when it's over?" He skimmed his hands up, cupped my breasts in his hands. "Because I'm going to be pissed off if I wake up alone again."

"You won't." I hadn't yet explained to him that I wasn't going anywhere yet, and I wasn't going to. Although maybe I should.

I pressed my mouth to his and caught his lower lip between my teeth. "I'm waiting..."

And then I wasn't waiting anymore.

For a mortal, he moved damned fast. So fast, the room spun around me as he turned and pressed my bare back against the bare concrete wall. Cold and hard, it was a shock against my system, especially compared to his heat.

His chest, wide and hot and slicked with sweat, crushed against my breasts. His mouth, hungry and hot and demanding, ate at mine. And his hands were everywhere.

I gripped his shoulders, certain that I could catch my breath if he would just give me a second...

He started to kiss a burning, blazing trail down my chin

and I sucked in a breath—yes, I could breathe. But then he went to his knees, catching my breasts in his hands and plumping them together, squeezing them, pinching my nipples. Each touch, each stroke...so much pleasure. Too much pleasure.

I fisted my hands in his dark hair, tried to hold on, tried to keep my balance.

Blood pounded in my ears.

He tugged on one nipple restlessly, teased it while he kissed and nipped a stinging trail over to the other. When he caught it between his teeth and bit down, the pleasure blistered through me.

I wanted to tell him to slow down—I needed him to. I needed a second...just five seconds to breathe...

Then he shifted his focus lower. He tore my panties off and dropped the shredded silk to the floor. When he caught me behind one leg, I started to wobble. I would have fallen if he hadn't braced me. Would have fallen all over him and I still might, because then he pressed his mouth against me and licked me. One long slow lick that opened me.

Harsh, panting breaths exploded out of me. He curled his tongue around my clit and sucked it into his mouth. Then he slid his hand up my inner thigh and pushed two fingers inside me. Still suckling on my clit, he started to fuck two fingers in and out of my pussy, and I shattered.

I keened out his name and my other knee buckled.

"Again," Jack snarled, surging to his feet and fisting a hand in her hair. He jerked her head back, covered her mouth with his and swallowed her groan.

Even though he'd driven her to shattering climax only hours ago—not that long ago, truly—it seemed like he'd been waiting years, decades, an eternity, to hold her. The hours they'd spent together earlier hadn't even taken the edge off.

He needed her so much it blew his mind.

He needed more. So much more.

"Damn it, I want to see that again...fuck, you're so beautiful."

She shuddered in his arms, that long, willowy body arching

against his, and he felt the press of her belly against his cock. He cupped her ass and lifted her up. Through the thin, worn cotton of his workout shorts, he could feel how hot she was and he was dying to be inside her, to feel her coming around him this time.

He put her down and had a moment's satisfaction as she wobbled and slammed her hands against the wall to balance herself. Then he was too busy dealing with his shorts and the aching burn in his cock. Long, agonizing seconds later, he reached for her, only to freeze and swear, long, viciously and raggedly.

"Fuck. Condoms. In the house...forgot them earlier, but..."

Perci's lashes lifted and she gave him a slow smile. "You don't need them. You're healthy. I'd know if you weren't. And you have no need to use them with me."

It should have cooled the fire in his veins. He knew who she was—*what* she was. Part of him still wanted to rage at her...why in the hell couldn't she just be *normal?*

Normal? You mean like you are?

And even as he held still, he saw the flicker of her lashes, saw the minute tensing of her shoulders as she braced herself. Almost as though she'd been following his train of thought, but could she do that?

Shit. He couldn't walk away from her. It just wasn't possible. For some reason, fate had put her in his life and right now, he needed her. Right now...always.

Swearing, he curled one arm around her waist and lifted her. She was so slender, so slim but strong. Her legs came around his hips, gripped him as he pressed the head of his cock against the slick, swollen entrance of her pussy.

"This is insane," he muttered against her mouth. "You know that? Insane..."

"Yes. Shut up. Just shut the hell up and fuck me," she panted.

It should have sounded so wrong listening to that pretty mouth making that demand. To his surprise, he managed a painful laugh and bit her lip. "Is that any way for an angel to talk?"

She bit his lip. "Jack..."

"Impatient." He leaned into her, pressed his brow against hers. "Damn it, you're hot."

"And you're too slow..." She wiggled against him, arched her back and tried to rock against him.

Deliberately, he pulled back. "Don't women like it slow?"

Perci swore and slammed her head back against the concrete wall.

Jack winced, but it didn't even faze her. A devious look crept into her eyes.

Instinctively, Jack shifted his hold, hooked her knees over his arms, taking her leverage away. "Don't rush me," he whispered against her lips. And then he started to sink inside. This time, damn it, this time he was going to enjoy it. Enjoy *her*.

"Watch," he muttered, tearing his mouth away from hers and lowering his gaze, watching as he slowly, oh-so-slowly sank inside her. She stretched tight around him, and the sight of it was so damn hot he could feel his balls drawing tight, could feel the burn, the need to climax already starting to build.

Perci's breath sobbed out of her and he shifted his gaze upward, saw that she'd been watching too. "Fucking hot, yeah?" he muttered, watching her face.

"Hmm." Her lashes, thick and black but tipped with golden-red, fluttered over her eyes and she lifted her head up. Her face was flushed, her mouth swollen from his. Her dark brown eyes glowed with heat...and she stared at him as though mesmerized.

A rush of tenderness swamped him and he released her legs, drew her close, cradled her close. "Damn it, you're doing things to me, Perci. What in the hell are you doing to me?"

"Nothing more than what you're doing to me. Kiss me, Jack." She turned her face to his, teased his lips with her tongue.

Groaning, he opened his mouth as he slid one hand down her side and cupped her ass.

She clenched around him, hot, tight—slick.

Her fingers trailed up his back, dipped in his hair, tangled there. The other hand curled into his shoulder, and as he stroked deep and hard, her nails tore into his flesh, a sweet, burning pain.

"Harder," she begged against his mouth. "Please..."

Jack shuddered. "Fuck, I don't wanna hurt you."

"You won't." She arched closer, ground her hips against his and his eyes damn near crossed.

Too fucking hot—too much. Damn it, damn it, damn it. His muscles bunched, his body ached with the need to drive hard...deep.

"Please..."

Aw, hell.

Control disintegrated, and with a savage growl, Jack slammed into her. Perci cried out. He froze—

"Are you okay?"

She curled an arm around his neck and jerked him close, sinking her teeth into his lower lip. "Don't you fucking stop," she snarled at him. "Don't you..."

The next words died in her throat as he drove into her again and again, slamming into her hard, fast, driving into her with a force he'd never dared use with a lover before.

Perci sobbed out his name and begged for more, pleaded with him not to stop. Her nails tore up the flesh on his arms and back, her mouth sought out his, hungry, avid and desperate.

She came once, twice—so hard, so fucking tight, he had to fight just to get back inside her, and it was bliss. Nirvana and perfection and torment, because when she walked away, he knew he'd never touch a woman without feeling her, tasting her, *wanting* her.

As she shuddered around him, he felt the warning burn race down his spine, knew he couldn't fight it any longer. "Damn it, Perci."

She plunged her tongue into his mouth and he bit her. As she bucked against him, he started to come, hard, vicious...unending.

"All my life," he muttered blindly against her mouth. "I feel like I've been waiting all my life for you...longer."

It was insanity, he knew it. And he'd never meant anything more.

Chapter Ten

We finally did make it to the shower. Jack insisted on washing me, and I was fine with that. As long as I got to return the favor. He had the most amazing body. Those wide shoulders, that deep, muscled chest...why in the hell was I so hot over him? Guys like him had never done it for me before...

Of course, guys *like* him weren't *him*.

And there really weren't guys *like* him. Jack was one of a kind, and his body was only the beginning, I suspected. But it was such a nice beginning. I could have spent hours, days, longer enjoying it. And I would, I decided. Wasn't like we wouldn't have time together. We had plenty of time—

Time.

Oh, my dear one. You have plenty of time.

Those words echoed through Persinette's head as she paced her prison. Locked away in the tower, sick in both body and soul, each day, she prayed that Luc would return.

Even as she feared it.

What would happen if he returned and found Cosette mad?

Mad.

Mad didn't describe her. The woman's grief had driven her insane, and it was pushing her to grievous sins. Like Jacques—

Persinette wanted to weep as she recalled what had been done to him. He had been so focused on her—yet another sin Persinette must bear. His death was at her feet and his blood was on her soul.

He had tried to help her.

Tried to take the healing from her, and somehow, Persinette knew that Cosette had planned that. The child had been so hurt though.

So grievously hurt...

Persinette hadn't been able to turn her back on that battered, broken body. So small. The boy had been so small, and the pain had wracked Persinette, screamed through and torn into her with angry claws. Yet she had known, in the depths of her soul, she *could* save the child.

Despite the baby she carried, she hadn't been able to walk away. But the healing had taken a terrible toll.

When Jacques had come to her, rested his hands on her shoulders and told her, "Push the pain into me, madam. Release the pain into me."

She hadn't wanted to do it—hadn't thought she could.

"You can...take my hand, release the pain. It will flow into me. You cannot bear this pain without risking your health, the health of your child."

And so she had tried. With tears in her eyes, she had taken his big, scarred hand and she had tried...tried to release the pain. It had been so simple. So very simple.

For a few, brief moments, then his body, strong and powerful, had crumpled.

Persinette had been rising from her sickbed, had watched in horror as four of Cosette's men had come in and held Jacques's helpless body in place. Another had welded an ax. She hadn't moved with enough haste to stop them. Two more men had emerged, catching her as she screamed, heedless of the child she carried.

And Cosette had stood there, laughing, as Persinette stared in shock at Jacques's lifeless, beheaded body.

No...

"My dear one. You have plenty of time now. And no protector to keep you from me while you think about what you have cost me. When my son returns, perhaps he'll suffer the same fate. Perhaps he will not."

Then her gaze dropped to the ripening swell of Persinette's belly. "I have not yet decided what I shall do about the child you carry. Something I must think on..."

Persinette stared at Cosette. "You cannot do this."

"Yes. I can." And then she glanced at her men.

Persinette was dragged kicking and screaming out of the room, and when she landed one solid blow on one of her captors, she was struck in the belly.

Cringing inward, she went still.

The child...she had to protect the child.

Jacques was no longer there to protect her. And Luc...Luc was still away. She was alone—

I was crying, I realized. Lying in Jack's arms and crying.

"What's wrong?" he asked me softly.

I shuddered and blew out a breath. "Memories."

Old, *old* memories...where had they come from?

Poison...

Will had spoken of releasing the poison. But I didn't want to release this poison.

Shaking it off, I sat up and wiped the tears from my face. Over my shoulder, I looked at Jack's face. He was in shadow, all but those misty gray eyes. So familiar, those eyes.

"Bad memories," I murmured.

He sat up and curled his big body around mine, rested his hands on my thighs, a sheltering, warm cave. "I imagine you got a lot of those."

"Bad memories?" I didn't have to think about it. "Not as many as some. I've never let myself get close to many people. All these come from...well, before."

"When you were still human."

I sighed and covered his hands with mine. "Jack, how do you know so much about us?"

"I already told you. I just know."

Resting my head against his shoulder, I stared off into the darkened room. He didn't *feel* like he was lying. If he *was* lying, I think I'd glimpse something of that—I was good at that. All of us were. But nothing on him tasted of a lie, felt of it.

It felt like truth.

"How can you just know?"

I felt his shrug. He reached up, toyed with my pendant. "I just do."

He sighed and I felt it against my back. Although my gift had never been keyed into emotions, I felt a weight in his chest when asked, "How come you're in my life right now, Perci? How much longer until Will pulls you away?"

Closing my eyes, I searched inside myself for the answer.

How did I tell him this?

Gently, I eased out of his arms and then turned and knelt across his thighs. I slid my hand through his black hair, once, twice, fisted in it. Then I let go and smoothed it back from his face. "You know what I am. And you know I was human once. Right?"

"Yeah." He shrugged, a restless move of wide shoulders. "I gotta admit, I'm kind of wracking my brain trying to figure out just *who* you might be too."

I narrowed my eyes, studying his face. *Interesting...* "Damn, you really do know a lot."

"Don't ask me how." He slanted a grin at me. "I just know. I don't *know* how." He stroked a hand up my back, one of those absent, gentle touches that said, *I'm touching you just because I need to.*

It made me melt inside. It also made it damn hard to concentrate on what he saying.

"I was going to get online and figure it out, but you keep showing up."

"Figure it out?" I echoed. Then I snorted. "Shit, you think you'll find a bio of me online?"

Jack's eyes came back to me. "Will called you by your name. Your real name. I think I'd find something if I looked around some...Persinette."

Shit.

Interesting? Hell. That didn't even touch it. How did he know so much?

Tired, I snuggled against him and rested my head against one wide shoulder. I'd figure that out later, I guess. I didn't really have to know—I *wanted* to, but it wasn't crucial.

However, the talk we needed to have, that *was* crucial, and it would be easier if he would trust me. Maybe the best way to establish some level of trust would be to give him...something.

I reached up and stroked my finger down a scar he had over his chest—all too close to his mortal heart, I thought. Too, too close.

"So you want to know who I am, huh?"

"I'm curious, yeah."

I remembered a few days earlier when I'd gotten my hair cut. I don't remember when I'd started doing that—growing it out just to get it whacked off. There was something weirdly satisfying about it, although I don't know what.

Cosette hadn't let me bathe, hadn't allowed me clean clothes, or even bath water. By the time Luc found me I was barely a step away from an animal. After, when I became a Grimm, the first thing I did was cut my hair. Short, as short as I could. For years after, that was how I kept it. Sometime in the past hundred years or so was when I'd started growing it out just to cut it off.

And Luc teased me, just to see me smile a little.

The similarities between the tale of Rapunzel, and the earlier adaption of Persinette and my own story weren't really all that similar. But they didn't need to be, not really. The point of the fairy tales had always been to draw attention away from the real events.

And Sina had been quite clever spinning the tale of Persinette the way she had. It had been written just a few years before my entire life went straight to hell, but I'd much rather people think my mother had some cravings and that's what led to me being locked up in a tower than the truth. I didn't want anybody knowing the truth.

I didn't even want to know the truth.

But I'd have to share some of it with Jack.

Sighing, I said, "You ever heard the story about Rapunzel?"

Jack lifted a brow. Then he combed a hand through my shorn locks.

"As in *'Rapunzel, Rapunzel, let down your hair'*?"

"Yeah." I smirked. "I bet you're thinking, *what hair?* Although, really, Jack. People can get haircuts, you know." I continued to trace the scar on his chest.

"There was an older story before that one. Rapunzel was based on that story. It was called *Persinette*."

Persinette...

Her voice, soft and low, reverberated through him. Her accent had thickened, but Jack had no trouble understanding her.

Persinette...

Blood roared in his ears. His heart raced. Every muscle in his body tensed and he squeezed his eyes closed, tried to focus, because Perci was speaking.

But he couldn't hear a damn word she said.

Suddenly, he was seeing her on a bed, her body wracked with pain and face tight and contorted...

"Push the pain into me, madam. Release the pain into me. You can...take my hand, release the pain. It will flow into me. You cannot bear this pain without risking your health, the health of your child."

And she had gripped his hand.

Pain gripped him, shuddered through him...and her face eased.

Then abruptly, horror flooded her eyes and pain tore through him again. Then everything ceased—

"Jack?"

Swearing, he shook his head and made himself focus on her face, stare into her eyes. They were dark, dark with worry, with regret and fear... Fear of what? That he'd walk? Yeah. He suspected that was exactly what she feared. But how in the hell could he walk away from her?

"Rapunzel, huh?"

It was the only thing he could come up with, and once more, he found himself staring at her close-cropped, red-gold hair. And thinking that he knew exactly how she would look if that hair hung past her slender hips.

Perci cocked a brow at him. "Persinette's tale came first, but yeah. That's basically the story."

Jack wiped the back of his hand over his mouth, the remnants of the story coming to him. A tower. There was a tower. The long hair. "She was locked in a tower by a witch," he murmured.

Perci looked away. "There was a tower, yes. But she wasn't a witch. She was my husband's mother."

"Your..." He set his jaw. Even as he tried to wrap his mind around that bit of information, he had an image in mind. A man, tall and slender—the one he'd seen with Perci before—in images that seemed like memories.

Luc. She called him Luc.

"Your husband," he finished, his voice rough as gravel, tight and harsh.

"Yes."

"His mother." Jack closed his eyes.

Another image slammed into his mind. This time a woman...older, but not unattractive with it. Grief lined her face, and then the grief pushed her to madness.

Cosette.

Her name is Cosette and I must protect Persinette from her.

"Why did she lock you in a tower?" He sat rigidly, but Perci barely seemed aware.

She slid off his lap and stared off into the distance. "Because I wouldn't heal her husband. Not Luc's father. He had already died. This was her new husband and he was ill. I've always been able to heal. But he had an illness I couldn't heal. I didn't know what it was at the time, but it was cancer, deep, deep inside him and trying to heal that would have killed me...and the child I carried."

The child.

Luc.

Abruptly, Jack didn't want to hear anymore. But when he looked up, he saw there were tears rolling down her pale cheeks and her eyes were a silent, screaming hell. "You were pregnant," he said. He knew that—he *knew*.

And somehow, he knew how the high, hard mound of her belly felt under his hand.

"Yes. It was our first...twins, although I didn't know that until later." A sad, bittersweet smile curled her lips and she turned her head toward him. "Too late."

I don't want to know this.

"She kept me locked away. My husband, Luc, he was fighting in the war." The sad smile on her face turned bitter and angry. "Such a useless war. So many useless wars, you mortals fight. It took my husband away, because it was the *noble* thing for him to do. And when he returned to me, that crazy bitch of a mother had killed our children while I still carried them in my womb."

She closed her eyes and bowed her head. "It was slow, you know. I did not even know how to recognize the symptoms of illness in my own body. I never took ill and I thought it was just being with child, and what she was doing—locking me away…"

"What are you talking about?"

Perci lifted her head and stared at him. Her eyes glittered, with grief, rage, and a pain that all but stole his breath away. "She was poisoning me. Not enough to kill *me*…but she was a wise woman. Far wiser than many of the time, and she knew whatever I ate or drank would affect the children. I'm not sure, but I think she was putting arsenic in the water that was brought to me. Slowly, over time, it killed the babies, and it weakened me. When Luc returned…"

A sigh shuddered out of her. She walked to the window and stared out at the endless expanse of blue water. With her brow pressed to the glass, she said, "She knew he was coming. And she lay a trap for him. She had all of his men killed. I heard him fighting, struggling to get to me…and then I went into labor. While I struggled to deliver the babies, he was struggling to get to me."

Jack came off the bed and came up behind her, wrapped her in his arms. A harsh, bitter sob wracked her body and then, her voice eerily calm, she said, "The babes were stillborn. And…then…I lay there, and I was dying, listening to Luc scream. They kept him alive, just to torture him, so I could hear him screaming, and I knew Cosette would keep him alive as long as *I* lived."

She was silent for the longest moment.

"So I decided not to live anymore."

He tightened his arms. Dread gripped his heart.

"I was climbing up to jump out the window… Cosette never thought I would do that. But she didn't know me well, I guess. My death would end Luc's suffering and I wasn't going to listen to her torment him." She spoke in a monotone now, her voice so dispassionate and empty, it was as though she discussed the weather. "That was when Will arrived. I hadn't met him before that and he caught me just as I would have made that jump. He told me my life would be worth more than that, and that by ending my life, I let her madness win. Did I allow her to win, or did I try to save my husband?"

Perci turned in his arms and rested her head against his chest. "I wanted to let her win. More than I can explain, because I wanted that pain to end. But if I could save him...if there was a chance. So I listened. I...I already knew about the Grimm. One had already come to us, told us about them. But I'd...well, forgotten."

Gaze locked on her face, he stared at her, waiting.

"We're given a choice...do you know about that as well?"

He gave a short, terse nod.

"Why am I not surprised? Okay, then. So I made my choice, and then..." Perci grimaced. "Then I jumped. Will was pissed. Apparently that wasn't quite how he'd planned it, but since I was grieving, ill and not entirely right in the head after what Cosette had done, well...the lines of communication weren't all that clear, I guess. He brought me back, but—"

"You *jumped*."

In his mind's eye, he could see that tower.

Whether it was real or not no longer mattered, not in this moment.

He could see her hovering there, lost in grief and despair, and his heart wanted to shatter. Closing his hands around her upper arms, he eased her back and stared at her face.

"You *jumped*," he said again.

"Yes. I don't remember much of it. I think I thought that was what I needed to do to pay Cosette back, although it wasn't about paying her back."

Paying Cosette back—how many years of my life had longed to do just that?

A snarl twisted my face and I pulled away from Jack to pace the bedroom. "I wanted to pay her back. She'd killed my babies. Driven me to madness...and by the time I emerged from Will's healing, Luc was past anything *I* could do to help him. I tried, but..." I reached up, touched my face, remembered the brutal punch of pain that had wracked me when I'd tried to heal his eyes.

That was what she'd done first.

After she'd managed to capture him, she'd used a scalding hot blade and pierced his eyes with it. Blinded him. The same blade had been used to carve up his chest like a Thanksgiving turkey.

Blinded, tortured...and the sad thing was, he would have done it all again because he loved me.

Sadly, I whispered, "I failed him so miserably. Luc, my babies. Everybody who depended on me. I failed them."

"You're wrong," Jack murmured, wrapping his arms around me and pulling me back against him.

The feel of his nude body against mine didn't send shivers of want and lust and need running through me this time. It was warmth...and comfort. And I desperately needed both.

"I did fail them."

"How?" He pressed his lips to my brow. "You were victimized by a woman who went mad with grief, and after she murdered your children, she murdered your husband. You were sick with grief yourself, but you didn't go mad and decide to kill innocents, or torment an innocent woman. You hold no blame here."

"People have told me that for years," I said quietly. "And I still can't let go of the guilt."

"Maybe it's high time you do." He swept me into his arms, carried me back to the bed and settled down against the headboard with me in his lap. There, he wrapped the blanket around me before he cupped my chin and made me look at him. "How long ago was it?"

I looked up at him. "A long time ago...and only yesterday."

The compassion in his gray eyes was enough to nearly level me, and I didn't know how to handle it. It could have leveled me. Almost did. Reaching up, I laid my hand along his stubbled cheek and forced a smile.

"Three hundred years ago," I said quietly. I watched his eyes, waiting for the disbelief, the shock.

It didn't come.

He just nodded. "You've kept all that pain, all that guilt hidden inside. All this time." He tipped my chin back and kissed me gently. "No wonder I keep seeing this heartbreak inside you."

Heartbreak.

He saw heartbreak inside me? And I thought my shields were so thick and solid. But he saw deeper than I'd realized—there was more to him than I'd suspected. A lot more.

Drained, emotionally and physically, I rested my head on his shoulder. I wanted to curl up around him and sleep for weeks. Just sleep. But although my heart and my body were weary, my mind wasn't ready to shut down.

I still needed to address some things with Jack. Things that I had been putting off too long. Sighing, I reached up and stroked a hand down across his chest, once more stroking the scar over his heart.

Under my hand, his heart jumped and his muscles flexed and rippled. And although I had the best of intentions, I couldn't help but stare a minute.

I guess I was feeling better.

Man, but I loved his body. What in the hell was up with me? *Nobody* had ever reduced me to a puddle of drooling female flesh before, but Jack was pretty damn close.

"You're doing bad, bad things to my head, Jack Wallace," I said softly. "You know that?"

"Am I?" A grin slashed across his face and he dipped his head and kissed the tip of my nose. "Can't say I mind hearing that, because you've totally managed to screw my head up to hell and back, Perci." Then he eased me off his lap, pausing to tuck the blankets around me.

The show of consideration touched my heart in the weirdest way. It wasn't that it was cold in his house. It wasn't. The misery of the memories and my grief had left me chilled through. There was just something comforting about having the blankets, warmed from our bodies, wrapped around me.

Small kindnesses. At first glance, somebody who looked at him might not expect them from him. I closed my eyes, smiling a little to myself. Those small kindnesses didn't surprise me.

Something flashed through my mind—

Lying in the bed, sick with the babe I carried...the man at my side wiping down my brow with a cool, wet cloth. "It will pass, Persinette. It will pass."

Beautiful, misty gray eyes that watched me so very closely—

With a gasp, I tore myself out of that memory.

Jacques.

"Perci?"

I blinked and looked up at Jack. He was staring at me, his gaze worried, a scowl drawing that rough-hewn face tight. "Are you okay?"

Breathing raggedly, my heart pounding in my chest, I rolled out of the bed and stumbled to the bathroom. "A minute," I muttered over my shoulder.

Between my breasts, my pendant suddenly felt terribly heavy, terribly cold.

What the hell...

Kicking the door shut behind me, I made my way to the sink and bent over it. It took three tries to get the cold water on, my hands shook so badly.

What the hell...

What was going on? So familiar. Something about him had seemed so familiar, almost from the beginning. Not his face, even though his eyes had captured me from the beginning. No, it had been something deeper.

"Am I going crazy?" I muttered.

The door opened and I lifted my head and stared at Jack's reflection in the mirror.

"What's wrong?" he asked flatly.

Numb, I shook my head.

"Then why in the hell are you staring at me like you just saw a ghost?"

Chapter Eleven

For the briefest minute, when she'd looked at him, it had been like... Hell. Jack had *felt* like a ghost. Felt like everything and everybody and everywhere...shit, even *time* had fallen away.

Only Perci had remained and she hadn't been sitting on the bed in his room.

She had been lying on a bed in a dark chamber, a long, white gown twisted around her, clinging to her. She had been ill. Her face was pale, slick with perspiration, and her eyes were glassy.

Nausea had gripped her and although Jack didn't know *how* he knew, he knew she'd been pregnant—it hadn't shown, not yet. But she'd been sick from a child, and even though he had known she shouldn't have tried to heal anybody while she carried the babe, he had also known she wouldn't turn away from a child she could save.

"Push the pain into me, madam. Release the pain into me. You can...take my hand, release the pain. It will flow into me. You cannot bear this pain without risking your health, the health of your child."

His heart had broken for her, even as it swelled for the love he felt for her...for the child she carried. A child that wasn't his. He had no right to her, to that child, and yet he'd wanted—

Then the moment shattered and she was sitting on the bed in his room, staring at him. Like she'd seen a ghost. And her mouth had formed a name...

Jacques.

Fuck.

She had all but run into the bathroom, leaving him there to stare at her back and wonder what in the hell was going on.

Acutely, he was aware of the pain in his neck, slashing through his throat.

Acutely, he remembered the dream.

And Will's words...

The mind forgets... But the body doesn't.

The body doesn't forget what?

Dying.

Dying.

Feeling savage, half-insane—and although he wouldn't admit it, somewhere deep inside, there was a flickering warmth—Jack stormed to the bathroom, shoved the door open and stared at Perci's reflection in the mirror.

She was pale, and when she looked up and met his reflection, he saw that she looked as shaken as he felt.

"What's wrong?"

She just shook her head.

"Then why in the hell are you staring at me like you just saw a ghost?"

"Was I?" she asked, and her voice was just a little too cool. A little too controlled.

He advanced on her. She watched him in the mirror, her eyes unreadable, her face calm. Between her breasts, the pendant she wore was beginning to glow ever so slightly.

"What did you call me?" he asked gruffly.

"When?"

Gently, he reached up and lay his hands on her shoulders. "Don't play dumb with me, Perci." He stroked his hands down her arms and gripped her wrists. "It doesn't suit you and I won't buy it."

"I don't believe in playing dumb, Jack," she replied. Then she leaned back against him, holding his gaze in the mirror. "Stop the brooding, intimidating male bit. I've seen it too many times to be impressed. You wanted to know my story, and there you have it. Now...there's more talking we need to do. Or would you rather fight?"

He bent down, bracing his hands on either side of her, and stared into her eyes in the mirror. She had that damned smirk on her face now—the one that made him want to haul her against him and kiss it off. But not right now. She was trying to distract him and he wanted a fucking answer.

Jacques.

She had called him *Jacques.*

And it was like she'd thrown a stone in a still lake. The ripples were still echoing through him, but instead of fading, each ripple grew stronger, weighing down on him, pressing on him, harder. Harder. Harder.

"Perci, what in the fuck did you call me?" He was hard-pressed not to haul her around and force her to look at him.

She straightened away from the counter, reached up and twined her arms up and back, curling them around his neck as a smile curved her lips. "I don't know what you're talking about. But if there's something you'd *like* me to call you, just tell me. Want me to call you something special, lover?"

Blood roared in his ears. His heart pounded.

Jacques.

Gripping her waist, he muttered, "Damn it, Perci. I want an answer. I don't want..."

She wiggled her hips, pressed her ass snug against his rigid cock. "Want to bet? You definitely want."

But then she sighed, and let go, disentangling herself from his hands.

"We have things to talk about, Jack, and it's important we get it done *now.*"

And before he could press *his* issues any further, she dropped a bombshell in his lap.

"Why in the hell do you think I've put in your life, Jack? Have you taken five seconds to *really* think it through?"

Those dark gray eyes locked on my face, and if I had been the type to *get* intimidated? That look would have done it. There was just something about the way he stared at me. Something about being the focus of that heavy-lidded, intense gaze. It was...disturbing. It was almost eerie.

And damn it, I have to be sick, because it was also erotic as hell. As my nipples stiffened, I folded my arms across my chest and tried to think why I'd thought I could have this conversation while the two of us were naked.

Clothing, or the lack of it, hadn't ever much bothered me in the past few centuries, but then again, in the past few centuries, I'd rarely felt the draw of sex and when I did...

No, not thinking of that right now.

I was trying to face too many demons, own up to too many wrongs today. Instead of thinking about the fuck-ups of my past, I faced the present dilemma of my future and tried not to think about how much I wanted to shelf the conversation.

He wasn't going to take this well. I already knew it.

"What are you talking about?" he demanded, his voice a harsh, demanding snarl.

"I'm not here just because I want to see your pretty face or take advantage of you again," I said. Then, because I couldn't stop myself, I added, "Although I got to admit, I really do like taking advantage."

A gleam lit his eyes, and despite the tension mounting in the air, he said, "You feel free to take advantage of me all you want, princess...*after* you explain what you're talking about. And after we finish the conversation you just put off."

Damn. He wasn't going to let that go and I had no idea how to answer him either. How could I answer him though? Looking into his eyes was like...shit. I felt like I'd done it before. The face was all wrong. The body wasn't exactly right, although he moved the same.

The eyes though...those misty, beautiful eyes. I felt like I knew them, had known them a long, long time ago, in a memory hidden by the mists of time and the pain I'd spent too much of my life shying away from.

Something weird was going on...too weird, and until I understood it, I couldn't give him any answers.

"I'll hold you to that," I said, forcing a smile I didn't feel.

Unable to keep standing in front of him naked, I turned away. From the corner of my eye, I saw a shirt hanging on the doorknob and I grabbed it and tugged it on. It smelled of him, and as it warmed against my flesh, I was hard-pressed not to bury my face in the faded cotton and breathe it in.

"You know so much about us, Jack. I'd be freaked out about it, but Will isn't worried," I said, padding into the bedroom and settling down on the edge of the bed.

Jack followed but stopped in the doorway. With one shoulder braced against the doorjamb, he stared at me. "Why would you be freaked out? It's not like I'm any kind of threat to you."

Oh, he had no idea. He was all sorts of threat...to *me*. I kept quiet about that part though.

Absently, I stroked my hands down my thighs and frowned. "I'm not overly worried about *you* specifically. More about the general idea of a mortal knowing about us. Can you imagine what would happen if some of those conspiracy kooks got wind of us? The hell they could make our lives?" Then I sneered and added, "Or worse...imagine the hell we'd get if it came out what we have to *do*. You know what we hunt, and why...and you understand. The typical mortal doesn't. They'd look at us and see us as murderers. They don't realize the lives we save when we kill the demonic hosts. And none of us are about to go to prison for doing what needs to be done. Nor can we *stop* doing what must be done."

"Okay." He nodded slowly. "I get that. But it's not like I'm going to take out a front-page ad."

I grinned at him. "I know that."

"And if I did, people would just assume I was insane."

"Yes." Swiping my damp palms down the sheets, I sighed. "But that's not even what I need to talk to you about. I'm definitely still curious about *how* you know."

Jack blew out a frustrated breath and shoved a hand through his hair. "Damn it, Perci. I just *know*. Okay? I always have. *Always*."

Always. How could he always know...

I closed my eyes and in the back of my mind, I saw Jacques. The first time I had seen him he was riding toward the chateau where I had lived with Luc. The first time I'd seen him, I remembered thinking he looked like some tarnished knight from some old tale...and he had frightened me.

Forcing myself to look at Jack, I let myself wonder.

Could it be...? It would explain—

I looked down and crossed my legs, folded my hands. I couldn't think about that now. "Fine," I said, my voice husky and rough. I couldn't believe I was even *considering* the idea.

Couldn't believe it.

"Jack, why do you *think* I'm here?"

He was quiet for so long, I wasn't sure if he'd answer. From under my lashes, I looked at him.

As our gazes locked, a crooked grin slanted his mouth and he shrugged. "Beats the hell out of me. Either you're here to torment me or I've really, really got some trouble coming after my ass, I figure."

"Why would you think that?"

"If Will thinks I need a full-time guardian-angel bodyguard? Yeah, that would mean there's trouble coming after me." He jerked a shoulder again.

"Why would you have trouble coming after you?"

He snorted. "Princess, you got any idea how many of those things I've killed in the past seventeen years? It's a miracle one of them hasn't gutted me already, and unlike you, I don't have any of the supernatural hiding skills. I'm just me and sooner or later, they'll catch up with me."

A chill ran down my spine.

"And what do you plan on doing when that happens, Jack?"

He shoved off the wall and sauntered off to the nightstand. "As long as I'm able, if they show up?" He pulled open the drawer and pulled out the gun.

The sight of it made my heart clench.

"I'll die before I let one of them take me. And if I can't stop it? I just hope one of you are around to put an end to me fast."

Shit.

I shoved off the bed and started to pace. The words boiled up my throat, blasted out of me before I could stop them. "I'm not here to be your *bodyguard*, Jack. I'm here to train you. You're supposed to be one of us."

The look on his face was one of poor bewilderment. If I had taken the gun from him, pressed it to his brow and pulled the trigger, I don't think he would have been any more surprised. But the shock passed quickly, bleeding over into anger.

"One of you?" He raked me with a contemptuous glare and shook his head. "I'll pass. Just make sure you're close by when my end comes."

It was a blow to my heart, and my soul. He'd rather die...no, he'd rather a demon take him, and me have to kill him than be one of us.

But I didn't blink, didn't so much as flicker an eyelash. Keeping my voice calm and steady, I held his gaze. "Why? You already do what we do. What's so bad about being one of us?"

"You abandoned my mother—left her to suffer, to rot from the inside out. And you want to know what's so bad?" His lip curled and he shook his head. "Fuck it, Princess. Just fuck it."

He stormed past me out of the bedroom. As he left me alone, I stared at the wall. Once again, I'd royally screwed up. Toying with the pendant I wore, I whispered, "This job should come with a handbook." Then I sighed and stood.

I needed to get dressed. Needed to figure out where to go from here. Outright *leaving* wasn't an option. And somehow, I didn't think Jack was up to more discussion just yet.

I had a bag stashed in his living room. He hadn't noticed it yet. I grabbed it and I tugged out a pair of black BDUs and a snug black sport bra and tank. Without looking around for him, I took another quick shower and got dressed.

My gut told me that Jack was going to be itching for a fight tonight and unless I was reading him way wrong, he wasn't going to take the easy way and have that fight with me. He'd leave. And since he was pissed off, and distracted...

Nope. He wouldn't leave alone. If he did decide he had to have a fight tonight, he could damn well have it with me at his side... The hair on the back of my neck lifted. The cloying taint of evil flooded my entire being. I felt something pressing closer, and closer. Closing my eyes, I lowered my shields minutely and reached out.

Vankyr.

Orin.

And more.

With a hiss, I jerked my shields back up and stormed out of the bathroom. I found Jack striding into the kitchen, his hair hanging down to his shoulder in wet ropes. Apparently, he'd taken a plunge in the bay.

As he stalked through a small door off the side of the

kitchen, I followed him.

"Out of sheer curiosity, *lover*," I drawled. "Just how many of those things have you killed in the last seventeen years?"

He swiped a towel over his damp, naked body and then started to rub it over his hair. "Lost count after the first couple of years. A lot."

A lot.

As he reached for a pair of jeans, I knocked them out of his hands and grabbed a pair of black cotton instead. A little looser, easier to move in.

"What the—"

Baring my teeth at him in a mean smile, I said, "Maybe I get to play bodyguard for a while after all. Until you get your head out of your ass. You *do* have trouble coming. A lot."

Too much for me to handle, actually. Especially with nobody but a mortal at my side.

Even if he was a damned talented mortal who moved with more skill and speed than any mortal *I* had ever seen.

Reaching for the pendant, I met his gray eyes.

"What are you talking about?" he asked.

"You seemed to think they'd come after you. You're right."

"They're coming? Now?"

I nodded. "Yes. We have a few minutes. They are miles away still. But it won't be that long."

His eyes darkened to black and he looked past me, as though he could see through the window. His home was isolated and I suspected he'd picked it, in part, because it *was* isolated...and he had always known a day like this would come.

"Will." I knew he'd hear me. The pendant warmed under my hand, a single pulse. What that answer meant, I didn't know.

"What are you doing?" Jack asked, as he tugged the pants on. He stormed past me and I watched as he headed into the living room.

"Calling for backup."

"Like that will help," he muttered and flipped open the lid on the trunk that served as a coffee table.

"It will. Regardless of what you think, we don't abandon our own," I said quietly. "And you're one of us...even if you won't claim us. We'll still help."

My heart ached as I said it. For the first time in long, empty years, I really didn't *want* to be quite so isolated, but this man didn't want me with him. Perhaps this was karma, I thought. I was reaping what I'd sowed with Luc all those years.

"Nobody's going to help me. Will may or may not, but he can shove his help if the price tag is being like you. Which means I'm probably on my own," Jack said, shaking his head. He had emptied a small arsenal onto the floor beside him and he gave me a tight smile. "Hang around if you want. Or just come back when the blood bath is over and deal with me then."

I narrowed my eyes and sneered at him. He actually thought I'd leave him?

"Yes."

I looked up as Will stepped through the arched doorway that led to the kitchen. And he wasn't alone. I'd been so focused on Jack, I hadn't even paid attention. *Stupid, stupid.* At least it wasn't the demons yet.

Krell caught sight of me and wagged his tail. "Hi, boy," I said, smiling at him.

Luc stood next to Will and on his other side was Sina. Greta and Rip were there, and now that I was focused, I could feel others.

Jack stood and glared at Will. "Why you here now, old man?"

"I always told you that if you had a need, we'd be here," Will said quietly.

Jack snorted, still more focused on his weapons than anything else.

"He seems to think we would abandon him." I narrowed my eyes as I gazed at Will. "He feels we abandoned his mother."

"His mother owed him a life...and once she'd paid that debt, her time was done," Will said cryptically. "And now..."

There was no more time for talking. Glass shattered and I whirled, putting my body between Jack and the *vankyr.*

Just come back when the blood bath is over, Jack had said.

Oh, yes, there would be a blood bath.

I kept myself locked at his side. If he fell, I'd do my

damnedest to heal him, even though it was suicide with this many demons. At least I wasn't alone. I knew my friends would lay down their lives to protect me.

An *orin* lunged for me, struggled to get past me. Judging by the look in her eyes, she wanted to get her hands on Jack. I was just the obstacle. Problem for her was that I was one very skilled obstacle. I used my dagger to destroy her heart, and as the demon's essence faded, I watched the mortal's body die. Pity stirred my heart, but there was no time to pause. Already another was coming at me.

They'd overwhelm us by sheer numbers if this kept up. I heard a hideous bellow of pain—felt it tear through me. I screamed and went to my knees. Behind me, I knew Jack had done the same.

One of them had gotten to him. And because I hadn't shielded against him, I felt it.

Blood rose in his throat, and I tasted it. I heard Luc, saw him fighting to get to me. Krell bit and tore through everything that blocked him, and although Luc's eyes no longer functioned, it didn't slow him. He used a bladed staff with a speed and skill no sighted mortal could ever hope to duplicate.

But he wouldn't reach me in time.

Then, brilliant, blistering white-hot light ripped through the small cabin. The demonic hosts screamed...and all went gray...then black. And silent.

Luc saw her fall through Krell's eyes. He watched her sway, then falter and go down. A bellow of denial rose in his throat, but he bit it back as he hacked his way through to her side. He wanted to send the dog to her, but he needed the canine with him to see as he fought to get to her.

Perci.

White-hot heat scalded him. Instinctively, although he had little fear from injury, he lifted an arm and shielded his face.

As quickly as it came, the heat faded.

And his sensitive ears detected no sound of the demonic. He tried to see through Krell's eyes, but the dog couldn't see anything...just a blinding, brilliant light.

Chapter Twelve

Jack was bleeding out. It was amazing how he could feel that. Even more amazing was how he could *see* it as he hovered over his own dying body.

"You're not supposed to die."

A familiar voice spoke to him and he looked up, saw Will striding toward him through a misty, insubstantial world.

"Everybody dies," Jack said. He bent down and tried to touch his own body out of some morbid fascination, but his hand just passed through, and it was like touching fire.

"Yes, everybody dies, you fool. But *you* weren't supposed to. Not yet. Why didn't you accept what Perci offered you?"

Jack looked at Will. "I don't want to be one of you."

"You are already *one* of us. Or you *were*."

Jack realized that Will looked pretty fucking pissed off. Those weird eyes of his all but burned and his face was a cold, hard mask. It was easier to focus on that oddity than what Will was talking about—so much easier...

"By God, you will *listen*," Will snarled, and he reached for Jack.

Jack smirked, expecting Will's hands to pass right through him.

But the silver-haired man's hands gripped Jack's arms, solid, certain and unrelenting. His grip was too strong to evade, too strong to break, and as Jack struggled, Will said, "You need to *remember*, Jack...*Jacques*. Remember, because you won't get this chance again. Cosette has made amends for the mistakes she made, and now you have a chance at the happiness you couldn't have in life. But you have to *remember*..."

And even as Jack struggled, he was already falling.

"Why are you doing this?" Jacques stared at Cosette and

tried to understand what had changed the woman before him. Although he knew. Love could do strange things to the mind, and this woman had loved. Grief had turned her love to madness.

She gave him a wide-eyed, innocent smile, but it didn't reach her eyes. Nothing reached her eyes. Nothing changed that pale blue gaze. Always, a madwoman lurked there.

"What do you mean?" she asked, her voice husky and soft.

"I saw the woman you tried to take to Persinette. You cannot continue to bring her these people to heal. She is too ill with the child. Do you wish to kill your grandson?"

"But Persinette is a healer. God has given her this gift and she must use it to do God's work," Cosette said quietly, her voice soft, pious...and under it, so very malicious.

She went to go around him.

Jacques caught her arm. "You will stop this." The woman before him once had kindness in her. He had seen it. He had to find it again, for Persinette's sake. "You *must* stop this, before you destroy her...and yourself."

For long, tense moments, Cosette stared at him.

And then, abruptly, tears flooded her eyes and she hissed, "I *am* destroyed, because *she* would not give me aid. Because she would not heal my husband. Have I not lost enough? What else must I lose? What else is left that I *can* lose?"

"How about her love? The love of your son? Your people? What about your soul?"

Cosette snorted. The demure, refined image she presented to the world fell away and she stared at him with flat, hard eyes. "My soul? And what do you care of my soul, Jacques? You do not truly believe there is a god watching over us, do you? If there was, he would not have taken all from me. Again and again. No, there is no god. But there is a cruel, heartless wretched woman who will pay for what she did—and she *will* pay."

She tried to pull away from him, but Jacques only tightened his grasp.

"If you harm her, you will know cruel and heartless, *woman*," Jacques warned. And although it was forbidden, he lowered the mask he wore around mortals and allowed her to see the man he was, not the man he pretended to be. "She has done you no ill and could not have saved your husband."

As he spoke, he drove the words into her mind, knowing she did not just hear them, but felt them, ached with them, shuddered with them. She would hear those words in her sleep. They would follow her and haunt her.

But Cosette was no simpering, shy miss, and although she flinched under his power, she didn't buckle. Instead, as he released, she jerked away and glared at him. "So...you are like her." Cosette stared at him. Then she shook her head. "I do not care. She will pay, and I do not care what the cost is."

"And if the cost is the life of an innocent child?"

Her lids flickered. But then her face hardened. "She made her choice." Cosette turned and walked away.

Jacques murmured quietly, "As have you. And as have I."

"Choices, Jack. Life is about them," Will said.

Jack tore away from Will and stumbled into the wall. Or rather...*through* it. The moment Will wasn't touching him he lost whatever solidity he had. "What in the fuck...you're messing with my head," he muttered.

"No. I'm showing you the truth you've hidden from for too long. Your mother always knew." And with that, Will grabbed him and once more, shoved him hurtling back.

Back into the past...

Only this time, it was just years, mere decades, not centuries. Jack even remembered the moments.

Sitting by the bedside as his mother breathed through a machine, watching as she wasted away.

"Why are you dying?" He hated that he sounded like a little kid...he wasn't. He was twelve fucking years old. Practically an adult.

But his mother just smiled sadly. "We all die, Jack. It's part of life."

"But you're too young. And...and I need you," he whispered.

"I'll always be around," she murmured. She reached over and caught his hand, squeezed. Although her body was weak, her grasp was still strong, still steady. "I love you, baby."

He tore his hand away. "You shouldn't have done it."

"Done what?" she asked.

But she knew. He saw the answer in her eyes. She already knew.

"Stop being one of them. You wouldn't have gotten sick then."

Mom sighed. "And I wouldn't have you. All along, I was meant to have you, Jack." She held out a hand.

Jack stared at it, and then lifted his eyes and stared into her pale blue eyes.

They looked nothing alike. He must have inherited his dad's looks, but he'd never know, because he'd never met his dad.

"Jack, come here," she said quietly.

Reluctantly, he walked over and placed his hand in hers. "What?" he asked sullenly.

"Sometimes I hated how you always knew the things you've known," she said.

Blood rushed to his cheeks and he looked away. They never spoke of this, but he knew she didn't like it, knew it made her sad.

"And sometimes I wish I knew just how *much* you knew..." Then she brushed his hair back from his face. "But you can't know all, because then you would hate me."

She leaned in and pressed a kiss to his brow. "The time will come when you *will* know all. I just hope you can forgive me, although I don't imagine you will. But know this—I lived *this* life with no regrets. I made this choice and I'm glad of it. I wouldn't undo a moment I had with you."

Confused, scared, Jack looked at his mom. "What are you talking about?"

But she just shook her head and moments later, Will entered the room.

And later that night, his mother died quietly in her sleep.

Leaving Jack alone.

Jack tore away from Will and stared at him.

I hope you can forgive me...

He remembered his mother's pale blue eyes. And her strange, cryptic words.

I lived this *life with no regrets. I made this choice and I'm glad of it. I wouldn't undo a moment I had with you.*

And then he remembered Will's words—words he'd said to Perci, but Jack had heard them nonetheless.

His mother owed him a life.

"Shit," he muttered.

He went to rub his face, but his hands passed through his insubstantial flesh—*not* a pleasant feeling. Glaring at Will, he said, "Please tell me this isn't real."

"Oh, it's quite real...and you're running out of time." Then he looked down.

That was when Jack saw Perci.

Perci's still, pale body.

"And so is she."

And Jack's world seemed to come to a complete and utter stop.

He sank to his knees, and this time, he didn't pass through the floor. Staring at Perci's face, he reached out to touch her. And he touched warm flesh, warm...but cooling.

She breathed, but not well. Her heart beat, but somehow, he could hear it faltering. Shaking his head, he went to look up at Will and found himself staring at a face that he *knew* he had seen before.

"*Luc,*" he rasped out.

The man stilled, then reached out.

Jack saw the sightless eyes. But as Luc's hand came toward him, somehow, he *knew* the man could see him. Somehow. And he knew the man saw more than just what lay on the surface. He tried to fall back, even as he wondered if the man could touch his incorporeal form.

But he didn't move fast enough, and yes, Luc could touch him.

For a moment, incomprehension rolled over Luc's face. Then, like a movie reel, the memories Will had dumped inside Jack's head started to roll. And Jack knew he wasn't the only one seeing them.

Shock flickered across Luc's face.

"Jacques," Luc whispered.

"Jack," he snarled as he jerked away. This time, his hand passed through Luc's, as insubstantial as a wish.

"What..." Then Luc shook his head. "It does not matter."

He turned, his gaze unerringly seeking out Will. "I don't know what is killing her, but she's fading. Save her."

Will's gaze rested on Jack.

"I can't," Will said flatly. "Only Jack can. She's connected to him and he chooses to die. That means when he dies, she will die with him."

Those words hit Jack square in the chest and he found himself staring at Perci's still face. And then he looked up and stared at Luc.

Luc... Memory after memory rolled through him.

Luc. The man Perci—*Persinette* had married all those years ago.

Back when Jack had asked who she was, and she'd told him, he'd just assumed her husband had died as well.

But he hadn't.

"You're a fucking bastard," he said to Will, and then he looked back at the ripped meat that was his body. Oddly enough, no blood flowed, and he really didn't look any closer to dead than he had a few minutes ago.

And although Jack said nothing out loud, Will knew exactly what thoughts rolled through his mind.

"That's because I'm keeping you alive. Giving you a moment to decide. Is it death you want? Or are you going to come back to what you are?"

Shifting his gaze to Perci, he focused on her face. Now he had a lifetime of memories swarming inside him, and he remembered the love he'd had for her. He could have done without that. Especially as he stood there just a few feet away from her husband.

Without looking at Luc, he said grimly, "I'll do it."

But damn it, Will was damn well going to find somebody *else* to train him, or whatever the fuck Perci was supposed to do. It wasn't like he really needed training now anyway, did he?

And then, before his thoughts could even complete, he was being sucked back into his body...and it *hurt*.

It *hurt*.

I came awake with a scream, curled into a ball and whimpered, all but ready to beg for mercy.

Luc was there and he caught me in his arms, pulled me against his chest. "Hush, Perci...just breathe, the pain will pass. It always does. Just breathe, just breathe..."

Breathe...I can't...it hurts...

"You have to breathe." His voice was firm and hard.

I curled my hands into his thighs, arched against the fiery pain tearing through me. I tasted blood in the back of my throat.

"Breathe...breathe..."

A hand touched my brow. "Perci. I could use your help."

I knew that voice.

Will.

At his touch, a cooling, comforting rush washed over me, and I tried to open my eyes, tried to look at him. Hard though. So hard. Through cracked, dry lips, I whispered, "Hurts."

"I know." His eyes were grim and he slanted a look past my shoulder. "It's not helping you that your new partner isn't letting me help *him*. You're feeling his pain, and until it passes you know you'll both suffer. He might let you help."

Will lifted a hand, let it hover over me. "May I?"

"Shit, if it will stop this..." And even if it didn't, I'd let him. My partner...did he mean Jack?

Tears blurred my eyes. Jack hadn't wanted to be one of us. He'd wanted to die.

"Jack isn't dead," Will said quietly. Then he placed his hand over my breastbone. "Choices, Perci. We all make them and he made his."

I sucked in a breath as his power washed over me, undoing whatever damage had been done. I could still feel the pain though, and now that the hideous agony wasn't blinding me, I knew why. My shields...I'd lowered them and when the *vankyr* had torn into Jack, it had just about killed me as well.

Overloaded me.

Not smart, not smart.

"Can you stand?" Luc asked.

My legs were rubbery, watery. I knew that even without putting any weight on them. "I don't know."

I felt eyes on me and I looked up, realized that we had an audience...a large one. Greta, Rip. I saw Elle and although I didn't see him, I knew Michael must be somewhere. Sina stood just beyond Will and there were others. I could sense them.

Sina's eyes, dark, dark blue bored into me and I looked away. Something about her stare had always unsettled me and today was no different. I braced a hand on Luc's shoulder and tried to push to my feet, but I couldn't.

"Let me help," he said.

Shame flooded me as he helped me to my feet. The times I had hurt him, all the times I had failed him. Like always, Luc knew what I was thinking. He stroked a hand down my arm. "You must move past this, Perci. If we were meant to be, we would. And if you failed me, then I failed you as well." He kissed my brow. "Let it go...and go help your man. He needs you now."

My man. Luc nudged me along toward Jack, and when I saw him lying there, still bloodied, still broken, my heart all but stopped.

I ran to him. "No," I snarled. I didn't even know who I was talking to. "You can't do this. You *can't.*"

Finally, the cold aching knot that was my heart had thawed and I could feel something beyond grief and pain...or at least I *had* felt something. For a few days, I'd felt...something.

And now Jack lay here—

"No." Sinking to my hands, I covered the bloody, torn flesh of his sides.

But he knocked me aside, even as battered and broken as his body was. "No," he rasped, glaring at me.

I would have argued with him, except I was too far across the room and staring at him in utter shock. He wasn't that strong—mortals *weren't.* Not even him, and he was definitely the strongest mortal I'd ever known.

Dazed, I looked across the room to Will.

"He is as he is meant to be," Will said obliquely.

I wanted to tell him to shove the cryptic shit, but I could feel Jack's pain even through my shields, and it hurt so bad—so bad.

"How?" My question came out through gritted teeth.

But there was no answer and just then, I couldn't try to pound it out of Will, even if I had a chance at that. No, I had to take care of Jack.

"Fuck how," I muttered. "Just hold him."

Luc caught one thrashing arm, evading Jack easily despite his lack of sight.

Will caught the other one. Rip and Greta pinned his legs.

Rip shot me a wide grin and said, "He's a strong one, eh?"

Strong...yes. And he'd have to be, because the wound in his side would have killed even one of us. And *how* could he be one of us...

"Don't," Jack panted as I knelt down. "Don't you fucking dare. It will heal."

"You're too weak," I said. I could feel the energy, the life seeping out of him. And below that was my own nagging weakness—no, none of this was good. I had to heal him, take that pain away...or we were both screwed.

My weakness concerned me, but it wasn't enough to kill me. I knew that, could sense it. Besides, Will was here. If I faltered, Will could steady me. He'd done it before.

When my hands covered the hot, pulpy mess of his side, blood gushed out. I ignored it. I'd felt worse. I'd had my hands buried in blood and guts more times than I could count and it hadn't ever bothered me. The only thing about this that would slow me down was if I failed...and I wouldn't fail.

Not now. Not this time. Not with Jack.

Pain arced through us. We both screamed. Jack stopped screaming long, long before I did.

Chapter Thirteen

"Where are you going?"

Jack flicked Luc a look and then resumed the task of buttoning his shirt. It shouldn't take this long. Really, it shouldn't. But he wanted to concentrate on it. The longer it took, the more thought he put into *each* detail, the less he thought about...well, everything else.

Like the fact that Perci's husband stood just a few feet away from him.

Like the fact that Perci lay in his bed, still unconscious.

After more than twenty-four hours.

It had been quite a while since he'd done this bit, but he knew that wasn't normal. Will had assured him that she was fine, and despite the fact that Jack was still madder than hell at the other guy, he knew Will wouldn't lie.

Oh, he'd withhold secrets—like the fact that Jack was living out his second life. Like the fact that his *mother* had been living out *her* second life...after she'd *killed* him in her first life.

Cosette.

Fuck. None of this made sense.

"Have you no answer?"

Through slitted eyes, he looked at Luc. "I'm leaving," he said succinctly. He grabbed his work boots, shoved his feet into them and sat on the edge of the couch to tie them.

"Leaving..."

It wasn't until he was striding across the room that Luc made another sound, made another move. And then Jack's next move was to go flying head first into the ground.

"You selfish bastard," Luc said, his accent growing thick and heavy. "Leave her, will you? After all she has suffered?"

Jack shoved upright and glared at Luc. "Yeah. I'm leaving. And I never asked her to help me. I didn't ask for *any* of this."

He hadn't asked to come back...hadn't ever wanted to fall in love with her to begin with, not then. Not now.

Especially not now, when he had endless, empty years stretching out before him.

There was a harsh intake of breath behind him. And then, to his surprise, Luc started to laugh. It was a bitter, ugly laugh...hard and wrenching. "You go on then, Jacques. You run. Fool."

Waking is rarely pleasant after doing a major healing. This time, it was even less pleasant. The worst pain wasn't in my side though, or my gut, despite the fact that my guts had all but been ripped out as I took Jack's pain.

The worst pain was right in my heart.

Even before I opened my eyes, I knew he was gone.

With a sigh, I rolled to my hip, lifted my lashes and stared out the window.

He didn't want to be with me.

Didn't even want this life, and I couldn't blame him. Chances were that Will had somehow manipulated him into it. Maybe even used me to do it, although that wouldn't have set him running. Although it would certainly harden his resolve.

For long, long moments, I stared out the window at the moonlight sparking off the water. I would have stared at it for hours, except I knew I wasn't alone, and the woman with me wasn't going to tolerate being ignored for too long.

"How long will you remain here feeling sorry for yourself?"

Blowing out a breath, I sat up. The sheet fell to my waist, but I was too tired to care.

I met Sina's level gaze with one of my own. "Why don't you go hump a dwarf, Snow White?"

A cool smile twisted her lips. Her midnight-dark eyes flashed. Eerie power rolled from her.

But I wasn't afraid of her. Tired and aching, I shifted on the bed. "Save the theatrics for somebody who might be impressed." I waited a beat and added, "Unlike me."

"Always so strong," Sina murmured. "So unwilling to need somebody."

"I'm not *unwilling*."

"You never let yourself need Luc."

That might have hurt. Except she was wrong. Frowning, I climbed out of the bed and looked around for my clothes. They weren't anywhere to be found. Tucked in the corner was a closet and I headed over there. I found a worn, white polo that smelled of Jack and it made my heart hurt as I pulled it on.

"You're wrong," I said, keeping my back to her. "I did need Luc. Maybe I didn't love him the way I would have liked—and the way he deserved, but I did *need* him. And I do still need his friendship. I just can't love him."

Turning, I faced her. I crossed my arms over my chest. That ache inside, it still lingered. "Not that it's any of *your* business."

"Hmm." She reached up and stroked one of the chains around her neck. One held her medallion. The other, I couldn't see. Her hair fell to her shoulders, framing her face.

She wasn't lovely—not the way the fairy tale portrayed her. But she also wasn't stupid enough to eat a poisoned apple, and as far as I knew, she'd never had a prince kiss her out of a drugged slumber. Most of the men I knew were more than a little scared of Sina.

She had a way of cutting people off at the knees...or the balls.

Sina might not be lovely, but she was exotic, sensual...and when you looked at her, it was hard to look away, especially if she was looking back.

And right now, she was looking back at me with a faint smile curling her ruby red lips. She wore no make-up. Never had, not in all the years I'd known her. Rising from the seat by the window, Sina strolled over to stand at my side. "This *Jack*," she said. "Do you love *him*?"

"I hardly know him."

"Not an answer."

"I..." I blew out a breath and stared into those eerie, insightful blue eyes. Then I shifted my gaze elsewhere. Inside. Jack made me feel again. For the first time in *this* life. "I don't know. But I think I *could*. If he lets me...if he stays, I think I will. But he doesn't want me."

Sina looked past me.

I already knew why. Looking up, I saw Luc standing in the doorway. Krell was at his side and the moment I looked at the dog, he wagged his tail. Out of habit, I snapped my fingers and he bounded over to me. Crouching down in front of him, I buried my fingers in his fur. "Hey, boy."

He went to lick my nose and despite myself, I smiled.

"Your man thinks we're still married, Perci," Luc said.

My smile wobbled. Died.

"He...he what?"

Luc came inside and knelt by Krell. His hand came up, rested by mine. "I saw in his mind. All the memories...Jacques." A spasm of grief tightened his face and he whispered, "I cannot believe what Cosette did..."

I covered his hand with mine. Some of those memories I had never shared. I hadn't wanted him to know, and now he knew anyway. "It is over," I said.

He turned his hand over, gripped mine. "Over," he echoed. Then he tugged his hand away and stood. "I saw it in his mind as he was leaving. He hasn't remembered how to shield, or perhaps he never learned. I do not know. But I saw it, heard it all. He remembered who I am, that we'd been wed. And he thought I had died. Then he saw that I still lived and he..." Luc shrugged. "He wouldn't stay. It felt to me like he couldn't. He thinks we are together, and it hurts him."

"Oh, shit," I muttered, my gut clenching. I looked at Luc and saw the pain he tried to hide. No matter what, I was hurting these two men.

Luc combed his hand through my hair. "Go, Perci. Find him."

"Luc—"

He pressed his finger to my lips. "Go," he said again.

And I went.

The door closed behind Perci before Sina said a word. Luc knew it was coming. Unspoken words carried a weight, a heavy one.

"You still love her."

Luc made his way to the window, relying on the imagery

he'd gleaned from his link with Krell. Before he answered, he opened it and leaned out, breathing in the fresh sea air. He thought he might like to walk the beach for a while. Perhaps.

Sighing, he turned back to Sina. "Whether I love her or not changes nothing. She doesn't love me, and more than anything, I need her to be happy. And at peace."

"So selfless," Sina said. "Always so selfless."

"If I was selfless, I would have walked away from her years ago, instead of taking whatever scraps she would give me. But because I kept clinging to a useless hope, I held her tight and neither of us healed." Luc shook his head. "Both of us are to blame, Sina. I don't know why you are so angry with Perci, but it ends. Now."

Then he turned and strode away.

As he left her alone in the room, Sina turned to look out the window.

Such a clueless man. He'd loved a woman for years. And Sina had loved him for years. Why shouldn't she be angry? Of course, he had never seen it. Nobody saw it. And that was how it would remain. It was safer that way. Much, much safer.

Chapter Fourteen

It was hard to trail him. I'd been after him for weeks. Two, at least. Maybe three. I was losing track, and running on too little sleep. I think it had been four days since I'd slept, and almost a week since I'd eaten. Where *was* he and how was he moving so fast?

He was still too new. He shouldn't be able to move like this. But he did. I followed the ache in my heart, knowing it would lead me to him.

Before it had been a burn...a buzz. Now it was pain, hot and lashing.

I was in Maine now and somehow, I wasn't surprised. The ocean seemed to draw him, and right now, the wild, turbulent waters echoed the chaos in my heart. It would echo his as well. And when the tears clogged my throat, I knew I was close. I pulled off the road and found myself close to the shore.

There was a small, rickety looking cabin, but he wasn't in there. The path under my feet kept trying to crumble as I headed down to the rocky beach.

I saw his silhouette even from nearly half a mile away, and I knew the exact moment he sensed me. I was almost a quarter mile away when he did, and I wondered if he would leave. It would be harder for me to catch him now, but damn it, if he thought he'd just run away...

But all he did was turn and watch me approach. Words crowded my head, leaped into my throat. What was I supposed to say?

Why in the hell did you leave like that?

I'm not married. Technically, both of us died so the marriage was null, but I wanted it more official and we're not married, haven't been for more than three centuries. Is that why you left?

Are you angry?

The distance between us closed all too soon, and I found myself standing in front of him and staring into those misty, beautiful eyes...and I had no idea what to say to him.

He broke our little staring contest and turned away, looking back out over the water.

"I don't need a trainer. So run on back to Will and tell him you tried. You did your job. You can go back to your husband now and leave me the hell alone."

I scowled at him. "I'm not here because of Will. And for your information, Luc hasn't been my husband in over three hundred years. We were divorced *before* it was the *in* thing to do."

If I hadn't been watching him so closely, I wouldn't have seen it, wouldn't have seen how his shoulders went rigid, wouldn't have heard his harsh intake of breath.

And as quickly as that, he relaxed and shrugged. "Whatever. I don't want a trainer and in case nobody clued you in, I've done this gig before. I was doing it before you were even a thought, princess, so I think I can handle it. Now get the hell away from me."

"Are you *trying* to piss me off?" I asked. "Or does it just come naturally?"

He looked back at me. "No. I'm not trying. I just want you gone. So...go."

His eyes...they were so fucking cold. Glacier cold. It hit me square in the chest. I could have screamed it hurt so bad, and that was when I realized.

I *did* love him.

I'd been wrong when Sina asked me. I couldn't *grow* to love him, because I already did. But he didn't want me here. Karma...talk about karma. As the pain twisted inside my heart, I pasted a false, bitter smile on my face. "Yeah, fine."

He didn't want me here. He didn't want *me*. Oh, the irony. Luc had been wrong.

Sadly though, I knew I wasn't going to get much relief by pointing that out to him. As I made my way across the sharp, jagged rocks, I focused every last bit of energy I had on that single task.

I didn't think about anything else, because I couldn't.

The rocks, they were all that mattered.

And then I was clear of the rocks...but there was the path ahead. It was a twisty path, and eroding something terrible. I didn't want to fall, right? So I concentrated on that. Just that. After all, it wouldn't do for me to fall, because the way *my* luck was going, I'd break my ankle and then I'd be stuck here long enough to get Will out to set it. Stuck here with Jack—

I hissed out a breath.

Don't think about him.

Just like that, he was in front of me.

"What's wrong?" he demanded, his craggy, rough face darkened in a snarl.

I edged around him and tossed back over my shoulder, "Nothing. Going now."

The path. Focus on the path. And after that, I'd find something else—

Jack's hand, hard and hot, closed around my arm and swung me around.

"What's *wrong?*"

I stared at him. What's *wrong?* He wanted to know what was wrong. I spent three weeks trailing after him, I find him, and he pushes me away and he wants to know what's wrong.

But I wasn't going to tell him that I'd just realized I was in love with him. He didn't get that from me. He didn't care enough. Carefully, I said, "Nothing is wrong. Would you let me go, please?"

He shook me, staring down at me with intense eyes. Eyes that glowed. Shit. His gift. It was his gift—

"Don't tell me that," he muttered. He laid a hand on my cheek. "You're hurting somewhere. I feel it. What's wrong?"

Hurting.

I jerked back, so hard and fast I ended up on my butt with the sharp rocks digging into my tender flesh. *Now* I had some real physical, if somewhat minor pain.

But that wasn't the pain he'd felt.

No. Oh, shit, no.

Shoving to my feet, I skirted around him. "I'm *not* hurting," I told him.

"Yeah, you are."

I sneered at him. "You a healer now? Fine. I just gouged my ass on the rocks over there. You come kiss it and make it better."

"Perci—"

He tried to reach for me again, but I was prepared this time. Yeah, he was fast. But I was just as fast. I moved away, evading him. I stood with the cliff at my back as I faced him. The wind slashed across my face, stinging my eyes.

"You have a nice life, Jack. Sorry you got stuck with this deal again—I know you didn't want it." Then I started the climb up, moving as fast as I could. And it was pretty damn fast. It should have been fast enough. But even as fast as I was, he caught me. I was nearly to the top, but he still caught me.

"Wait," he muttered, catching me and crowding up against me on the narrow trail.

"Sorry. I need to be gone."

"Why?" he asked baldly. "You just got here."

"Yeah, and *you* just told me to get the hell out."

He didn't even respond to that, he was too busy staring at me, like he'd see something on me, in me. *Why* was he staring at me? "Damn it, what do you want?"

"What's hurting you?" he demanded and his eyes looked slightly wild. "You're not still hurt, are you? Damn it, it's been more than three weeks."

More than three weeks.

Those words circled around in my head as he reached up, touched my face, tipped my head back and peered down at me. His touch, his nearness, it numbed me, dazed me, made it so hard to think.

But I had to think. Damn it. Tearing free from him, I back away, edging closer and closer to the edge of the trail. If I got to my damn car, it wouldn't matter how fast he was. None of us moved faster than cars. We might be a little more than human, but we were basically still human under the fancy trappings we'd been given, and we weren't prone to things like Superman's skills of "faster than a speeding bullet".

"I'm not hurt," I said, forcing the words out through a tight, raspy throat. "I'm not hurt and you can stop

251

worrying...although why in the hell you feel the need, I don't know."

"If you're not hurt, why does it feel like something inside me is..." His voice trailed away and he stared into my eyes.

Broken.

He didn't say it out loud.

But he didn't need to. He felt broken inside because he was feeling *my* pain. And I was broken inside. Shit.

I slammed up heavy, thick mental shields, layering them as thick as I could and hoping it would block him. Empathy—why in the *hell* had they gifted somebody like *him* with empathy?

I had to get away before he figured it out. Damn it. I was going to leave here with *something* intact, and the only thing I had left was my pride.

"I'm fine," I said again with a sharp-edged smile. "Chances are you didn't *have* this gift before..." And I was still trying to get my mind wrapped around that. "It's all new and weird and *more* when you change over. So it takes a while to adjust. So you stay here and adjust and have fun with it. *Ciao.*"

I turned on my heel and rushed for my car.

I had my hand on the fucking *handle* when he reached over my shoulder and slammed down on the door. I jerked against him and he shoved the door with so much force, I saw the metal crumple under his hand.

"Damn it, Jack."

"Why are you here, Perci?"

Desperately, I jerked on the door. I needed to get away. *Now.*

He brought a hand up and curved it over my hip. "This pain, it's just in one place, you know. Right in my heart. Like somebody has a knife there, twisting it. But you aren't hurt there." He lowered his head, pressed his mouth to my shoulder.

A shudder wracked me from head to toe.

"If it's not something I can *see*, then what was I feeling? And why can't I feel it now?" He pressed his lips to my hair. "What's going on, Perci?"

"You're too new to your gift," I snapped. "Nothing's going on. Learn your gift, how to use it. And take your hands off me."

But he didn't. All he did was breathe me in. Strangely...I *felt* that.

"I don't really want to take my hands off you, Perci."

He dipped his head and kissed my nape. The brush of his mouth against my flesh jolted through me, making my nerve endings sizzle and my knees weaken. My heart slammed against my ribs, beating at a speed that might have been dangerous had I still been completely mortal.

Too damn bad—passing out just then might have been handy.

"You wanted me gone, Jack," I said, keeping my voice hard and flat, even though all I wanted to do was melt against him. "Now I want to be gone. I've got things to do, people to see, and it's easier for me to do that if you would let go."

"People to see...like Luc?" Big, rough hands curled over my shoulders. His voice was a ragged snarl in my ear as he said, "You know what it did to me when I saw him? It was like somebody had punched a hole into my chest and just ripped my heart out. I remember, you know—that other life. I remember the way you used to watch him, how he watched you. It was...beautiful, and even though it hurt me then to see it, it was what you needed. And all I could think was that you belonged with him, you needed that beauty back. I hate myself for thinking I had taken what belonged to another man...and I kept wondering why in the hell you didn't *tell* me."

"There was nothing to tell—not to you, at least, Jack. Luc and I don't belong together." I blinked back my tears, struggled to maintain whatever shields I could to keep him from feeling my anguish. This was torment. This was hell. And I wanted, more than anything that blissful numb state I had known for years. It was better than this. Better than this gut-wrenching agony. Keeping my voice neutral, I stared off over my car as I said, "Luc and I aren't the people we used to be. What happened during our mortal lives, at the end of them, changed us—*too* much and we can't go back to who we were. A part of me has known that ever since it happened, and Luc has come to see it as well."

He tugged on my shoulders, tried to make me face him, but I couldn't do that—wouldn't. Swallowing the knot in my throat,

I added, "And like I said, Luc and I haven't been married in years. So you weren't fucking a married woman. You haven't sullied your precious honor."

I still didn't understand completely what had happened, but I knew back during my mortal life, honor had been important to Jacques. It would matter to Jack as well. Thinking he had been sleeping with a married woman had probably been weighing on him. Although if he *had* been sleeping with a married woman, and I'd kept that secret—the sin would have been *mine*, not his.

Men. I swear, they made no sense.

"You think this is just about honor?" A harsh, grating laugh escaped him. "Yeah, I don't like the idea of fucking a married woman, but it was more than that...and damn it, will you look at me?"

This time, when he tried to turn me around, there was enough force in it. It was going to look pretty foolish if I resisted. I didn't want him knowing *why* I resisted, after all. Didn't want him feeling anything from me, didn't want him guessing that it hurt too damn much to look at him.

Setting my jaw, I turned around and met his eyes. Even though I'd prepared myself, my heart still leaped, still jumped and danced inside my chest. And now that I *knew*, I could see it...Jacques. Yes, the face was different, and the body...but those eyes. Those eyes were the same, and as I stared into them, I knew the soul was the same as well.

Jacques.

He'd frightened me, intimidated me in that first life.

Dear God, how was this possible...

But there really wasn't any need to ask that. I'd learned that nothing was impossible, not really. After all, here I was...some three hundred years after I'd been born. I'd fought things that never should have existed. Why shouldn't I be standing in front of the man who'd fought to protect me all those years ago?

"You're hiding something," he muttered, lifting a hand to touch my cheek.

I turned my head aside, evading that light touch—couldn't let him touch me now. Not now. From the corner of my eye, I saw his fingers curl into his palm, watched until his hand fisted and fell away.

As I looked back at him, I fixed an impassive mask firmly in place. But it didn't do much good. He was one of us. He could hear my heart rate, could hear the miniscule catches in my breathing that I *couldn't* regulate, no matter how hard I tried.

He lifted an arm, braced it over my shoulder and rested his hand on the car behind me. I felt surrounded by him and it did bad, bad things to my mental state. Bad, bad... As my heart accelerated, I saw his eyes widen, watched the misty gray of his pupils darken.

"What's going on, Perci?" He didn't touch me, but he leaned in close, so close I could feel his heat all along my body. "What are you hiding from me?"

"Nothing you need to worry about," I said. "You want me gone, right? So get out of my way."

Those sad, sad eyes... They'd gutted him, right from the first. But now they weren't sad. They were carefully, deliberately blank—just like everything else about her.

If it wasn't for her jacked-up heart rate and the slightly erratic cadence of her breathing, Jack would have thought he was staring at a stone statue. That was how much emotion Perci showed—how much emotion she put out.

It was too fucking much—from the moment she'd stepped foot on his beach, he'd felt the pain radiating from her, like a vicious, burning wound, and then, as quick as a blink, it was all gone.

In the back of his mind, a voice whispered the answer, but he didn't want to listen to that voice. He wanted the answer from *her*, because then he could trust it.

"I wanted you gone because it hurts too much to look at you and think about how you belong to somebody else," he said slowly, forcing the words through a tight, tight throat. He didn't want to tell her that, didn't want to strip himself so completely bare.

Staring into her dark eyes, he lifted a hand and rested it on her waist. "I saw Luc and it was like everything inside of me just ended. I knew what would happen—somehow, I just knew.

You'd be back with him and your world would be right again. I...my head's been fucked up since then, can you get that?"

She didn't say anything, just shifted her gaze away from him and stared off over the cliff toward the water.

"Perci"

"My *world* hasn't been right in so long, I can't even comprehend what right would be like. I don't know what *right* feels like." She sent him a look from the corner of her eye. "I'm messed up, okay? I locked everybody, everything out and I've spent the past few centuries hurting Luc because I couldn't drag myself out of the pit I'd dug for myself. But I don't love him the way I need to, and I never will. He's not a part of my life anymore, except for being a friend." She paused, then opened her mouth. "I...no. You know what? Fuck it. I'm leaving. I'm out of here, Jack."

She shoved against his chest, but Jack just reached up and caught her wrists. "Not yet," he muttered. "I don't want you leaving yet."

"And what if *I* want to?" she demanded. She glared at him. "Damn it, I've been on a roller coaster ever since I met you and I can't do this. It hurts too much. I'd rather go back to not feeling *anything* than to feel like this. Either you want me or you don't—stop jerking me around."

"Ah, hell, Perci. That's the problem." Still holding her wrists, he dipped his head and gently rubbed his lips over hers. "I've always wanted you. Even when you belonged to somebody else and I had no chance in hell of ever *having* you. I wanted you then. Dying didn't stop that. All the years between didn't stop that. And the minute I saw you...I wanted you then. I want you now. I'll always want you. Want you...need you."

Her hands, balled into fists, abruptly loosened and curled into his T-shirt. Daring to let go, he cupped her face in one hand, angled it back and slanted his mouth over hers. "You're my heart, princess," he whispered. "I must have been sent back to find you. We can't live, or even rest in peace without a heart, I guess. And you're mine. Always have been."

Her lips parted on a sob and he took another chance and eased his tongue inside. Her rigid body went lax and she all but fell against him. Jack groaned and caught her weight in his arms. She wrapped hers around his neck, her mouth moving under his.

And the shields—that solid, cool wall that had come between them, evaporated. As her emotions crashed into him, he sagged, might have fallen, but he didn't want her on the rough, unkind ground. So he shifted and crashed into the car, keeping her cradled against him as the weight of her emotions washed over him.

Tearing his mouth away from hers, he whispered, "Perci?"

She pressed her brow to his, her narrow shoulders shaking.

"You wanted me to leave," she rasped.

"No. Hell, no. It was just killing me to think I couldn't keep you." His heart clenched in agony as the pain inside her washed over him.

"I don't want to leave you," she whispered. "I haven't felt alive, felt *real*, until I met you. I...shit, Jack. I think I'm in love with you."

Shaken, he cradled the back of her head and stared up at the dark gray skies over head. Words he hadn't thought he'd ever hear...not from her.

"Perci..."

She lifted her head. "Don't go freaking out," she said, forcing a smile. "I'm not going to get all clingy and desperate. I just—"

He fisted his hand in her hair and hauled her against him, silencing her words with his mouth. He stopped just long enough to mutter, "Three hundred years. I knew I loved you then. And I know I love you now. If you're not going to get all desperate, and even a little clingy sometimes, I'm going to get pissed. I waited two lifetimes to hear you say that. I think a little desperation is just fine. I'm sure as hell desperate. And I plan on clinging to you a lot. Starting now."

"Oh...um. Okay." Tears gleamed diamond bright in her eyes, but she smiled and a hiccupping laugh escaped her. Her teeth caught her lower lip and she glanced around. "Now? Right now?"

"Yeah."

Without waiting another second, Jack swept her into his

arms, grinning as a surprised giggle escaped her lips. "You know, I've never had a chance to do that."

"You do it really well." She snuggled against his chest, absently stroking her finger over his chest as he carried her across the uneven ground to his small cabin.

It wasn't much, and just then, he wished it was. He'd love for it to be a palace, a mansion, something with a wide, luxurious bed, silken sheets that would glow against her skin. But she didn't seem to even notice, and once he got her inside, Jack didn't much notice either.

He barely even remembered carrying her to the bed. The cabin had just two rooms. The bathroom was separated from the rest of the cabin and the bed was tucked up under a window that faced out over the water. He lay her down on it and stretched out beside her. As he lifted his hand to her face, he realized his fingers were shaking.

This was real.

A few days ago, he hadn't even known this woman. And now, his head flooded with memories of another life, and his heart ached with the love he'd had for her then. She stared at him as though she needed this as much as he did.

"You're really here, right?" he whispered. He stroked a hand down her side, gripped the hem of her shirt and slid it up, baring the smooth, soft skin there. "You're not going to disappear when I wake up."

"I'm really here. Really here..." She pressed her lips to his throat, breathed him in. "And so are you. Touch me. Would you please just touch me?"

"I am touching you." He cupped one small, firm breast in his hand, stroked his thumb over the silk-covered nipple and when she shuddered, he did too. Her pleasure became his and he groaned. "Fuck, this might kill me."

"No. It won't—promise." Her hands dipped into his hair, tugging.

Obliging, he lowered his head and caught the tip of her breast between his teeth, hissing out as the pleasure arced through him as well. *Too much, too much, too much.*

Swearing, he sat back on his heels, grabbed the hem of her shirt and tore it away. His hands, usually so steady, fumbled with her bra, her jeans and panties. Her jeans and panties tangled around her ankles and for about two seconds, he contemplated just ripping them off—he could—he knew he could, especially now.

But instead, hands shaking, he fought the tangle of clothing off and then closed his hands around her ankles. Sliding his gaze along the long, pale length of her body, he rested his gaze on the tight curls covering her pussy, then along her flat belly, along her torso and higher, until he was staring into her eyes.

"One of these days, I'm going to be able to take my time, make love to you soft and slow, the way you deserve. But right now, I can't," he said, his voice harsh and rough. "I need you too much."

A drowsy smile curled her lips. "Then have me. And I don't need soft and slow—just need you."

Pushing upright, he grabbed his shirt and wasn't quite so patient with it when his hands got clumsy. Fabric ripped and he threw the remains off to the side. He fumbled with his jeans and managed to get them off without tearing the sturdy denim. When he looked back at Perci, she was lying there with a smile curving her lips and a light of amusement dancing in her eyes.

"What?"

"You're impatient."

A dull red flush crept up his neck. Levering his body over hers, he fisted his hand in her short, red-gold hair. "Damn straight. Didn't think I'd ever have this...have you." Pressing a hard kiss to her mouth, he whispered, "Open for me, Perci...open for me."

She opened for him, arching her neck and giving him access to her mouth even as she brought up her knees and squeezed his hips.

He pressed against her, groaning as he felt the slick wet heat of her. She slid her tongue along his lower lip and he caught it, bit her gently.

"Want you," he muttered.

She arched her hips against him. "Stop waiting already, Jack."

With a harsh growl, he braced his arm on the bed and lifted

up, staring in her eyes.

It left him stripped bare. Completely bare.

But he needed to see her...needed her to see him.

Somehow, it felt like the first time. And maybe in a way it was. He knew who he *was* now. Abruptly, that driving, burning need eased and he found some of the gentleness he'd needed, wanted to have for her.

Holding her gaze, he sank slowly inside her. Her breath caught in her chest, and he could feel that, just like he could feel the spirals of heat spreading through her. Her pleasure was his, and it was bliss and agony, heaven and hell... "Killing me," he whispered. "Fuck, you're killing me."

"Hmm. If I am, just make sure you take me with you." She tugged him down and slanted her mouth over his.

Heaven. Hell.

Cupping her cheek in his hand, he angled her head back and took the kiss deeper. His heart squeezed in his chest as she stroked her hands along his sides, then dipped into his hair. And all the while, she watched him from under her lashes, watched him the way he watched her, like she feared he'd disappear.

Savage, desperate need twisted through him and he drove into her deeper, harder. Perci cried out. Jack stiffened and swore. "Are you okay?"

"Don't stop," she whispered. "Fuck, please don't...please."

Gathering her close, he braced an arm under her shoulders and drove deep. Her nails raked down his shoulders and neck and each sweet pain had him gritting his teeth, nearly insane from the pleasure.

She tightened around him, the silken muscles of her pussy clenching around him, milking him.

"Fuck, that feels good," he growled against her mouth. Cupping her ass, he tilted her hips up, rode her deeper, harder.

Perci mewled and started to shudder, his name coming from her in ragged, whimpering cries. And when she squeezed down around him, tighter...tighter...the top of his head felt like it was going to come off. Shifting, he reached between them and stroked her clit. He was going to lose it—going to lose it, and damn it—

She came, shattering under him.

Jack growled, taking her mouth in a savage, rough kiss. Pleasure so sharp it hurt blistered through him and he lost himself in it, fell into it...and she fell with him. He could feel her. Not just her body...but *her*.

And as they drifted back, her arms wrapped around his shoulders, her fingers stroking through his hair, he could still feel her through some tenuous, vague connection. Reaching up, he caught one hand and laced their fingers.

"You're staying, right?"

A smile, brash and cocky, curled her lips, but he could feel the nerves and pain inside her now as she stared at him. "As long as you want me."

"Then you're staying for always, Perci," he whispered. "Always."

"I could go for that." She turned her face into his neck and breathed him in. "Yeah, I can go for that."

About the Author

To learn more about Shiloh Walker, please visit www.shilohwalker.com. Send an email to Shiloh at shiloh_@shilohwalker.com or join her Yahoo! group to join in the fun with other readers as well as Shiloh: http://groups.yahoo.com/group/wicked_writers.

So you think you know fairy tales? Guess again.

Candy Houses
© *2009 Shiloh Walker*
Grimm's Circle, Book 1

Greta didn't get her happy ending her first time around. And now that she's a Grimm—special kind of guardian angel and official ass-kicker in the paranormal world—romance is hard to find. Besides, there's only ever been one man who made her heart race, and the fact that he did scared her right out of his arms. Now Rip is back. And just in time too, because Greta needs his help.

On a mission he knows is going to test all of his strengths and skills, the last person Rip expected to see is the one woman who broke his heart. Working together seems to be their only hope. But, when faced with a danger neither of them anticipated, the question is, how will they face the danger to their hearts—assuming they survive, of course.

Warning: Dark, sexy, a little bit scary—this fairy tale is only for grownups and is best saved for bedtime.

Available now in ebook and print from Samhain Publishing.

SAMHAIN
PUBLISHING

It's all about the story...

Romance

HORROR

www.samhainpublishing.com

CPSIA information can be obtained at www.ICGtesting.com
Printed in the USA
BVOW071058090412

287209BV00003B/5/P

9 781609 288648